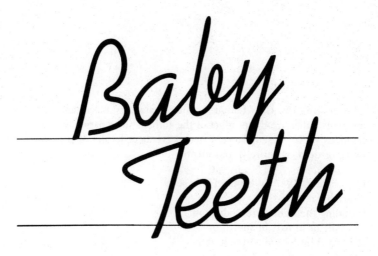

a novel by

Blythe Holbrooke

SIMON AND SCHUSTER
New York

Copyright © 1987 by Blythe Holbrooke
All rights reserved
including the right of reproduction
in whole or in part in any form
Published by Simon and Schuster
A Division of Simon & Schuster, Inc.
Simon & Schuster Building
Rockefeller Center
1230 Avenue of the Americas
New York, New York 10020

SIMON AND SCHUSTER and colophon are registered trademarks
of Simon & Schuster, Inc.
Designed by Levavi & Levavi
Manufactured in the United States of America
10 9 8 7 6 5 4 3 2 1

Library of Congress Cataloging in Publication Data

Holbrooke, Blythe.
    Baby teeth: a novel.

    I. Title.
PS3558.0347744B3   1987   813'.54   86-31620

ISBN: 0-671-63284-1

The author gratefully acknowledges permission from the following
publishers to reprint the line of poetry from "Out of the Sighs" that
appears in the epigraph:

Dylan Thomas, *The Poems of Dylan Thomas*. Copyright 1953 by Dylan
Thomas. Reprinted by permission of New Directions Publishing
Corporation and J. M. Dent & Sons Ltd.

For Donna, Barbara, Francis,
Kitty, Greg and Stephanie

"How much was happy while it lasted"
—Dylan Thomas, *Out of the Sighs*

Baby
Teeth

Chapter One

"**G**o entertain Daddy," she said, leaning back against the glass doors in her cross-strapped sundress. Her copper hair was curled and fell in shimmering waves on her bare shoulders, making her look just like the grave yet earnest college sweetheart in the silver-framed photo on Daddy's desk. Like most grown-ups Mom mostly looked irritated, but when she smiled she was as sublime as the girl in the photo, who smiled as if she knew a secret beyond the power of her smile.

It was Sunday afternoon. Mom never wore dresses at home on Sunday. But there she was in her cross-backed sundress. It was hot and sticky outside with mosquitoes buzzing like bad static, still Mom looked cool as her iced tea as she gazed out at the lake.

That was the summer Marilyn Monroe killed herself,

the summer after Dad hired Bruce, a summer I would remember for the rest of my life.

"This late bulletin just in from the WQXR newsroom,"
said the man who broke into the Living Strings' movie
theme medley with the news. She was thirty-six. Champagne and sleeping pills, he said. It all sounded very sad,
mysterious, and important, but I didn't understand it.

"Monroe was the funny blonde who lived upstairs in *The
Seven Year Itch*," Mom explained. "You know, the movie I
let you stay up to watch last Sunday on TV."

I didn't think it had been a whole week, but that's part
of summer's magic, how the days melt into hazy weeks
when folks take off their watches and time stands still as
the dead air you plunge into the lake to escape. Summer is
heaven. You can get away with murder. Everything is per-
mitted. Even the sun stays up late.

That was the summer after we had the patios built. The
summer we had the backyard re-landscaped. The summer
I won the diving championship and Dad made me take
tennis lessons, the summer of my hopeless crush on
Howie, the lifeguard, and his beauty queen girlfriend.
The summer *Life* magazine featured two-page color
spreads of London call girls Christine Keeler and Mandy
Rice-Davies waving from their limo after testifying about
their meetings with British defense minister Profumo and
a Soviet military attaché. The two girls smiled bright as
stars, and Christine Keeler's shoulder-length flip was as
perfect as my cousin Donna's. Week after week, *Life*'s big
pages told the story.

"What's a call girl?" I asked.

"A what?" said Mom. Like most grown-ups Mom was
always busy—even when you thought she was doing
nothing.

"Why did she kill herself?"

"Who?"

"Marilyn Monroe."

"I really don't know, darling. She didn't tell me," Mom said, blotting her lipstick as she watched Dad walk slowly up from the lake.

August fifth, the announcer had said. August already. A month that sometimes stretches like forever. Still it's the last month before school, so however endless it seems, you're always worrying it might end.

"Come on, baby. Run along. Go make him take you sailing. Don't come back before six," Mom said, giving me a quick hug that sent me out the door.

So I left Mom smiling—not a flashy smile like Christine Keeler's, but the smile of a girl expecting someone, not knowing quite what to expect.

"Oh, Daddy!" I cried, racing down the lawn to meet him. He was wet and tired. He'd been sailing all morning. He didn't want to go back out on the lake again. He wanted a drink. "But you promised to take me out to the far point!" I cried, taking his hand. Dad looked down at me, then up to the house where Mom had disappeared from behind the glass door.

"You really want to go sailing?" Dad asked.

The winds were against us and we weren't back home before seven.

You know people and they disappear, maybe even not wanting to leave you.

That was a while ago.

"Life is just life," some say. "Why should it matter?" Yet to me it matters so much I sometimes see it all as clearly as if it were happening right now. At least, I *feel* as if I see it all so clearly, but there were actually two summers. There was the summer Bruce did the patio. Then there was the summer we had the backyard re-landscaped and *Life* featured Christine Keeler with her perky blond girlfriend who wasn't that pretty. Still, *Life* ran her picture too, since *Life* liked blondes, and it was all over with Marilyn Monroe the summer before.

That first summer, at least, everyone but Dad seemed fairly happy. But the second summer was different. That was the summer that changed things. I know these were separate summers, yet they seem so connected they sometimes bleed into each other like badly dyed T-shirts. I was ten when Bruce did the patio, eleven when we had the backyard re-landscaped. Still, I didn't feel as if the whole thing was really over until after I said goodbye to Frankie when we'd sat out back waiting for Sam that third summer I was finally twelve.

You can think about things a lot. Sometimes you can think of them so much, they seem as clear as the crow's cry bouncing like a skipping stone across the water. Only once the cry ends, or the stone drops back into the lake, you're suddenly uncertain, maybe even half panicked, like when you redo the main problem on your math test two minutes before the bell, only when you add it up once more, you get a different answer. But there's no time to check again.

The summer I was eleven was a busy summer, what with the lake and running after Howie, the lifeguard, and avoiding getting killed by my older brother, Tad. Not that he really would have killed me, but you know how it is with big brothers. They almost act as if they terrorize you as a favor. For Tad didn't have to bother with me. He had everything—grades and girls and being first in free-style on the swim team. He was such a good fighter none of the other boys dared cross him. And Tad was rich because every week he stole my allowance and my little brother

Sam's. Tad was so good at finding our money, I don't know why we still bothered to hide it.

Sam was four going on five. I'd just turned eleven. Tad was eighteen months older than me, still twelve. He and his best friend, Dave, were the bravest kids around. They even set fire to the woods once, but only Dave got blamed. That's because Tad was such a fraud the grown-ups liked him. I didn't like him, but sometimes just seeing him made me feel all sorry, like you feel for the kids who get picked last, which was crazy, since, like I told you, Tad was the boss. He and Dave would split the gang into two armies for war and organize tag games so big the whole neighborhood played. Tad always had some game you were supposed to be playing. Then, besides all the games and hanging around the beach, I had diving practice and tennis lessons. I also spent a lot of time walking up and down the back path calling my dog, Stormy, who was only mine because Mom felt guilty about the accident, for there I was sitting in the car waiting for Mom one day two summers before when I heard this screech like raging elephants on TV. You know how it is when you sense something awful just around the corner, but you feel like an idiot because you can't see it? I heard that noise and sat there wondering what to do for half a second that felt like hours before I threw myself down on the seat to pray.

Smash! came the truck. Bang! into the car and, suddenly, I was buried in broken glass with the engine right beside me. I leaped out of the crumpled station wagon, my mouth all sticky. People came running up from all over, but I couldn't ask anyone where Mom was since we weren't allowed to speak to strangers. Besides, the people were all staring past me at the wide-eyed truck driver stuck on his windshield. It was so gross I thought I'd throw up but, instead, out poured this blood and lots of teeth like when you slice a whole row of corn off the cob.

I didn't know what to do. The crowd started swirling around me like girls playing ring-around-the-rosy during recess as the world exploded into sirens. Then the nice policeman came.

"Don't wait for the ambulance," he told his partner, tucking me into the back seat.

They were just closing the car door when my mother wandered over.

"You're her mother? Get in," said the policeman. But Mom said she'd stay and get some witnesses' names for the insurance.

"Get in," the policeman repeated. Mom began to explain, but the cop cut her off.

"You're an unnatural mother," he said, shoving her into the squad car like she was some kind of criminal. The policeman was young and nice-looking, and nice-looking young men usually liked my mother, but this one didn't like her at all. He just sat in back holding me, getting bloody, while Mom sat up front next to his partner making small talk. At St. Mary's Hospital the nice policeman told everyone how I'd thrown myself on the seat to pray and the impact had buried me in the upholstery, which was what saved me. The nuns were mad about the story.

"It's a miracle she's alive," they whispered, passing the trays full of shiny instruments.

"She's just real lucky," the doctor laughed, stitching me up.

I didn't feel so lucky. I had cuts all over, and Mom was still angry at the policeman. Then a pretty nun brought me some orange juice that tasted funny and I fell asleep. I didn't wake up until after dark when I lay very still watching the wide green hall where nuns passed pushing carts full of bandaged people.

Mom looked less angry than sorry when she came back to the hospital that night to visit.

"Maybe I shouldn't have left you in the car so long, but it was legally parked. How could I have known a runaway truck would jump the divider? Now you've lost all your teeth!" Mom cried, exaggerating like always. So I shook my head and showed her the handkerchief full of teeth the nice policeman had picked up. Which only made Mom worse.

"How could I have known? How can I ever make it up to you?" she said, almost as if she were to blame. Mom felt so bad she hadn't even bothered switching on my light, but there was a fluorescent glow from the wide green hall.

"It wasn't your fault," I said, but Mom wasn't paying strict attention.

"How can I ever make it up to you?" Mom repeated, squeezing my hand with such a guilty look you might have thought I was some guy.

"I want a dog," I said. That woke her up.

"We already have a dog."

"I want a dog of my own," I insisted. For you know, there's a big difference. Mom said nothing, just released my hand and gave me the "Be reasonable, dear" smile she usually saved for Dad. Why does "Be reasonable" always have to mean "no"? I wouldn't take "no." It's not easy talking with your mouth full of stitches, but if you want something bad enough you can't just lie there. I started to open my mouth again, but the nun standing by the bed began to threaten Mom I'd hemorrhage.

"Okay, you win," said Mom, who was late for an appointment. And that's how I got Stormy, my black labrador, because of an accident, which wasn't so bad for me, at least, since most of my stitches were inside and the tooth fairy left ten dollars for the handkerchief full of teeth I put under my pillow. That's more than a dollar per tooth. And they were only baby teeth.

Mom wasn't a bad person. She could act worse than Tad sometimes, but I think she was just heartbroken over something, like the ladies in the fairy stories and the musty black book called *Victorian and Later English Poets* Mom read.

"'That's my last Duchess painted on the wall, / Looking as if she were alive. I call / That piece a wonder...'" Mom would begin, appearing before me like a ghost as I lay waiting for her to come tuck me in. "'She had a heart—how shall I say?—too soon made glad,'" Mom would murmur, turning the page like she was reading, though we both knew the poem by heart. "'I gave commands. / Then all smiles stopped together,'" she'd continue, taking the Duke's voice, for that's how the poem goes. The Duke speaks, telling how he murdered his last Duchess for nothing more than her wanting to live.

Mom wanted to live. Mom and I went everywhere together. Dad was more interested in staying home drinking, so he had three bars built into the family room, rec room, and library even before he had Bruce do the special outside bar for the patio. Dad built four bars, but he did most of his drinking standing over three bottles on a silver tray in an entrance hall corner that gave him a clear view of the front and back doors.

"All right, go! You and your daughter," Dad would say, shaking his drink as we walked out to the car. "You and *your daughter*," he'd sneer as we walked out past him.

Mom and I went everywhere together. Well, almost everywhere. And even when she didn't take me along I usually knew where Mom was going since she liked to ask me what she should wear. Mom told me everything always—family secrets, money secrets, even other people's secrets. I was her best friend, and had been ever since I could remember. Mom had a square face, blank as an angel's, which she always hid behind dark glasses. Still, whenever she came to fetch me, all the men turned to watch.

"Now there's a knockout," said Bruce, smiling.

"Pretty poison," said Barry, Bruce's brother.

"A killer, all right," said Frank the foreman.

"I'd kill myself if it weren't for you," Mom said, turning back to stare at me one night as we stood poised before her closet.

"What should I wear?" she'd sigh, then we'd talk about her choices as I searched her wardrobe for the inspiration while she watched.

Come to think of it, Mom was a lot like the angels in church paintings, always milling around God like so many gold-winged moths. For there they were, all grown up, still looking to Him for all the answers. Of course, Mom wasn't exactly like that. She didn't believe in God, and besides having no wings, Mom was a brunette. I'd never seen a picture of a dark angel, though one is mentioned in a sonnet Mom sometimes read.

"That's different," Mom said. "Shakespeare means 'dark,' not brunette."

I'm dark myself, though I was named for Mom's older sister who was pretty and blond and had all the friends.

"I would have hated her," I told Mom.

"It never occurred to me," Mom said, explaining how Alice-Marie wasn't just the life of the party. She was the party. Then one day Alice-Marie got sick with a fever and a stomachache. The doctor came over and said take aspirin. Alice-Marie's playmates came over and Alice-Marie said come tomorrow. But that night Alice-Marie's stomachache got worse and her fever got higher despite the aspirin she took every four hours until she died.

"She died of ruptured appendix and a bad diagnosis," said Mom, who explained how when your appendix ruptures they have to take it our right away and give you antibiotics or you sweat like crazy, get peritonitis and die within hours. That's why Mom got so serious about our stomachaches.

"Which side hurts? Let me take your temperature. No, it won't wait till after 'Walt Disney Presents,'" Mom would say, really meaning it for once. For there Alice-Marie was, laughing like always one day and they were carrying her out dead the next. That left only Mom. Her dad never got over it. He wouldn't even go downstairs for the funeral.

"She looks so alive," everyone at Alice-Marie's funeral marveled.

"Alice-Marie always looked alive," Mom told me.

"Go get your father," Grandmother told Mom since my grandmother couldn't reach him. No one could reach him. Mom's uncle had to make all the funeral arrangements while her dad just sat upstairs. After a while, the guests began to whisper.

"Go get your father," Grandmother repeated. So Mom went upstairs and found her dad sitting in the corner chair where he always used to read to Alice-Marie, not reading or weeping.

"Dad," Mom said, touching his shoulder. Then she stood there looking at him until she saw she could have gone on standing there like that forever. So finally she took his hand and said, "Dad, everybody's here."

"I know," her father said, not moving.

"Everybody's waiting," Mom repeated, because she couldn't go back downstairs without him.

At last Mom's dad stood up. He wasn't tall, but even hunched over with grief he was still a whole lot taller than she was. At the top of the stairs he paused to look at Mom. "You know, I wish it was you who died instead," he told her.

"I know," Mom said. She was only nine.

"I know you wish you were blond now, but all that soon changes," Mom promised, for she was already a beauty at twelve when she was sent to live with an uncle who owned half of Columbus he'd bought for cash in the Depression. Mom's dad was long gone and Uncle Ted was pretty strange, but Mom didn't care. All that mattered was no one in Columbus knew her as Alice-Marie's kid sister.

"So I became Alice-Marie," Mom said, making her face into a smile as she told of the dreams and dances and how she kept the boys all waiting for nothing, though none so bad as poor Jake, who drove twenty miles each day just to watch her cheerleading practice, when she wouldn't even let him drive her home after. "Can you fathom that!" Mom laughed. A heart breaker by twelve, she told me. And twelve was just the beginning, she said.

But twelve still seemed ages away the summer before Dad first hired Bruce. That's when the playhouse was doing the musical *Gypsy*, about a girl named Louise who isn't as pretty as her blond sister, June. Mom taught me Louise's lines because she wanted to see a friend and needed a reason to go to rehearsals. But it didn't work. The director from New York was impressed that I knew the lines, but he said I was simply too young for the part.

"Allie's old for her age," Mom insisted. But the director just laughed and cast another girl. Then one day he called and asked, "Does Allie still remember the lines?"

"Of course," said Mom. "She remembers everything."
So they took me after all.

I don't know if you've ever seen *Gypsy*, but it's mostly a
story of courage because the little girl finds a way to take
care of everyone. But it's also a true story, so it's still sort of
sad in the end.

Nobody cares about young Louise in the first act and I
have to sing "Let Me Entertain You" very badly. But it's all
right, because in the second act I grow up to be Gypsy
Rose Lee, the famous stripper. (Not me personally, of
course, but a pretty lady from New York in a sparkly cos-
tume.) The lady from New York sang "Let Me Entertain
You" so well, just watching her was such an inspiration,
that after our third performance the director forbade me
ever to watch her again.

"You're *supposed* to sing it awkward. You play 'before,'
she plays 'after.' You're just a little girl," he said.

That was the summer my boyfriend Billy's father died. I
was the only girl on the block who wasn't a sissy, so lots of
boys came to the door, but I especially liked Billy. He was
a whole year older and always helpful, like when he taught
me how to ride a bike. No one else would bother to take
the time, but Billy took me to the top of the big hill, put
me on his bike, and pushed. I made it all the way down to
the bottom before discovering I didn't know how to turn
or stop.

"What if a car had been coming? Look at you, you're a
mess!" Mom said, spraying Bactine, which stung like
crazy, on my scraped knees. "Now stay in the yard and
stay away from Billy!" Mom called as I ran off to pick up
the fine points of turning and stopping.

But about Billy's father. Billy didn't much like him. Not
that Billy talked about it. Billy never said much about any-

thing. The other boys all asked you to marry them, but Billy made no promises. He just came to the door for me every day until he and his mother moved away. I guess they left pretty sudden, but then his dad died sort of sudden. I know, because he dropped dead on stage beside me during *Gypsy*'s previews.

We were both standing there listening to Mama Rose talk when Billy's father gave this great gasping slurp like the blob makes when it gobbles you up—only different. Someone's last gasp is like the sound of a bone breaking. Even if you've never heard that crack before, to hear it is to know it. It was the same with Billy's father. I just knew he was dead.

The lady playing Mama Rose kept on talking as though nothing had happened. I looked to the wings for help, but there was only the prompter staring back speechless as Billy's father collapsed, toppling onto me like a limp truck. We came down with a thud, the same second as the curtain. Then people came running up from everywhere along with the doctor who opened Billy's father's shirt and two more doctors who tried all sorts of banging and thumping on his chest before they quit and covered Billy's dad up.

I always thought a sheet stretched over your head was the end, but people kept milling around like the show wasn't over. And sure enough, Mom appeared looking pale and pretty as the nights she read me poems. The doctors crowded around her. That was too much for Billy's mother, who was standing beside me on the sidelines. She stared straight at Mom and laughed real mean, so I stared right back at Billy's mom. At first she pretended not to notice. But Billy's mom couldn't ignore me forever. At last she looked down at me, face full of regret. "I know it's not your fault," she said, touching my shoulder. "I hear my son's in love with you," she added, trying to smile, only she cried.

At first everyone was worried about finding a replacement, but we got me a new father from the city and the show went on to a nice run.

I believe my mother dreamed of doing many things before she settled on just living. That must be why she went to college all those extra years. That's where my parents met—in college. You go to college to meet people, then in graduate school you finally settle on just one. Dad went to law school, which he hated. Mom got a doctorate in English. There were tons of books upstairs and I was dying for Mom to tell me what they taught her, but Mom mostly talked about her beaux. Mom talked so much about her suitors I almost felt as if I had chosen with her. I knew that Erich was rich but a foreigner, and that Donnie had been the nicest, only he was too short if you wanted to have sons.

"And I did have two sons," Mom said, as if maybe I hadn't noticed. So many boyfriends got the same answer, Mom's rejects made husbands for half her sorority.

"So why did you marry Dad?" I asked, and Mom just smiled like she was about to let me in on some big secret. Then she showed me an old snapshot which seemed no answer at all. Still, the more I looked, the more I got the picture.

"Whatever you do, don't get married," Mom said, handing over the picture of a handsome navy pilot in dress whites patting the nose of his favorite plane.

The war was long ago. Landing on aircraft carriers like Dad did was dangerous. You had to put the plane down on a moving ship and catch the tripwire at the end of the deck. If you didn't catch the tripwire you went skidding

off into the water. Lots of guys Dad knew won their dog-
fights only to get killed landing, so it was a good thing
Dad's bosses in Washington decided to call him home.

"That was lucky for you," Mom said. And it sure was,
since I wasn't born yet. In fact, Dad's bosses called him
home because they were thinking of the future—not my
future, of course. They were getting ready for their new
fight with the Russians, who were already busy spying on
us, only we had trouble spying back since native-born
Americans can't speak Russian without an accent. Dad
spoke perfect Russian because he wasn't born in America.
He was born in London, which is why it was so funny
when Mom claimed Dad spoke English with an accent.

Mom says that's how Dad got hooked up with J. Edgar
Hoover, whose FBI fought spies. She told me that Dad
had to sneak around and sometimes even break into
houses. I thought he must be pretty brave to do that, but
Mom said it was just an excuse to be violent. "Using a gun
doesn't make you brave," she said, only she wouldn't explain. And Dad didn't talk about his spying any more than
he talked about the war, so I don't really know if he was
brave. All I know is that before Dad quit he wound up on
the wrong side of some bad people who swore they'd get
him. That's why he was still supposed to carry a gun, only
he often left it lying out next to the green dish full of
change and bullets on his dresser upstairs.

I don't know how Mom and Dad finally found our
house. I know they traveled some after the war and lived
in Washington, New York, and another country. I don't
know why they moved—whether it was because of Dad's
work, or if they did it hoping to be happy. I don't know if
it made them happy. All I know for sure is that they ended
up in a big gray stucco house with black shutters and a
back lawn you could roll on all the way down to the lake.

"The backyard used to be just woods. Fawns came right up to the door. Deer hunters too. I used to dress you in red for fear they'd shoot you by mistake," said Mom, who was so afraid of water, heights, and guns I sometimes thought she imagined things.

"There were hunters right on the back path," she insisted, but I didn't believe her until she found a picture of me in a red snowsuit crawling past a "No Hunting" sign. Even then it was hard to imagine men with rifles stalking our woods, for the back path was special. It was nobody's yard, and all the neighbor dogs knew it. The path wound all the way around the lake before disappearing. It was the shortest way to almost anywhere, but no one I met had ever walked clear to its end.

Mom said Spring Lakes used to be pretty wild. It could still get wild. There were hurricanes with thunder and lightning that zapped trees and knocked out the electricity so that we had to use candles to find our way upstairs.

"Be careful, or your hair will catch fire," Mom warned, lighting mine.

"Watch your sister," Mom told Tad, but he never listened.

I took the candle upstairs and didn't notice anything, even after Tad started screaming "Her hair's on fire!"— because that's just the sort of trick Tad likes to play. Then I smelled something burning and saw strands of hair flare up like sparklers beside my eyes. I couldn't move. I just stood there screaming, paralyzed, like in a nightmare, until Mom raced up, threw me on the bed, and covered me with blankets. She nearly smothered me, but I stopped screaming. Mom almost seemed a different person. She knew what to do.

"Look what happened to your pretty hair!" Mom said,

digging me out from the singed blankets. True, my hair was singed and my pajamas were scorched, but I would have forgotten the whole thing by now if only everyone didn't keep talking about "the night you caught fire" like it was hell, when it was just my pajamas.

Hurricane Hazel came and went. It changed nothing. But the summer before everything fell apart was also the summer Dad built a bilevel stone patio big enough for a whole party to watch the sun set over the lake. Actually, Bruce and his men did the real building. They came for a week, and ended up staying the whole summer.

"Just like a builder—they're all alike," Dad would say, shaking his head when he walked out back to check their progress each evening after fixing his first drink.

"Bruce was the best outfielder ever," said Dave, my older brother Tad's best friend. Dave was always in trouble, yet he never fought me. Most people thought that was out of respect for me as Tad's sister, but it was from fear, not respect. Most girls don't fight, or if they do fight, fight fair. But you can't fight fair with boys, because they're stronger and they'll beat you. So whenever a boy tries to punch me out, I bite and scratch.

I'm not saying I'm brave. I used to let Tad push me around just like everybody else. Then one day I came home and found a pile of shredded paper on my bed. At first I couldn't figure what it was. I sat down on the bed and sifted through the pile like you might sort pieces of a puzzle. Suddenly, I saw the face of my favorite paper doll in one of the scraps. That's when I just went crazy. Tad was so mean he didn't just destroy my dolls, he tortured them!

"I'll get you new paper dolls," Mom said. But I didn't want a new paper doll for Tad to shred. I wanted blood. I went looking for Tad and just threw myself on him—temporary insanity, like in the movies. The whole neighborhood came to watch.

I wanted blood and I got it before they pulled me off and raced me to the emergency room for needles and catgut.

"At least most of the stitches are in your eyebrows," sighed Mom, who didn't see you have no choice fighting a bully. There's no hope of justice, no hope of getting even. But there's also no surrender. That makes you strong. Even my getting murdered was nothing beside my hurting Tad a little because Tad was such a good fighter he'd forgotten what it was like to get hurt.

I'm not ashamed of biting Tad, only of biting all the other boys who were my friends. It wasn't fair that everybody called them crybabies. I don't know why they never told on me.

"How could Allie hurt such big boys?" all the neighbor ladies would say, shaking their heads.

Nobody guessed the truth, except my mother.

"Why do you bite those poor boys?" she'd ask.

I don't know why I bit them any more than I know why I slapped the baby-sitter. But I did. It was right after my bath. Mrs. Hanson stood me on a chair and, just like that, I reached over and smacked her. We stood there eye to eye a second. Then she slapped me back.

"The poor woman was so upset. She kept saying you'd always been such a good little girl," said Mom, who thought it funny Mrs. Hanson was less upset that I'd slapped her than that she slapped me back.

That was years ago, of course, when I was just a baby of six or seven. I got out of the tub and Mrs. Hanson stood me up on a chair. It was the first time I remember ever having seen a grown-up's face at eye level. There was no reason. It was just like the biting. Mrs. Hanson started to dry me and I slapped her full in the face with all my might.

Chapter
Two

*I*t was the perfect place to grow up, our parents told us, what with the club and tennis and the fresh green lawn that rolled down to the lake. The lake was green too, clear emerald green by the rocks and slimy green around the edges. But there was nothing greener than the leaves outside my window, where I had what Mom called "a balcony worthy of Juliet."

Spring Lakes was full of lawyers and their families living year round in big stucco houses that were once summer homes for the rich. The town sprang up back in the twenties when they'd just invented cars and everybody made a fortune in the market. All the houses had three floors. Some even used to belong to famous people. Tad said World War One ace Eddy Rickenbacker used to fly in for his girlfriend's dances and land his helicopter on her roof.

Mom said that Tad was just kidding. Dave told me the big stone house on the hill was haunted, but Dad said it was still vacant because the estate was tied up in court.

Mom and Dad bought our house because Mom loved the balcony, but Dad liked the mahogany paneling on the third floor, so they lived up there in a dark bedroom looking out on the lake in back and a room full of books facing the front. Other houses' top floors had lower ceilings, but ours were still a full ten feet. The landing just outside my parents' door had a tall window like in church and made a great lookout. You could see half a mile down the road each way even in summer when the trees were out. Still, I didn't much like the third floor. It was too big really, full of empty guest rooms and abandoned baths that would have been great for playing hide-and-seek, since the floors weren't too creaky. But even the squirrels who crawled in from the attic were quiet because the third floor was built around the library, where Dad slept more than he worked.

My parents' bedroom had big windows blocked by heavy curtains and was full of the black lacquered furniture Mom bought from the widow who used to own our house. Everyone admired the strange octagonal chests and big round mirrors.

"They're Art Deco, too," Mom said. Still, I thought they only made the dark room look even creepier, casting all kinds of shadows, so every corner was alive. The room was dead by day, though the floors creaked nights when we heard my parents fighting, their voices loud enough to wake us up, yet too far off to understand.

"What should we do?" I'd ask, creeping into Tad's room, Sam trailing me tight as a shadow.

"Get lost," said Tad, who was busy sorting his comics into cartons by brand name and superhero.

"What should we do?" I'd ask, and Tad would just look at me like I was stupid, because he didn't know the answer.

Upstairs was scary. But my room was full of sunshine.

"You're a very lucky little girl," Mom said, because my windows opened out into the trees like you were sleeping in a treehouse.

"Look," I said, reaching out to touch a branch. "I could climb out my very own window."

"They're not windows, they're French doors," said Mom, who'd been to Paris. But it didn't matter what you called them. All that mattered was that when you leaned out my window at night, you could see lights dancing in a corner of the mansion owned by a lady who was once the girl a famous ace flew in to see.

I believe what Dad said about the stone house not being haunted, but I also believe what Tad said about the girl and the ace, because the old lady's house really did have a ballroom. It's all closed up now. The crystal chandeliers are draped with dustcovers and only white sheets thrown over the furniture still dance in the breeze. Still, the ballroom exists. I know because Tad, Dave and I sneaked past the gardener and looked in the windows once to see.

Spring Lakes is a funny town because it isn't really a town, just a beach, two clubs, two churches, and some houses. Not everyone could live there, but everyone who did needed a station wagon because there was no place to buy anything besides sporting equipment at the club pro shops. Dad said there was even a law forbidding you to build a house on less than two acres. That's why the tag games were so good. Those big lawns and fat hedges were just made for our dodging and hiding. Sometimes Tad would have two dozen kids tearing around the neighborhood ignoring the strings supposed to keep us off newly

seeded lawns. This made some people very angry, but Tad
didn't care. He thought having to dodge both the kid who
was "it" and the people in the houses made the game more
fun.

"Who trampled this lawn?" Dad would say, getting
angry whenever he noticed new muddy patches tracked
with sneaker skid marks.

"Some neighbor kids, I guess," Tad would say.

"What do you know about this, Allie?" Dad would ask,
turning to me for a straight answer. But there was nothing
I could say, for I was not a tattletale.

"Goddammit!" Dad would swear, whenever he came
home enough before dark to see how many patches needed
replanting. It was like an endless war. We'd have a great
tag game. Dad would reseed. We'd play again. Dad would
go crazy—as if the lawn weren't there for running, but
only to look at, like Mom's antique blue-on-white Chinese
rug.

The battle with Tad finally wore Dad down so, he
couldn't face the lawn himself and called in reinforce-
ments. I think that's why Dad first hired Bruce. He
wanted Bruce's men to put terraced gardens in the lawn so
we'd twist our ankles, only Mom got ideas about building
patios and the lawn had to wait. Mom was going to throw
parties on the patios. Labor Day parties. Fourth of July
parties. But Mom never used the patios for parties. In fact,
Mom stopped giving parties altogether by the time Bruce's
men started re-landscaping the far back.

"What do you want that son of a bitch to plant?" Dad
asked Mom over dinner once at the start of that second
summer. She just looked at him, and Dad went right on
talking since he was only asking because he knew Mom
didn't know the first thing about flowers. Even when he
wasn't drinking, Dad loved to make you squirm.

My dad was a lawyer like everyone else's dad, only he didn't wear glasses. The neighbor ladies called him dashing. I know that he was tall and could play good tennis. He taught me how to sail and dive like a champion and he could shoot guns and fly airplanes. Sometimes he'd rent a little plane and take me flying, which is beautiful, only it makes your heart beat faster than a mad hare thumps. Other days Dad would go off to target practice and bring back posters of shadow men shot full of holes. Our neighbor Mrs. Baskin said my mother should consider herself lucky. What more could she want, asked Mrs. Baskin.

I guess I wanted not to feel sorry each time that I saw Dad.

"You want a lot," Mom told me, sipping her iced tea as if it were champagne. I always thought Mom should be in the movies, smoking long cigarettes and eating chocolates, but she never ate chocolates, smoked, chewed gum, or drank much of anything besides iced tea. "Unladylike," Mom said, not seeming to notice she swore worse than Dad.

It was pretty bad at home. I'm sure other kids' parents also had their problems. Still, my parents didn't like each other much, although they sometimes went out to parties and the theater with other parents who stopped by for drinks. Not that my Dad needed much company for drinking.

"Aren't we starting the party a little early?" Mom would say in her fake cheery voice as the ice crusher started up Saturday morning. But her remarks only made Dad drink more, so Mom gave up the helpful hints and just kept worrying about what would happen. That's what made having people over so tense—Mom worrying, Dad drinking, Mom getting all wound up watching Dad drink.

Mom shouldn't have worried so. Dad was amazing. He

could drink all day and never act sloppy with outsiders. Mean, yes. But Dad was always mean, and whenever grown-ups stand around drinking long enough someone is bound to get nasty. Dad wasn't even always the meanest. Yet no matter how many couples came by for drinks, Mom always looked the prettiest with her red lipstick, gypsy earrings, and rustling taffeta dresses in half the colors of the rainbow, though I liked the red one best. We kids hated how Mom and Dad fought when they were dressing, yet we knew the fuss was worth it once they'd left. My parents used to go out every weekend, but they still didn't like each other much when they came home.

Mom started getting dressed right after making us kids eat dinner. "Don't forget the Dickersons' party tonight," she'd remind Dad.

"Come on," she'd say, after a few more hints.

"I don't know if I'm going," Dad would answer, still standing around in his blue terry robe.

"They're your friends too," Mom would say, smiling, eyes wide from the strain of not screaming.

"Are they?" Dad would ask, picking up his drink and a magazine. Mom would look at him settling into his chair, then stalk off on her high heels.

"Eight forty-five. Christ!" Mom would say, walking into my room to pace by the window, leaving a cloud of perfume when she went back upstairs.

"Come on," she'd plead, watching Dad eye himself in the full-length hall mirror.

"Why are we doing this?" Dad would ask, fixing his tie with a sharp yank to show he'd had his fill of suits during the week. Dad studied the crease in his pants and adjusted his jacket. Mom stood there, thinking he was almost ready. Only once Dad finally got dressed, he fixed another drink.

"Nine thirty. Jesus!" Mom would say, racing back into

my room and throwing herself down to cry on my extra bed. Ada hated to bleach the white cover, but it was the only way that she could get out the mascara marks Mom left.

"All right, I'm leaving," Dad would yell from downstairs, slamming the door as Mom jumped up, calling to me for her purse and a cold washcloth.

"I can't stand this," she'd say, racing downstairs, her gold earrings tinkling. "What can I tell them?" she'd ask, all worried since she'd already used up the good excuses like injured children and car breakdowns. My parents used to go to parties, only they kept leaving home later and later. Then they finally stopped going out.

Weekdays Mom had to sit with Dad while he had dinner. Then he would talk and it was trouble if you interrupted, even if you said "Excuse me" first. The smart thing was for us kids to eat fast and disappear upstairs as soon as possible. If Dad came home after seven, we'd pretend we'd already eaten. I'm sure Dad knew that we were lying. But he didn't much care about having dinner with us kids. All he wanted to do was drink and complain.

Yet I remember how once, long ago, we used to wait dinner for Dad, and Mom would make us get cleaned up for him like he was something special. Then I'd go sit out at the end of the driveway, watching the road till he came.

"What's this?" Dad would call, flicking his headlights as he drove in. "What are you doing out here?" he'd ask, his voice friendly, not yet suspicious. Then he would pick me up and carry me inside, since I was even lighter than a bag of groceries then.

"Oh, hi," Mom would say as Dad set me and his briefcase down. "Did you have a good day?" she'd ask, sort of nervous since she was always scared she might do the wrong thing. Mom still tried to share things at dinner. It wasn't like later when she'd just sit there.

"Come feel the baby kick," she once said, touching her big stomach when she was pregnant with Sam. Tad and Dad just looked at Mom like she'd burped, so I had to walk over and hold out my hand, which Mom took, guiding my fingers along her stomach.

"There. No, here!" she said, all excited, like it was some great mystery, when I'd been kicking inside her myself just a few years before.

"What's this mess?" Dad interrupted, pointing to some boxes the delivery man had left that morning after unloading the new dining room chandelier Dad hadn't even mentioned.

"Nothing," Mom said, falling silent. Back then Dad didn't have to hit Mom to make an impression. He could still hurt her with a look.

I remember some summers Dad used to come home early enough to play tennis. Then he started coming later and later. As far as we were concerned, he couldn't come late enough. Dad was home evenings and holidays, which are supposed to be the happy times but were really the worst. We were all a lot happier when Dad was gone. Dad left each morning around eight thirty. Bruce's crew began drifting in a few minutes later. By then my little brother Sam and I were already on the back path to the beach. The lifeguards didn't start till nine, but Howie always came a little early because he ran the beach.

Howie was my best friend. He wore a whistle, a stopwatch, and a baby blue bathing suit with LIFEGUARD stitched in big red letters on the side. His whistle hung from a braided blue plastic lanyard I gave him. His girlfriend, Christine, said the lanyard was so ugly he had to get rid of it, but Howie said it went fine with the suit.

Howie was tall, brown-haired and tan except for his

sunburned shoulders and his nose, which was pink as a rabbit's when you could see it. But most of the time Howie's nose was white with sunblock, which made him look so funny Tad couldn't figure why Howie rated a pretty girl like Christine. I'll tell you why. Howie had the world's best personality. He was real smart yet still sort of nice, like he cared about everyone, though you could see right away he cared most about me and about our kitten Fluff.

Christine was just Howie's girlfriend. She drove to the beach each afternoon to talk with him. Then she'd sit just there on the guard stand between us, trying to look cool. "Don't you have to go home?" she'd finally ask me, and Howie would frown at her because she kept forgetting I never left before Howie closed the beach. That's the best time of all, when the guards get off and hang around to play a game of tag under the docks, which isn't allowed when the guards are on duty.

"Just for ten minutes," Howie would say, 'cause all the lifeguards' girls were waiting. But those games were so great we'd keep playing long after everyone was dying of hunger and had missed dinner so that all the mothers in town would be mad. Sometimes we played so late all the girlfriends gave up and drove off.

"Okay, you guys, everybody out of the water now, it's dark," Howie would say at last, and we'd groan and swear we could still see, making Howie laugh when we had to borrow his flashlight to find our towels. Then Howie would walk Sam and me home up the back path, even though we hadn't asked him. Walking along we heard the frogs begin to croak and the sound of sprinklers starting up each night, "like vespers," said Howie.

"What are vespers?" I asked Mom, who was worried when Howie first became my friend. Then she discovered

Howie was Mrs. Barton's son who went to divinity school in Boston.

"It's a sin you're too young for him," said Mom. For Howie was rich. You could never have guessed it from the way he acted. But Christine probably knew. I bet that's why she came around, acting all ladylike and quiet. Whenever Christine was around Howie got quiet too. Sometimes I'd get so bored I'd put Fluff on Howie's shoulders like a parrot and she'd crawl around his sunburn.

"That's disgusting! I'm leaving!" Christine would say, glaring at me as she jumped up.

"Patience," said Howie. Mom told me she thought Howie was more patient than God. I thought I was pretty patient myself waiting around for him each morning. The lifeguards didn't start until nine. That's hours after sunrise when I got up with nothing to do but walk Stormy, who always ran away to hunt. The paperboy didn't come till seven. Even the TV was only snowflakes before six thirty when Sam finally crawled out of bed and "The Modern Farmer" came on. The show's credits would just be ending when Mom came downstairs to fix the eggs Dad never ate because he felt awful mornings. Sometimes his stomach felt so bad he couldn't even drink his coffee. Still, he sat in the breakfast room skimming his paper, while Sam and I went out to look for Stormy until we saw Dad's car was gone.

I think breakfast is important. That's why I always waited for Dad to drive off before I sat down at the breakfast table, poured the milk on my Rice Krispies, and put my ear to the bowl. You always get a few Rice Krispies in your hair if you get too close, but I love to hear them murmur like a conch shell that listens to the waves so long it ends up sounding like the sea. I'm not sure why Rice Krispies whisper like there's a fairy locked inside them, but

I do know that if you listen to them too long they get soggy, and while Grape-Nuts taste better soggy, soggy Rice Krispies are just gross.

I always ate very quickly once I got started, but Sam liked to study the box, pretending to read the special offers, so that no matter when we started breakfast we always had to rush to be at the parking lot waiting when Howie drove in with milk for Fluff.

Fluff was a little gray and white girl kitten with long hair soft as my pink angora sweater. Fluff wasn't a hunter like Stormy. All Fluff ever did was sit in my lap. "Isn't she good?" I'd say, because I knew it was Howie's influence. That summer I found dozens of stray cats I brought Howie, but it always turned out they already belonged to someone else.

"She just has sunstroke," said Christine, who was mean by nature, for there was no reason she should have hated me and Fluff.

"She's only joking," said Howie. Still, from that day on I made him cover Fluff with his pith helmet. Then Howie's forehead got burned too, yet I don't think that he much minded. Fluff was such a good cat that she never did anything. But the best thing about Fluff was that her real owner never came to pick her up.

"Allie must be bothering you," Mom would tell Howie whenever she dropped by the beach.

"She doesn't bother me," said Howie.

"Still, her cat must, scratching your sunburn."

"Oh, the skin would peel off anyway," said Howie. He was nice that way.

Not that Mom stopped by the beach much after Bruce started work.

"Just wear a smile and a Jantzen," said the tag on Mom's powder-blue striped suit, a one-piece with a built-in bra that made her feel like a turtle when you gave her a hug. Mom said she was a perfect size nine, and I know she never grew an inch the whole time I knew her.

"But I've changed," she said. And it was true.

"It happens to us all," she explained, telling me about a little yellow wool bikini she gave away because of stretch marks. "From you kids," she sighed. "It's the way of all women: stretch marks, varicose veins, then death." That would have scared me if Mom had varicose veins, but her legs were as white as Christine Keeler's. My legs were just a mess of mosquito bites and scratches. "How do you find a place for the new ones?" Mom asked.

I didn't know. That was the bugs' problem. But if what Mom said was true, my grandmother should have had stretch marks and varicose veins—for Grandma was old. So old she liked to say, "How can you do that, when I may never see you again?" as her eyes filled with tears. But it was impossible to check Mom's theory by looking at Grandma. Grandma wore gloves and pearls. Not just pearl buttons on her Sunday gloves like me, but whole strings of pearls around her neck and layer upon layer of clothes, even in summer, so that even if she agreed to show you the stretch marks, you'd probably end up having to go before she peeled off all those clothes.

Even with all the clothes, Grandma was thin as paper. She had very light skin, no wrinkles, and always smelled old as a box of clothes from the attic.

"Chantilly," Mom said, but I don't think that it came from a bottle. I began to suspect no one had ever seen Grandma's stomach. She always wore cream-colored stockings, so I'm not even sure she had real legs. Sometimes I wondered if Grandma was secretly a mummy. She looked brittle, like if you touched her in the wrong place she might break. She wouldn't travel by airplane, which is also very suspicious, since I understand vampires prefer to travel by land. Grandma always came by train, stepping out of the sleeper with a present for Tad, not looking a bit like the jolly grandmothers you saw baking in all the cookie advertisements. I never saw my grandmother in the kitchen, though I once saw her taking off her stockings. Real silk stockings she rolled up so carefully I could see it was an art. Underneath the stockings were more stockings, but she spotted me before I got to see her take those off.

"Isn't she pretty?" Mom would say, whenever Grandma stepped onto the platform followed by a porter and some gentleman who'd adopted her for the trip. "Because she's a lady," Mom said. And so Grandmother would introduce the stranger to "Mrs. Gardner, my daughter," and he would compliment Mom on Grandmother and they'd all shake hands and say a few words before he disappeared. In all the times I went to the station to meet her, Grandma never introduced me. In fact, she always looked a little hurt to find me still there.

"Isn't she pretty?" Mom would say each time we spotted Grandma. She was okay, I guess, but Grandma hadn't been a beauty like my great-aunt Ella, who was so pretty she was already a legend at twelve—and that was before telephones.

"I never saw her myself," Mom said, but there was a boy who moved out to Oregon with his family when Ella was still little who came back by wagon train braving Indians and everything just to see Ella at fifteen. He became sort of a legend too, though some people thought that what he did was crazy. He rode into town, cleaned up, and had tea with Aunt Ella and her parents. "I just had to see how she turned out," he said. Then he turned around and rode all the way back to Oregon alone.

"For of course she wouldn't marry him," Mom told me,

though I don't know why Mom said "of course" since my
great-aunt Ella married three times, always moving west,
getting richer and leaving her children behind until she
finally ended up in Los Angeles owning half of Brentwood. Brentwood was just farms when Ella's third husband first bought land there, but it's full of people now,
according to Mom, who said Aunt Ella's last husband was
a famous bandleader. He died before Aunt Ella divorced
him, which may mean she ended up happy. I can't say for
sure because no one in my mother's family would speak to
Aunt Ella, though everyone still talked about her. That's
because Aunt Ella was so beautiful and had three husbands
back when nobody nice did that.

"She looks a little like Ella," Grandma said, frowning at
me. Mom said Grandma didn't mean to be rude by not
speaking to me directly. In the old days grown-ups never
used to talk directly to kids, but hired other grown-ups to
speak for them. It was just a custom, Mom said, like "children should be seen and not heard," only Grandma was
much too refined to say that. Grandma was so refined she
still wore a corset. I don't know how she managed to
breathe.

Grandma was the last besides Mom of an old family that
came from England and helped finance the Revolution.
They also fought in the Civil War for the North because
they were all Republicans and, besides, that's where they
lived. Mom's people didn't like change and thought Frank-
lin Roosevelt was the devil. They were all born Republicans and they died Republicans, even the uncle with the
estate where they held their family reunions each year before 1929, when he went into the garden and shot himself.

"He bought on margin," said Mom, which is maybe
what Marilyn Monroe did. I wanted to know all about that
uncle, but Mom only remembered swinging in his garden.

"I was very young," she said. And besides, a whole lot of her family killed themselves over the Crash. That's why Mom went to live with Uncle Ted, who'd kept his cash at home, bought real estate, and was very rich before half his money was stolen by a friend who went to prison. When Uncle Ted's friend got out of prison, Uncle Ted took him back and his friend stole the rest. Mom said it was a monster scandal. Still, that's what I liked about Mom's family. They financed revolutions which, even when they won, they lost.

"Thank God your great-grandmother was already dead," Mom said, for Uncle Ted had been her favorite. Mom said my great-grandmother Maria, pronounced Ma-RI-a like they called the wind, didn't look like anyone else in the whole family. She was near six feet tall and dark, not like her brothers or her brainy sister who was the third woman in the whole country to get a doctorate, but so plain she ended up marrying a professor and breeding Pomeranian dogs.

"Who are you looking for?" the shriveled Reverend asked my mother once, years ago, when she stopped by a country churchyard to find my great-grandmother's grave. For Maria Moody was dead then. She hadn't died young, or tragically. Still, she had died before my mother ever knew her, so I don't know why Mom risked going to a graveyard to visit a lady she never even met.

When Mom told the old man why she'd come he smiled.

"She's over here," he said. It was a big, haphazard cemetery, yet the old man walked Mom right over to Maria Moody's grave. Half of Mom's family was buried in that cemetery, so Mom got out her list and the old man showed her the plots and pointed out each headstone, telling Mom what happened to each person in between the chiseled dates. As the old man talked, the sky darkened and the leaves began to rustle. It may sound scary, but Mom says she wasn't frightened, even though the old man was a stranger and they were the only two living souls for miles around. Mom was just worried that she'd left the car windows open, so she told the old man she had to go and he showed her out.

Big, slow drops of rain had started falling and Mom was anxious about her car windows, but the old man didn't seem to notice as he took both Mom's hands in his and searched her face.

"Who are you?" he asked. They'd talked about a lot of dead people, but Mom knew right away what the old man meant.

"I'm Maria Moody's granddaughter," she told him, but he didn't seem to listen. That's when Mom said she finally got frightened, when the old man clutched her hands and stared at her like he was looking for something lost or half forgotten.

"Maria Moody was the most beautiful woman who ever walked through these church doors," the old man said at last. Then he turned and walked away.

It must make you very happy to be as pretty as Maria Moody, with cheekbones high as an Indian's and brown eyes deep as a dream. I only saw one picture of my great-grandmother, in an antique gold locket studded with diamonds and rubies, a locket with a story all its own. But the locket was stolen. Mom offered a big reward, no questions asked. Still, no one took Mom's money, and the picture was gone. That left only a book, old like the books of poems Mom got in college. Mom told me it was the family Bible. "David loves Maria with all his heart and all his soul," said the writing on the first page. The date underneath was October 5, 1867. David Moody was my great-grandfather and October fifth was my great-grandparents' wedding date. I liked the inscription very much, especially since there were no love letters from Dad to Mom for me to read. Mom said David Moody was very tall too. Even taller than Maria. I liked to think of the Moodys driving around in their carriage, tall and beautiful, with David loving Maria with all his heart and all his soul. I imagined them very happy, happier even than the Prince and Cinderella.

"They were divorced," Mom said, closing the book.

But my grandmother wasn't like that. She was too boring to be beautiful, yet pretty enough to marry well once, then again in her thirties, when her first husband died. Even Mom admitted Grandma was boring, "which is what made her such a good mother for young children." Grandma wasn't real nice to me. Maybe that's because I was too old already. But my brother Tad was even older and she always brought Tad a present, something special with a battery like they showed on TV.

Once, long ago, before I could even read, Mom's best friend came from far away where Mom grew up and brought each of us a present. Jane Wright was a pale, skinny lady with long red hair who just appeared at the door one day sort of nervous asking, "Is this where Jeanne Gardner lives?" She was so pale and thin I thought at first she was a fairy, but Mom said no, she had just come to New York to see some doctors and was her childhood friend. So Mom fixed iced tea and took her friend up to my room where they stretched out on the beds and talked till way past time Mom should have started fixing dinner.

There is nothing greener than the leaves outside my window. There's nothing softer than a summer evening with all the stickiness rained out. The only trouble is when I leave the windows open all the leaves blow in and get crunched up on the white carpet. You might think this

only happens in the fall. But the leaves start drifting in by
August. Still, you have to leave the windows open. That's
the whole point of the room.

Mom and her friend didn't come downstairs till almost
dark. The lady cried when she hugged Mom. Then she
gave each of us a present. I only saw her that once, but she
brought me my first storybook. The story was Cinderella,
but the book was mostly pictures of pumpkin coaches,
fairy godmothers, palaces, and party gowns with skirts big
enough to hide three children. I liked the story so much I
read it each night to Sam before the pages got all fuzzy
from my pointing to the pictures of the pumpkin coaches
and the small glass slipper that the prince took house to
house. It was such a pretty story that I wanted to believe
it. I asked Mom where Cinderella lived, but she wasn't
certain. The pictures of the palace made me think she lived
in London like Christine Keeler. Cinderella sure must have
been some dancer for the prince to make that fuss.

Chapter Three

"Ever wonder why we're here?" Howie said as we sat in the sun splitting a cherry ice so cold it burned your tongue. It was pretty clear I was there to take care of Mom, who was supposed to take care of Dad, only she kept messing up. She didn't think far enough ahead, making up jokes and songs to keep him busy. She didn't laugh right. She didn't smile no matter what. To see Mom laughing with some other man you'd think she'd be great at entertaining Daddy, but the truth is that she never much liked the job.

"I've got a migraine," she'd say. Dad said Mom was World Champion for migraines. Mom didn't care, she'd just go upstairs and take some pills. That left no one to talk with Dad but me.

"Dad," I'd say, sort of soft but steady, friendly yet wary like a lion tamer stepping into the cage for his routine.

"Come on, Dad," I'd coax, trying to remind him of our connection while he looked through me like a neighbor dog who pretends you're a stranger whenever he wants to bark.

"Hey, Dad," I'd say, starting a story, any story, just so it starred the two of us. "Do you remember the time you and I drove all the way to Princeton to go flying, but when we got there the plane wouldn't start?"

Dad barely grunted, still I could see he remembered how the blue sky above us had seemed to soar the whole drive out. But when we got to the airport there was trouble. Dad and the mechanic kept fussing over the engine while I stood in the crabgrass by the runway watching the other planes take off.

Dad, the mechanic, and me—we were all three hot and tired.

"It's just a gauge," said Dad, when I came to see what was taking him so long.

The mechanic was scowling. "It's more than the gauge," he said.

"Come on, get in," Dad told me.

"You can't take this thing up," the mechanic muttered.

"Don't tell me what I can do," Dad snapped.

The sweaty young man just shrugged. "Okay, it's your funeral," he said.

"Allie, you coming?" said Dad. The sky was clear as a dream and wide open as forever. I turned from the sky to the mechanic, who looked away, then back at me and shook his head.

"Come on, Allie," Dad said, gritting his teeth like trouble.

But there were people around, so I knew Dad couldn't kill me. I didn't have to go flying with him. I could always just never go home again.

"I can't go, I'm sick," I lied, holding my stomach.

"This whole damned trip was your idea," Dad said, pretending to be furious, when he was really happy for the excuse not to fly that plane.

"We can go back and find a safer plane," I suggested the next weekend. But Dad wasn't listening. He was still in his bathrobe, lost in his drink. Something in the way Dad wouldn't look at you announced the danger. Then you had to watch not to get caught in a room with just one exit, especially one like the kitchen, full of glasses and knives. Some days it was already hopeless by 10 A.M. Other times when he'd been drinking all day I could still get Dad over to the piano where I played an old song called "Chloë" with a dumb chorus we made into a joke. "Chloë," we'd sing, and I would laugh, but it wasn't funny. And I would sing, but I wasn't happy. Dad and I shared all these private songs and jokes, only we didn't share a thing.

Mom didn't teach me, so I don't know where I first learned that what grown-ups call listening is really saying the right thing so people don't hit you. I bet that's why I put talking off as long as I could. I said my first word. Months passed. My parents waited. I learned to walk and started to follow Tad around. Still, no second word came. I was so quiet Tad ignored me and most people overlooked me, which was fine, until the day when they forgot me during snacks.

"I want a cookie, too," I told a neighbor lady, who gave me the whole bag before rushing off to tell my mother. Mom thought it pretty funny I never bothered trying out a second word but went straight into sentences. She says that's because she has a doctorate in English.

I don't remember much from before I could talk, but I do remember standing under the dining room table watching my father smash a champagne glass in my mom's face and thinking, "I hate my father," and something inside me saying, "Little girls shouldn't hate their fathers." But I was standing there under the dining room table watching Mom bleed from a cut in her forehead. I don't think my parents even saw me. I was little, but I could see and I saw, so right away again I thought, "I hate my father." And this time the voice said nothing.

That makes it all sound clear and easy, but it wasn't easy, because it wasn't all like that. The hard part was, it wasn't all like anything. That was just one moment I would remember whenever I had to go and lie to Dad, even if he was being nice, so that I'd almost started to like him. Sometimes I dreamed of telling Dad the truth. Not for my conscience, but to give him one last chance to try again. That used to be my biggest wish, that one day I'd come in and say, "Dad, stop! Watch what you're doing. Look how you hurt us. See how we have to hide and lie."

In the dream Dad would stop screaming and just sit there silent, not even sipping his drink, since it's a shock to learn nobody likes you. Then, when he came back to his senses, he'd cry, saying, "Allie, thanks for telling me. I didn't know. From now on I'm going to be different." Of course, I'd wonder if he was just saying that so I'd come close enough for him to hit me. But in the dream Dad seemed as eager as I was for the nightmare to be over. "I'll stop drinking," he promised. "I'll change. I'll become another person. Even your mom will start liking me."

Mom smiled when I told her my dream. "That's about what he'd have to do for me to like him—die and come back as someone else," she said.

It wasn't easy lying to Dad when I kept wondering if maybe telling him the truth might change things.

"Of course it would—he'd kill us," Mom said, looking up from the mail she was opening in the garden. Then she went back to reading her letters because she knew she could always trust me not to tell. I suppose she was right. Dad would have killed her. It wasn't easy lying to Dad, but whenever I was tempted to really level with him I'd just remember standing under the table watching him smash that glass into Mom's face, then I could do what I had to do. That's what I was trying to think of that last night in the kitchen when Bruce thought I must be choking on a piece of cookie. I wasn't choking on a cookie. I was only choking on a memory.

It was always good talking with Bruce, but it wasn't heaven like raking the beach with Howie before the other kids came. It was so nice pulling the big rake along, even the sand made a purring sound. Sometimes a morning mist made the lake look gloomy, but you were always safe at the beach. The worst that could happen was you might step on an old nail and have to get a tetanus shot.

"Why don't you ever wear shoes?" Howie asked when the beach got so hot I had to run along behind on tiptoe.

"I like to feel the sand," I explained. Still, the next day Howie brought a pair of Japanese flip-flops, which I always carried but never wore because the only thing I liked more than sharing cherry ices with Howie was feeling the sand hot between my toes.

I don't know much about the "being happy" grown-ups fight for, yet I do know that whenever I walked the beach with Howie picking up candy wrappers I never for a single minute dreamed of being anywhere else.

But sometimes when we sat watching the water I'd remember.

"What're you thinking, Allie?" Howie would say, because he worried when I wasn't talking. I guess he thought I talked a lot.

But why talk about such bad stuff when the sun shone warm as a smile? Still, I sat in the sunshine dying to tell

Howie about listening and having no one to listen, and about how there were two Dads, one drunk, one sober, and how the drunken Dad was more dangerous, but at least he never talked about the office. He just raged and cursed, gritting his teeth as you sat there praying it would stop, but it didn't stop. He kept lurching around you, pouring another, his movements more jerky with each new Scotch.

"So how you doing? Are you happy?" Dad would jeer, tipping the bottle with one swift flick that set the Scotch sloshing back up against the glass like angry waves while you pretended not to notice because Dad was testing you for disgust. That's where my mom always went wrong. Mom used to try to seem cheery, but something in Dad always got to her. She was so cool in life, but she went to pieces whenever Dad stalked her, stumbling into end tables and slamming doors.

"A shame," he'd say, breaking a lamp Mom loved. Of course we all knew that he did it on purpose.

"Ruined. Can it be ruined? . . . like your mother ruined my life," Dad would say, voice rising, as he kicked the broken pieces while Mom straightened a picture still trying to pretend it wasn't happening again.

"Something the matter, Jeanne?" Dad would laugh, sticking his face smack into hers until she couldn't stand it.

"You're sick!" she'd hiss as he grabbed her by the hair and shook his drink in her face.

"Don't do that! It hurts!" Mom would scream, which only made Dad pull harder.

"Leave her alone!" I'd cry, grabbing his arm so that he had to turn and look at me. If Mom was smart she would have shut up then, but Mom was never a practical person.

"I wish you'd die," she'd scream, striking out at Dad just when I'd managed to distract him.

"Be quiet!" I'd whisper, but Mom couldn't stop scream-ing "You sick bastard!" She had great taste, but rotten judgment—that was the trouble with Mom. She didn't see that at home every move was important. You could get killed if you weren't smart.

"You bastard!" she'd scream, which only made Dad laugh as he kept pulling her hair so that all I could think of was how she'd cry the next day when whole clumps fell out in her brush.

"Come on, Dad, leave her alone. Come talk to me," I'd say, hoping Mom would just stay still until I could walk Dad upstairs.

"Stop that!" Mom would cry, arms flailing at Dad's face as he kept jerking her head. Yet in all the times she tried to slap him, I never saw her reach him even once.

"Come on now, Dad," I'd repeat, hoping he'd finally let me lead him back into the living room, where he'd go on about how bad Mom was as if he knew her, when it was clear from what he said he didn't know a thing.

I liked to think I was pretty good at handling Dad; still, some nights when we two sat alone I felt scared as a rabbit caught by its ears. A night is just a night, but time is funny. It goes so slow when you feel frightened. Some-times it seemed ten nighttimes before Dad finally slumped over in midsentence as I sat beside him watching the sun rise pink behind Mom's favorite chandelier. Then it was like you'd just survived a war, you felt so happy. And it was like you'd just half died, you felt so sad. I wanted to go to sleep, but couldn't before I told someone the night-mare. So I'd go stretch out in the hall where Mom had to trip over me first thing on her way downstairs.

"What are you doing out here?" she'd say without wait-ing for an answer. There was no one like Mom for forget-ting. Or maybe it was just the pills she took.

I wanted to tell Howie so I could forget it, like Mom seemed to forget when she came walking along behind her dark glasses and her wide, beauty queen smile. I wanted to forget, but having had trouble hanging over you makes it hard to really care about things like whether you'll get picked first for softball. You might say it helps give you perspective—but what's perspective? I don't think little girls really need perspective. Seeing things from far off is for dead people who can't get any closer, or for God. I think it's bad to know an awful secret and you can't say it. You can't say it 'cause you shouldn't know it, so the secret eats your insides out and kills you, only no one knows that either, so you've not only got to hide the secret but also what the secret has done to you. It's like you're really living in this nightmare and the beach is just a daydream and what matters to all the other kids seems silly. Your parents' problems are what's real, so you have to fake getting upset, like I did back when the young mailman ran over Nero, our first dog.

I was at the beach and didn't see it myself, but all the neighbor kids came running to tell me that our dog just got squished.

"Poor Nero. I always knew this would happen," Mom said when I raced home. But she couldn't blame the mailman for not seeing a little black cocker who liked to sun itself on a black road. Besides, Nero was Dad's dog, so it didn't matter, though, of course, we all had to act upset. The poor mailman never could look at us kids again without fumbling in his pocket for Hershey Kisses. We weren't allowed to accept food from strangers, but Mom made an exception of the mailman, saying we had to take his chocolates or he'd feel bad. That was years ago. We were just little. The young mailman isn't so young anymore and we're much bigger, but he still brings candy to console us for the loss of a dog we never mourned.

"Hi, Allie!" Howie would call each morning, waving to me as he drove in the lot, and every time I saw him I wanted to tell him. Not because I wanted him to feel sorry or because I thought he could change things, but because I just had to tell someone. I wanted to tell Howie about the fighting and screaming and having to sneak Sam out for walks so long you'd think we might grow up before we ever made it home. Tad could stay home. Dad never hurt him. Mom, Sam, and I weren't so lucky those nights my parents fought so hard Sam and I had to throw a raincoat over our pajamas and run. Then the three of us would walk all over town, Sam keeping up real well for someone who wouldn't be five until September when he started school.

It's strange walking around outside way past bedtime when the trees shake their branches as if they're angry. Even the road to school was scary. The streetlights seemed so far apart, you imagined robbers at each turn.

"You're going to get run over," Mom would say. Still, Sam and I walked close to the center of the road in terror of the wind and the robbers and being discovered with just a raincoat on over our pajamas. I wanted to hold on to Mom, saying, "What can we do?" I wanted to cry "Help!" but Mom was already sobbing, so I just said, "Don't worry. Someday I'll take care of you."

Howie thought it was crazy that I was dying to grow up, yet I knew he'd understand if I could only tell him. I didn't want to think about it, but it haunted me like fear of ghosts or the dark, only it didn't go away when daylight came. At the beach I had everything I wanted, except being able to tell him. Some days it got so bad sitting up there on the guard chair together, I could think of nothing else, except maybe watching Sam.

Sam came to the beach with me every morning. He was a strange kid, sort of quiet. In fact, most everyone except for his best friend Frankie and me ignored him, which was fine with Sam. He didn't care much about most people, but he liked his trucks and I liked Sam ever since the morning I found him singing to himself, strumming the spokes of an upside-down bicycle as if they were the strings of a harp. That's when I knew Sam was worth saving. So from then on, whenever Tad began bullying him, Sam would scream for me and I'd come running. Then Tad and I would stand there glaring at each other like two gunslingers on TV.

"I'm going to beat your head in," Tad would say. But I'd just laugh because I knew Tad wouldn't waste the time to kill me.

"Go pick on someone your own size," I'd say, flashing my nails to remind Tad how much he hated getting all scratched up.

"Don't push me," Tad warned, and I wouldn't. I'd just hold my ground till he got bored.

"You're both just stupid babies!" Tad would say, walking off in disgust.

Getting free of Tad's bullying changed Sam's life. Now he could bring his trucks out and they wouldn't get stolen. Sam and Frankie also could play more once Tad no longer tied them up for hours. The only problem now was that Sam and Frankie were so grateful for my protection, they wanted me to play with them.

"Come play monster," they'd say, pulling my arm. Monster is a stupid game like hide-and-seek, only when you're "it" you've got to make frightening monster noises. And I was always "it," because I made such a good monster. That's why Sam and Frankie liked the game. They were just little and didn't know that it was boring. Still, they were such good kids and so easy to catch, I almost always played. Besides, I'm pretty big now but I remember being little and asking Mom to play dolls with me and Mom always saying she was too busy and "Not now" until one day she finally said, "All right, all right, I'll play."

"Just tell me what I have to do," she said, staring at me as if she'd never played a game in her life. So we sat down together and I gave her a doll and made up a story, but Mom was as miserable as Stormy when she's all tied up and there's a rabbit nearby. Then I could see why Dad sometimes got cross when Mom would jump up to start doing chores when he was talking, especially since Mom never bothered to sort the silver when Dad wasn't around. I guess Mom was just no good at the pretending that you do for other people. All she wanted was to go, and you can't play dolls with someone who hates it, so instead of really playing I just made up a fast ending where the dolls all rushed off to meet a man.

"Is that all?" Mom said when the dolls ran off.

I nodded.

"Well, that wasn't so bad." She smiled and gave me a pat. For some reason Mom told that story to the neighbor ladies. She would tell them how I always asked her to play but she was too busy, until finally one day she did play and the game was over in no time.

"Five minutes was all she wanted. She never asked me to play again after that," Mom would say, yet she never really got it. She thought it was a happy story. It wasn't a happy story. That's why I almost always played monster with Sam and Frankie, though it was such a stupid game.

You may wonder what Mom was doing that she never had time to play with anyone. Sam and I used to wonder. Tad said he knew.

"You'd better watch out or I'll tell Dad," he'd warn Mom if she crossed him. Mom wouldn't even look at Sam and me before she rushed away.

But maybe she was just in a hurry.

"You don't appreciate how much work it takes to keep you presentable," she'd say. And it was true. We didn't. I don't know if Sam and I ever looked presentable, but when Mom went out in her crossed-back sundress she looked more beautiful than Cinderella.

The first night Bruce stopped by, Mom dressed me up in a scratchy pink nylon party dress and braided my hair so tight it hurt. Then she made Tad walk me to Melanie's birthday party three houses down because it was a cookout that couldn't begin until seven thirty when Melanie's dad got home from work to start the coals.

"You ready?" called Dave, whom Tad was bringing along for company, even though neither one had been invited.

"Ready," I called, rushing out, but the boys walked fast and paid me no attention.

When we got to Melanie's there was so much noise from inside no one answered the door. So we walked around back. The grill was inside the covered porch, but from the yard we could smell the hot dogs and hamburgers cooking and hear the fat dripping—zap!—on the coals.

We walked up to the back window where we could see twenty kids inside the rec room, only they couldn't see us standing outside looking in, because it was dusk.

"Hey, look!" said Dave, pointing to the double glass doors. "We could throw a rock."

"You do and I'll tell," I warned.

"You would, wouldn't you, because you're just a baby. Why don't you go inside with the other babies?" Tad sneered. And so I did, with Tad and Dave trailing me in

since you can't just walk away from barbecued hamburgers after you smell them up close.

"Hello, Allie," said Melanie's mother, Mrs. Foster.
Then Melanie saw me and we both started crying because
Melanie was moving to Texas the next morning. The cookout wasn't just Melanie's birthday. It was also her goodbye
party.

"Don't cry," said Melanie's mother. "We'll come back to
visit."

I sure hoped they would since Melanie and I were such
good friends I even slept over once.

Melanie was a lot like Fluff, real nice, yet quiet and
three whole years younger than me; still, at least she was a
girl.

"Have you seen the new family? Do they have a girl my
age?" I asked Melanie's mom.

"Just boys," said Mrs. Foster, patting my shoulder since
she knew it was hard for me to have no other girls close by.
At school there were so many girls to play with they sometimes fought over who got to be your friend, but come
summer I was stuck.

"I'll miss you," I told Melanie, who'd already forgotten
about moving away and was busy unwrapping the red-
striped jumper I brought.

Melanie liked all her presents, and it was a great party
with kids from school and one of those flat cakes from the
bakery with Melanie's name in red jelly, and blue icing
roses sweet as sugar but smooth as cream. There were only
four blue roses, but Melanie put almost a whole one on my
piece of cake because she knew I liked them. But we didn't
just eat. We played pin the tail on the donkey and I
couldn't even find the wall with the donkey's picture.
Then there was ice cream and we all got prizes because

eight is an important birthday. In fact, the party was so good Tad and Dave didn't go off like they'd planned, but instead hung around breaking birthday candles and popping balloons till the last kid from school had been picked up and it was time for Tad to walk me home.

I'm afraid of the dark. Tad knows it. I've always been a little afraid, but I've been a lot more afraid ever since I saw an "Alfred Hitchcock Presents" show on TV about a strangler who pretends to be a nurse taking care of a nice lady, only this nurse isn't even a woman. Beneath her dress she's a man! I'm not that scared of stranglers in daylight, but ever since seeing that show I've slept with my hands covering my throat, just in case.

It was a sticky summer night full of bugs and scary noises like the clicking of crickets that sounds like someone riding up after you on an English racer. Tad was supposed to walk me home but as soon as we left the party he and Dave ran off and left me in the dark. I was scared to be alone, so I started home as fast as I could. I ran so fast Tad missed when he tried to jump me from the big elm.

"Mom! Mom! Tad's after me!" I cried as I banged in the screen door and collapsed. What a relief to be home!

"*Now* what's the matter?" said Mom. "Go upstairs right now and change out of your good things. You too, Tad. Go!"

"I'm not dressed up," said Tad, who came in full of dirt from the flower bed where he landed.

"You both heard me," Mom said, sitting back down on the couch with Bruce.

"What's *he* doing here?" Tad grumbled, shoving me aside when I tried to go upstairs. But I pushed on past him. My dress was so scratchy I was desperate to take it off and hang it way in the back of my closet where Mom wouldn't find it. I couldn't wait to put on my soft, short-sleeved cotton pajamas with a pattern so faded you couldn't tell it was rows of ducks.

Once I changed, I called downstairs "Good night," then waited up what seemed forever. I wanted to tell Mom about the party and ask when Melanie could visit, only I couldn't go back downstairs in my pajamas with a stranger there. I called goodnight again and waited, but Mom never came.

Bruce was a lot taller than me, and a little shorter than my father. That first night Bruce just sat on the yellow sofa next to Mom, sort of quiet, but I knew he wasn't the quiet type. The guys all liked Bruce because he was always telling jokes that cracked them up. "You'll get it later," Bruce would say, patting my head.

Bruce was grown-up enough to drive a yellow convertible, but he still dressed in jeans like a kid, with a silver medal tucked in his shirt. Bruce told me it was a St. Christopher medal and that St. Christopher was the patron saint of travelers. I asked Bruce where he was going. He laughed and said my mom told him he was going nowhere fast. So I asked Bruce why he needed the medal. He said he didn't, but that he always wore it because it was the last thing his mother ever gave him. I asked him when his mother had died. Bruce said she hadn't.

Mom always said don't talk to strangers. Bruce wasn't a stranger, but right after he started work on the patio, Mom forbade us to talk with him. Mom said Bruce swore so much he'd be a bad influence—which was a pretty stupid reason when you figure Bruce swore less than Mom.

"So why don't you like me?" Bruce asked me later, long after Mom forgot what she'd said about not talking to him.

"But I do like you," I told him, for whatever Dad might say there was nothing wrong with Bruce. I'd liked Bruce ever since Dad first hired him. I liked how his smile made his blue eyes crinkle when he wiped the sweat from his forehead as he joked and swore.

"Don't lie. You didn't talk to me once last summer. What could that mean, but that you don't like me?" Bruce asked, watching me grow redder and redder, until at last he smiled. "Okay, have it your way, little girl," he said.

It was funny about that first night. Dad was away, which usually made things quiet, but already there was something buzzing like a mosquito on your pillow that you can't stop hearing but can't quite see.

Tad looked real disgusted when we walked upstairs together. He followed me into my room. "You want something?" I asked as he stood there looking at me like I'd just fumbled the fly that cost the game. "I didn't do anything, Tad," I told him, but Tad just shook his head.

"Grow up," he said.

Chapter Four

"If only he'd die," Mom would say when I asked about the future. And it was really surprising Dad didn't when you figure most of his brothers and sisters had died, not like Mom, who had only one sister to lose because her family had been shrinking ever since her ancestor Robert Morris signed the Declaration of Independence. Mom said he was "the financier of the Revolution," but he landed in debtors' prison when the states wouldn't pay him back. Eventually George Washington fixed things and Robert Morris married another one of Mom's relatives, only the poor man was so worn out from his first wife, debtors' prison, and the war that the family kept getting smaller with each generation until today there was just Mom.

Dad's family wasn't like that. There were a whole lot of them when they first came to America not so long ago. My dad's mom was really something. She'd been all around the world, even fled the Russian Revolution, going from Paris to London, then New York, Pennsylvania, and Ohio—always moving west like my mom's Aunt Ella. I think they might have liked each other.

"They would have killed each other," said Mom, who called Dad's mom "the Bitch" so as not to confuse her with her own mother.

Mom told all sorts of stories about the Bitch. In some she sent her husband to work in the Pennsylvania coal mines, then used his wages to buy the store she burned down to get the insurance that paid for a whole string of stores in Ohio, which is why she was so rich. But that's just one version. Every story about my dad's mom was different, like in the fables where the Lady of the Lake who takes King Arthur away is sometimes the Queen, his sister, and other times the bad fairy, Morgan le Fey. (In fact, my dad's last name wasn't really even Gardner before Grandma changed it from something long and foreign.) The stories varied so much it wasn't real clear what Grandma did besides go to church and call the shots. In some tales she was even a bootlegger, but in all the stories she sent each of her four sons to law school, although she refused even to speak English herself.

Dad's mom survived the Russian Revolution, Ellis Island, two world wars, the Great Depression, the Pennsylvania coal mines, and an alcoholic husband to end up a rich old lady pacing her garden talking about the things you can survive but not escape.

"Such a hypocrite," said Mom, who told me only a Catholic could reconcile arson and religion. Maybe that's because they think more about hell. Mom didn't like Dad's mother. I guess she did some shady things, but it wasn't real clear how Mom's Aunt Ella made do either. And at least when my dad's mom fled west she always took her kids.

Dad was the youngest. There is a sad story about how his older brother Al died of lung cancer just after graduating from law school, where he made the *Law Review* and was as popular as Alice-Marie. Al was as popular as Mom's sister, but Dad wasn't like Mom. He was jealous. Dad was still mad at his mother because she gave Al a car and Dad got nothing. It was like Dad forgot what happened next, Al dying this terrible death just when he finally manages to finish school and pass the bar. What could be worse? All that work and struggle, growing up for nothing. Alice-Marie was a lot luckier. She just played around awhile, then left.

It was bad what happened to Dad's family. If he'd cried about that, I would have understood why some nights he talked and sobbed like the sole survivor of some disaster who only lived to stammer it out. Yet Dad never talked about the big things. Mom was the one who told me what happened, so I know that at some point before they only argued, my parents must have talked.

Dad never told me about the accident and how his two older brothers and a sister lay in a bloody car while Grandma ran down the highway waving for help but no one stopped. I would like to tell you some nice man stopped or a whole family from out of town, but there's a special sadness to true stories which makes it a sin to change them, for all they have besides their sadness is the truth.

If it had been night, maybe you could say folks were afraid to stop because they thought there might be robbers. But it wasn't night. If it had been raining you might say they didn't see her. It was a nice day and people just kept passing Grandma till she staggered all the way into

town and came back with the ambulance to find her oldest
three had bled to death.

It must have taken a lot of guts for Grandma to make it
all the way to town injured herself, but you can always
manage when you still think you have reason. Dad never
forgave Grandma for having preferred the older kids. It
was just the way she felt, yet he never forgave her. Maybe
she didn't care.

When her three oldest died, then Al, Grandma gave lots
of money to the Church and turned her children into
stained-glass windows like in the fables where the maiden
dies and becomes a constellation. Mom said it cost
Grandma a fortune. Still, I guess it's the best she could do
for a happy ending. It was Dad's family, but it was Mom
who told me about all the moving and the crash and how
Al died of lung cancer like his alcoholic father while the
one surviving daughter married well and Dad married out
of the Church.

Mom told me the story of the accident like it was
Grandma's fault that no one stopped. Her fault for not
being a lady of such quality anyone would recognize her,
even bloody, like the princess in "The Princess and the
Pea." I think Mom thought people would stop their cars
for *her* even if her clothes were torn and her face was
bloody.

Mom called Grandma "the Bitch," but she always struck
me as sort of courageous. We only went to see Grandma
once after Dad's sister called to tell him about a priest in
Grandma's garden. My aunt said the priest hung around
Grandma like a vulture waiting for her to die so he could
take her money. Dad's sister didn't mean that the priest
would steal Grandma's money for himself. She thought he
wanted it for the Church. But maybe the priest just came
to walk with Grandma because she was old and sad and

because he liked her garden. But I know why Dad showed
up, and Grandma knew too, because she threw him out.

"Where did you get that?" Mom cried, seizing the rosary
Grandma gave me and hiding it away the way she took
Tad's dirty books. I was sorry because it was a pretty pink
necklace with gold balls like worry beads. "How can you
take things from someone who says you're illegitimate?"
Mom said, shaking her head in disgust like Tad.

"What's illegitimate?" I asked.

But instead of telling me, Mom explained about Catholics and Protestants and how the Pope said they shouldn't
marry each other, and that if they did, good Catholics
were supposed to make believe it never happened and that
the couple's children didn't exist. I could see Mom getting
madder and madder as she explained it. That's when I saw
Mom didn't hate Grandma because she was a bootlegger or
because she was Dad's mother. She hated her because of
religion, which is pretty funny when you figure that Mom
never went to church. Long ago Mom explained that she
didn't have to go to church because she was a Protestant
and they had a special deal with God. Protestants have to
send their children to church each Sunday, but the grown-
ups only have to go to church on Easter after buying new
spring hats. Only Mom didn't look good in hats. And anyway, she said that while showing up on Easter was nice,
the key thing was your relationship with God. Mom said
Protestants could talk to God whenever they wanted, not
like Catholics, who have to wait in line to go to confession.
Then, after all the waiting, all they get to talk to is a priest.

I was very religious myself once, only I was neither a
Catholic nor a Protestant because my parents kept fighting
over where we should get baptized. One week my father
would arrange to have us baptized Catholic, then Mom
would cancel that and set us up as Episcopalians, only Dad

would go crazy, so we couldn't do that either. I was just a baby, so I don't remember, but at least it gave my parents something to do on Sundays since neither one of them ever went to church. They used to have the religion fight every Sunday morning, and take it right from the start. Then they finally got tired and agreed that whoever drove us to church got to drop us off at the church he wanted. This was fine, I suppose. The only problem was when you're not baptized, you can't take communion either place.

It's a funny thing about religion. I used to be religious. I'd talk to God during the day to check things out before I did them and prayed a lot each night. I used to be religious because you want to believe in Him just like you want to have a nice father, only you want to believe in God even more, because if He's there He could fix everything. Besides, you need someone to talk to when the screaming starts.

At first you ask Him to help you make things different. Then you try and try for years, but it only gets worse. Still you keep on making every possible excuse for Him, trying to think there must be a reason for all the suffering, when there's no reason, there's only suffering and all your praying ever did was wear out the knees of your pajamas. After a while you finally figure you're the only one trying to fix things. Then you get a little angry when you think of all the nights you spent begging God like a hungry dog. In fact, you feel so cheated you want to hit something or someone. So I went running up to the third floor and burst into Mom's room.

"There's no God, is there?" I said, and held my breath waiting for the lightning to strike or for Mom to scream at me. I thought she'd scream because I didn't know about my mom yet. You know how you sometimes say "I can't do that dive" just so the coach will say "Don't talk that

way!" and make you try? I only said "There is no God" so
Mom would show me I was wrong. But Mom didn't
argue.

"For such a smart little girl," Mom said, "it sure took
you long enough to figure that one out."

I couldn't believe Mom was so calm. It was like the end
of the world, but Mom just kept sitting on the big double
bed flipping over her solitaire cards.

"But, Mom," I said, then waited, giving her a chance to
change her mind.

"Religion's a crutch," she said, smiling as she turned
over the ace of diamonds, which meant she could start a
new pile and finish the game faster. She didn't even look
up, but I was staggered. All the millions of stories she'd
told me. I couldn't believe she'd never even mentioned this
before. It was like she'd just announced we were all Com-
munists or something. It was so terrible I sat down on the
bed, far enough away not to upset the cards, and watched
her play the next three games.

"It's not so bad," Mom said at last, explaining the difference between agnostics and atheists as she played. "I'm an
agnostic," she said. I couldn't see why Mom was being so
nice about it. I was absolutely furious.

"Well, I'm an atheist," I told her. But Mom still
wouldn't bother to try to talk me out of it.

"At least I don't have to go to church anymore," I said.

"Of course you do. That has nothing to do with it," said
Mom.

It's very hard to understand grown-ups. Even when you
think you know them, they're full of surprises, like spies
with a whole other life they never talk about. It's scary
when you think how you need them and they know everything about you since the day you were born, yet they

only pretend to tell you everything, and then, when they finally do tell you the truth, you still have to go to church.

Mom was lucky. She didn't miss God. Did that make Mom braver than the Bitch, who could face everything but not nothing? Or was Mom just more comfortable with nothing than with something? But how could that be when it gets so lonely out walking and the headlights whoosh up on you like monsters? It gets so lonely you want someone big to protect you and make it better so that it's safe to go home to your room with a balcony worthy of Juliet.

That's what I wanted to tell Howie. Still, I guess it was all right. You didn't get used to it, but the night couldn't last forever and, besides, every single minute, day or night, I was growing up. That's the beauty of life—how every minute you're getting older. Not that I didn't still love the lake, Howie, Fluff, and swimming underwater so far that everybody thought I'd drowned.

Mom told me Dad was a lifeguard once himself way back before she knew him, and that he taught me how to swim by throwing me into water over my head. It was sink or swim, Mom says, but I don't believe there was ever a time I couldn't swim. Years ago, before Howie came, I was already getting beached for swimming across the lake to my swimming lessons. "What if you'd drowned?" the instructor asked, which is pretty silly since everyone knows that you can't drown if you grow up on a lake.

Mom didn't grow up on a lake. When she was a kid she'd learned to ice-skate at a rink and was so good she could skate all the way to the island without half trying, only Mom still didn't bother to skate that much. Summers she had less to do, so she used to take Sam and me to the beach. But Mom couldn't swim, so it never made much sense for her to come along, and the summer Bruce built the patio she finally stopped. That wasn't the only thing that was changing. They now let transistors on the beach. Walking along the dock, you were still hit by the smell of the big girls' Coppertone, but the older girls had also changed over the winter. Sometimes, when I went to shower at the clubhouse, I couldn't believe my eyes.

"Take a picture, it lasts longer," Gail snapped. Then all the big girls looked over like they expected me to cry. But why should I cry? What did it matter what she said?

My parents were right about the lake being just perfect. Nothing is as free as diving in and swimming all the way to the island and back before you're even missed. Of course, Spring Lakes wasn't half as much fun for Mom in summer, since she couldn't swim.

"The lake is dirty," she'd say whenever I asked if I could teach her. That wasn't true, but you couldn't argue with Mom.

Mom wasn't too happy at home. It was hard for her to make friends because eventually you have to invite your friends over to the house and having people over made Mom nervous. We couldn't even bring other kids by the house on weekends because we never knew what Dad might do.

Sometimes people stopped by, not knowing. The summer before Bruce laid the patio a man from down the street used to drop by Saturday mornings. Most people thought Mr. Edwards was Dad's friend because he sat and talked with Dad, but he really came by to help Mom keep Dad in line, and Dad suspected.

"You're crazy," Mom said when Dad told her what he thought. Still, whenever Mr. Edwards dropped by Dad started acting worse even than you'd treat a baby-sitter. So he drove the poor man out.

"You hate anyone who helps me, don't you?" Mom asked, not crying, just cold. It was around that time my mom stopped crying.

I tried my best to help, but Mom didn't much like her life.

"Alternately terrified and bored," was how Mom described it.

"Like the army," Bruce said when she told him. I couldn't believe she'd really tell him. I don't know when Mom first started talking to Bruce like she was telling him everything (which she wasn't), but it made Bruce happy. Still, it was bad of her. But Mom could be so bad sometimes.

"Or else," she'd say when she wanted you to do something. Or else she would slap you in the face.

My mom was never very happy, still I tried to think of things that might help keep Dad off her back—things like building the patio. What happened wasn't my fault, but building the patio was my idea. I thought it would help me do my job. I thought it would help me make Dad relax.

I worked hard entertaining Daddy, yet no matter how I tried to distract him, sooner or later he would end up drunk because he had these stories locked inside him. It was hard to have to sit and listen, but whenever my heart would start really going out to Dad, I'd just remember who he cried for. He never cried for his brothers and sisters left bleeding, or his dad and brother dead of lung cancer, or for his mother left with nothing but stained-glass windows to stand in for the family she dragged halfway round the world. Even Mom could cry for my last Duchess, but the only one Dad ever cried for was himself.

"You want to ask me something, Allie?" Howie would say as we sat together on the guard chair.

No. I didn't want to ask him, just to tell him. So many things I had to tell him. But when I looked over at the scratch marks where Fluff had clawed Howie's sunburn, yet he never complained, I could see how much he wanted me to be happy. I wanted him to be happy too.

"How come you always get sunburn?" I'd say.

Chapter Five

 ummer storms are sneaky. There was no hint
 of clouds that morning when the sun burst
through my windows, lapping my face like a happy dog. It
was still sunny two hours later when Sam and I started out
for the beach. Ada, the cleaning lady, was scrubbing the
patios. Dad said Bruce's men never did anything, but they
were already busy making the back lawn look like a giant
gopher's playground, digging holes for the rows of bushes
with their roots wrapped in burlap.

"Hey, Allie," called Ken, the youngest workman.

"Careful," he warned as we came closer. "Watch where
you step or you'll fall into a pit."

Ken was barely two years older than Tad and had just
gotten his working papers. He was nice, but dumb, with
too many freckles. Ken wanted us to stop and talk. Had

Bruce been working there with him, I would have stopped in a second. Bruce was always around the summer before when his men were building the patio. He made it fun. Even Mom used to come outside to laugh and talk with Bruce. Sometimes she'd go lie in the hammock and read until Bruce sneaked up and sprinkled her with rose petals to surprise her. He always sneaked up the same way, but Mom laughed every time.

Mom would smile once she'd spied Bruce. "Go get Ada to give you some iced tea and a beer," she'd say to me. So I'd jump up from the ground where I'd been sitting, brush the grass off my bottom, and rush off. Sometimes it took a while to find Ada, or Tad would try to trip me on my way, but when I came back from the kitchen Mom and Bruce would still be smiling. I never saw Mom smile so much. Even the next summer started out happy. Then in early July Mom went away for a week.

Mom said she went to visit Grandma, but she was never in when Dad and I tried to reach her. We only talked to her when she called back. Dad didn't feel like talking then, but I told Mom all about my day and Tad picking on Sam.

"You think she's really in Ohio?" Bruce asked when he stopped by our house to check the back one afternoon.

"Sure," I said, because Mom didn't start getting letters with strange stamps until about a week after she came home.

"Why is the paper so cheap?" I asked, fingering the tissue envelope.

"It's not cheap, it's light for airmail," Mom explained.

Nobody saw the letters but me because Mom hid them in my room. All summer long they piled up in my junk drawer, where I could have read them, but I didn't. I wasn't even interested in the strange stamps.

"Over here!" Ken hollered, always looking for an excuse

to stop working. It bugged me the way he smiled whenever he saw me. Still, it was Howie's day off, so there was
no need to rush.

"You hear about the sniper?" Ken said.

"What's a sniper?" I answered. Ken said a sniper was
someone who walked around with a rifle.

"How's that different from a hunter?" I asked. Ken
thought a minute, frowned, then said to forget it, it wasn't
all that serious anyway. So I asked Ken where Bruce was
and Ken said Bruce had mentioned stopping by later.
Then nasty old Frank, the foreman, who was drinking a
beer already, told Ken to get back to work, and Sam and I
walked on up the back path.

On the path we met two policemen. There were only
five in the whole town and no one paid them much attention because the patrolmen weren't even as powerful as the
lifeguards. The lifeguards could beach you and ruin your
life or even send you home, but the police could only say
"Hey, kids, stop making so much noise," or "Don't you
know you're not allowed to camp out on the golf course?"
Then all they could do was threaten to call your parents—
only they never did, since the parents might get angry and
it was a very easy job being a policeman in Spring Lakes.

"Hey, Allie. Sam. You see anything suspicious?" asked
Jim, the youngest cop on the force. Jim was tall and skinny
with mouse-brown hair and dried-up acne. He didn't look
like much, but Dave swore he once played fantastic basketball.

"Like what?" I said, just to talk.

"Oh, I don't know. Something you usually don't see,"
said Jim's chunky, red-haired partner.

"Something like a man with a rifle," Jim suggested.

"You mean the sniper?" I said, glad the day was turning
out to be fun after all.

"Where did you see him?" Jim asked, taking out his notepad.

"See who?"

"The sniper."

"What's a sniper?" I asked.

"But you just said you saw one."

"No, I didn't. I just asked if you were looking for the sniper. Ken told me all about it."

"What did he tell you?" the heavy redhead asked, mopping his brow.

"He told me you were looking for a sniper. What's a sniper?"

"Great. Terrific. Everyone's talking. We'll have this rumor all over town. You and your big mouth, Jim!" the redhead growled.

"What happened?" I asked.

"The old lady in the white house reported hearing a gunshot in the woods behind her house," Jim explained, as the old cop scowled.

"You talked to the old lady with the ballroom! Was she nice? What was she like?" I asked, all excited, because I'd never even seen her. But it turned out Jim couldn't say because another cop had taken her call.

"Look, it's nothing important. Just forget it. The old lady has probably started hearing things or the 'shot' was just the backfire of some car. Why don't you kids just forget you ever saw us," the big redhead said.

"Let's go. This is stupid," the chunky cop said to Jim. Tad said the big redhead once worked in the city, where policemen really have something to do, so I guess he was a bit ashamed.

"Did the old lady mention her parties?" I asked again. Then, since it was Howie's day off, we walked them back to their car.

The day started sunny, but it didn't stay sunny. Sam and I were playing on the swings at the far end of the beach when the storm came up sudden as a sunshower, only stronger. You could see a real cloudburst was coming because the sky got dark as ink. I love to swing high up where you can see everything, and it's even more fun when the wind whips around you and faraway thunder growls.

"Did you hear something?" the guards asked each other, smiling, since an electrical storm meant they could close the beach and go play cards in the guard shack.

I felt a raindrop on my nose and tried to swing faster so the rain couldn't catch me. Then I felt another drop on my ear. It was fun watching all the people on the beach grab up their blankets and turn to each other asking "Did you feel something?" all staring up at the sky like they'd lost their minds.

"Turn off your radios!" cried the guards, trying to hear the thunder, not a song called "He's So Fine" blaring from every transistor turned to WABC. Most of the other songs weren't so hot, they were just about cars. But "He's So Fine" was terrific because in it a group of girls sing "do lang, do lang" about a guy. The birds were going crazy fighting with the radios for who could sing the loudest. The radios were winning. They were even beating out the guards, who were blowing their whistles and screaming "Everyone out of the lake!"

"Did you see that?" asked a guard as lightning cracked just over the hill. Before I could even count the seconds between seeing the lightning and hearing the thunder the sky went BOOM and everyone ran screaming for their cars like the people in *Godzilla*. Then, *whoosh*, the sky ripped open and there we stood by the swings getting drenched.

I love to swim when the whole world is wet, magic, and melting, and there's so much rain you can barely see where the streaming sky becomes the choppy lake. But I couldn't dive in and set a bad example.

"Come on!" I told Sam. This was a serious storm that could last for hours, the kind we usually waited out in the guard shack playing cards with the rain on the roof pounding rat-at-at-tat.

The game was always the same. The guards played penny-a-point poker. The would have let me play, I suppose, but the guards were so good I couldn't afford it. Besides, it was more fun walking around checking everyone's hand. The guys all knew I could keep a secret, so they didn't mind my walking around the table behind them. They'd even point out their good cards with a slight crook of the finger. I guess they liked to have someone else know how they were doing.

Sometimes Howie asked, "Well, Allie, what do you think I should bid?" just to kid me, for, of course, I couldn't tell him. I just kept walking around looking, showing nothing, while the guys all watched me for some slip-up, with all the secrets like a game within the game.

The rain was coming down in sheets. I would have rushed to the shack for cards, but it was Howie's day off.

"Let's go home," I told Sam as we raced across the beach and on up the back path so washed out you had to skip over the roots that stuck out ugly as the veins in Grandma's hands.

"Come on," I said, grabbing Sam's sweatshirt whenever he wanted to stop and rest under a tree.

"We're almost home," I promised, though it wasn't quite true. So we sprinted up the back path, through the woods and on past the dock where our boats whined and pulled against their ropes like horses straining to break loose.

"We're here," I cried as we turned left into our yard, skirting the birch grove, on past the far back where Bruce's red handkerchief was still tied to a shovel stuck in the dirt.

"Hey!" I called, but no one answered. The guys had just abandoned their tools by the terraced gardens now flooded like the rice paddies in *Life*. The whole world had become a giant mud pie. Rain was battering the flats of flowers, tearing blooms apart like God was throwing a fit.

"Watch out," I said, grabbing Sam before he stumbled into a hole.

"This could be a graveyard from 'Creature Features,'" I said as we picked our way around the soggy ditches flanked by mounds of dirt.

"I'm scared," Sam said, so we forgot about being careful and ran the rest of the way past rows of dandelion-yellow mums, shocking-pink dahlias, and geraniums as red as Mom's lipstick, dodging the overflowing birdbath and rusting wickets of the croquet set still left up like a monument to the one time that we all played.

"Be careful, don't slip," I warned Sam as we reached the patio sudsing with Ajax left over from its morning bath.

The storm came up so sudden Mom hadn't even had time to bring in the pile of towels she usually left out by the back door for us.

"Hey, Mom," I said, banging the kitchen door open. We were both soaked clear through our sweatshirts. Sam's teeth were chattering. You'd think Mom might have heard all the racket. No one answered.

"Hey, Mom," I said again, checking out the front hall. But Mom wasn't in the living room, the dining room, or the den, where I found a half-empty beer bottle and a glass of melted iced tea.

"Hey, Mom!" I called. "We're wet!"

We were dripping, in fact, and had tracked in all sorts of grass and dirt.

"Come on," I said, leading Sam to the back stairs because the front ones had a white carpet.

"Hey, Mom," I whispered, tiptoeing into my room, where she sometimes napped.

My room was empty, with the French doors still propped open and two feet of white carpet before them soaked.

"What am I going to do now?" I asked Sam, kneeling to clear the leaves and twigs off my poor rug.

"We could play hearts," Sam said. "Tad has a deck."

"Wait a minute!" I said as Sam started to plop down on the bed by the window. "Do you see that?" I asked, examining the white eyelet bedspread for the imprint Mom's body left when she napped.

"See what?" Sam said, touching the bedspread.

"*Shh!*" I whispered, for I thought I heard a rustling at the end of the hall.

"Hey, Mom!" I cried, tracking the sound only to find Ada ironing in the laundry.

"Where's Mom?" I asked, bursting in. Ada didn't look up at first, then she just eyed me sort of funny. She was a tall, wiry black lady who always wore white dresses like a nurse and talked real fast, with all the words going up at the end. Other help had come and gone. Only Ada had been there in one of the maids' rooms forever, yet she only relaxed when my parents weren't there. Then Ada was happy and she'd talk about Trinidad and all her sisters and their husbands and her children and their divorces and her grandchildren and their sweethearts, and she'd tell me all about people knifing each other for love, or marrying two different girls on opposite sides of the island for money, or leaving the bride waiting at the church and running away and not marrying at all. The way Ada told it, Trinidad was like the fairy stories, everyone had more children than the old woman in the shoe and it was always summer. I wanted to hear all about it, but Ada talked too fast, laughing like crazy at all the mischief.

"What?" I'd say. And she'd tell me the same story all over again, from the beginning, with the same lilting accent at the same breakneck speed. I couldn't believe Ada had grandchildren, but Mom said Ada was much older than she looked.

Ada laughed about her family, but she was scared of mine. Maybe she'd heard that I slapped the baby-sitter. Only she wasn't just afraid of me. I think we all scared her—Tad, Dad, Mom, even Stormy, who bit her. "You best be careful, little girl," Ada would say.

"Careful of what?" I'd ask. But Ada only clucked and shook her head.

"Hey, Ada, where's Mom?" I asked. Ada just shrugged her shoulders and kept ironing the sheets.

"Hey, Mom!" I cried, racing up to the third floor where I heard creaking. No one was by the back stairs or in Dad's library. I looked down the hall of empty guest rooms, but the noise was coming from Mom's room.

"Mom?" I said, pausing a moment to study the footprints leading to her half-closed door.

"Not in there either," Sam said, walking out. "Now what?"

"Don't know," I said, standing at the top of the front stairs thinking.

"Allie, look," Sam said, pointing out the big front window to Mom's silver station wagon coming up the block.

"Come on," I told Sam, and we raced through the hall to the back stairs, taking them three at a time, grabbing on to each other whenever we slipped on the wet grass we'd tracked in going up.

Sam and I were downstairs in no time. We didn't dare track mud across the living room carpet, so we raced back out through the kitchen and around the house, hitting the driveway just as Mom drove up.

"Damn this rain," Mom said, killing the engine. Then she just sat there a minute, eyebrows knit like she was thinking.

"Oh, hi. What are you doing here?" she said, looking up.

"Hi, Mom," Sam said. But she wasn't looking at us.

I followed her gaze and spied Bruce standing by the peach trees dripping like he'd just stepped out of a shower.

"Just passing by," Bruce said.

"I see," Mom said, though it was hard to see anything too clearly in that downpour.

"I went shopping. Clothes shopping. Want to grab some of these packages?" Mom smiled, checking her lipstick in the rearview mirror. Mom was such a determined shopper she kept at it even though she had to keep calling the Salvation Army to take away last year's clothes.

"What packages?" said Bruce, walking up to the car.

"Oh, damn!" Mom sighed, slipping out of the driver's seat. In seconds she too looked as if she'd just stepped out of a shower.

"Let's see, I stopped by Kim Baskin's on the way home..." Mom said, leaning on the open car door, so caught up in wondering where she might have left the bags she forgot about getting soaked.

"Go inside and dry off," I told Sam, who scampered away.

"So call Kim," said Bruce.

"I will," Mom said, the same way she said "I'll be there in a moment" when she really meant "Forget it." Then Mom leaned so far over to grab the car keys, it was lucky she was wearing pants.

"Well," Mom said, straightening up, her wet hair falling in her face. "Damn," she said, brushing the hair from her eyes with her left hand as she slammed the car door shut.

I couldn't figure why she didn't just invite Bruce in. After all, it was pouring and his car was nowhere in sight. Only Mom didn't say a word. She just stood there wearing her soaking blouse and her "Run along now, dear" smile. But Bruce didn't run along. He just stood there too, staring at Mom like he was hungry or something, until she finally brightened her smile like she did before suggesting favors, tilted her face back to feel the rain even better, and said, "I bet this rain is ruining the lawn chairs!"

"Okay. I'll cover the chairs and check the boats," Bruce said as Mom ran for the house. Lightning cracked low over the hill by the next house, still I stayed to watch Bruce plunge back into the rain so heavy that I could barely see his white T-shirt bobbing along after a few seconds. Then the most embarrassing thing happened. I sneezed.

The white T-shirt stopped.

"Who's that?"

"Just me. Allie."

"What are you doing out here?"

"Nothing," I fibbed.

"Want to come along?" Bruce asked.

"Sure," I said, for I could see he needed help.

Chapter Six

*T*he day after the big storm it got nice again, so as soon as we heard Dad start downstairs Sam and I set out like always to find Stormy. We set out like always, only we didn't spend much time looking for my dog since we were really off to the old Walters place to meet Bruce because the day before I'd promised to let him know if I'd managed to convince Mom to go to Mrs. Baskin's house for bridge that afternoon.

I'd told Bruce that Sam and I would pass by around eight thirty.

"Can't you come a little later?" he'd asked as we fastened the boats against the storm.

"I'm sorry, I have to be somewhere before nine," I explained. For what would Howie think if I wasn't there in the parking lot waiting when he drove in?

Mom used to play bridge with Mrs. Baskin, Mrs. Dietz, and Mrs. O'Keith on Tuesdays. Then on Thursday they played canasta. Mom also sang in two different choruses —a small one that sang for fun, sometimes at weddings, and a large group that gave recitals on Christmas and Easter, though the recitals didn't count as church.

The bridge ladies were Mom's best friends, but Mom didn't like Mrs. Baskin. She was what Mom called "blond out of a bottle," only she must have kept switching bottles because sometimes she was a platinum blonde with brown roots and other days her hair was gold. Mrs. Baskin's first name was Kim, which is real pretty. She might have been pretty too, but she wore too much makeup and a phony smile. Mrs. Baskin talked more than Mom, and she didn't even tell good stories. All she ever talked about was men.

"Do you have a minute, Allie?" Mrs. Baskin would call out to me as I rode past. Then she'd offer me a cookie and tell me everything some man ever said to her from the very first second they met. Sometimes the man didn't say much of anything, but that didn't discourage Mrs. Baskin, who had a great imagination.

"Well?" she'd say, handing me a brownie when she finished her story. "What does he want? Do you think he'll call?"

"Will he call me?" she'd repeat, like she was ripping up some daisy playing "he loves me, he loves me not." Then my part was to say yes or no. If I guessed no, I had to make up a very good reason why Mrs. Baskin was lucky not to hear from the man, or she'd be sad. But not for long. Because Mrs. Baskin no sooner finished whispering to me about one man than she'd say, "Swear you'll never ever tell anyone?" and start right off talking about another.

"He will call me, won't he?" she'd insist, till I could see

why Mr. Baskin was always away on business. It could drive you crazy. When Mrs. Baskin called, Mom always had me say she wasn't in.

Mrs. Dietz had less personality than Mrs. Baskin, but Mom said she was a better bridge partner because she had greater powers of concentration. Mrs. Dietz came from the Midwest like Mom and had gray hair and two grown-up boys she missed so much she invited me to come along on a two-week trip to the Grand Canyon with her and her husband. Mrs. Dietz promised the trip would broaden my horizons, but Mom said she wouldn't dream of such an imposition. Was I ever relieved!

Mrs. O'Keith was more fun. Her name was Dot and she had three boys, red hair, and too many freckles. She also had two big front teeth which made her look a little like a rabbit when she smiled. Yet that didn't stop her from smiling. And I still liked her looks the best of all the neighbor ladies because no matter what happened Mrs. O'Keith was always as calm as the mother on "Leave It to Beaver." You'd stop by her house to visit and instead of fluttering around telling you how much she hated her husband she'd just say "How are you, Allie?" nice and easy like Bruce. Then I'd follow her out to the garden to watch her plant things or into the kitchen, where we'd talk. I stopped by every Wednesday on my way home from Brownie meetings, and in all my visits to Mrs. O'Keith she never told me a secret even once.

The ladies liked to play bridge on Tuesdays and canasta on Thursdays, only they couldn't always play because they needed Mom. Mom was their fourth, and while she liked playing cards, she also belonged to that small chorus which sang English folk songs like "Greensleeves" in parts. Whenever her group had to sing in public they called lots of rehearsals and Mom forgot about playing cards. Singing was better than playing an instrument for Mom because she didn't have to practice at home, she just had to make rehearsals. Mom had a good voice and liked to sing. Still, even when she skipped playing cards Mom kept missing rehearsals. That was the trouble with Mom. She'd start something, then she'd drop it.

I'd promised Bruce I'd try to convince Mom to come to Mrs. Baskin's, where his men were building a tennis court. Then Mom would be there playing cards when Bruce dropped by—at least, that was the plan. So I reminded Mom that she'd promised to play bridge on Tuesdays and canasta on Thursdays, and to sing madrigals on Mondays and to go to big chorus on Fridays, but that she rarely bothered showing up for anything. I told Mom she had all these responsibilities that she was shirking, and asked how long she expected people to be patient if she kept letting them down. I said this all for Bruce's sake. Still, Mom saw it made sense, so she promised to go play bridge at Kim Baskin's, but only if I'd come to fetch her by four thirty, before Mrs. Baskin bored her to tears.

I could hardly wait to tell Bruce. Sam and I ate breakfast early and took off with our towels rolled up over our shoulders so that we could go straight to the beach from seeing Bruce.

The way to the old Walters place is easy. You just go up Crescent, then down Oak, and over to the Boulevard, which is where skunks get run over since it's the widest road in town.

"Well, Allie, what are you doing up so early?" asked the big red-haired cop, who must have pulled over out of boredom. I saw him eyeing the rolled-up towels slung over our shoulders.

"Stormy got away," I told him.

"Does she have her tag?"

"I guess so."

"Well, if I see her, I'll send her home."

"I wouldn't try to corner her if I were you."

"You shouldn't keep her, if she's a biter. She should be destroyed."

"I didn't say she was a biter. I just said don't touch her mouth."

"What's 'destroyed'?" Sam asked after the policeman gave me a look and drove off.

"It's like 'passed away' for dogs," I told him. Still, I wasn't the least bit worried. Whole armies couldn't capture Stormy if she didn't feel like getting caught.

"Come on," I said, racing down the Boulevard past Mrs. Dietz's where Bruce had a job, only no one was there yet because everyone was next door at the old Walters place Bruce had just bought to redo. His men were tearing the insides out, making it all nice again, but different. Bruce said there wasn't much use for ballrooms. People wanted indoor swimming pools, modern kitchens, and saunas, so Bruce was turning the old Walters place into a model of what you could do with a big old house.

I'd never been inside the Walters place because they didn't have children. Sam and I knocked on the big, carved wooden doors. No one came. Still, I heard noises inside, and I kept knocking.

"I guess they don't hear us," I told Sam, so we just walked in. Downstairs at the Walters' was a big empty place like a gym, only it smelled of sawdust and you could still see the lines on the floor where there were once walls. The furniture was gone too, but the place was crowded with people. There were dozens of guys hanging around, because that's where Bruce had temporary offices for his crews to check in before they went off to other jobs around town.

There were lots of guys I didn't know, but I also saw Tim, John, and Phil, who were doing Mrs. Baskin's tennis court, Pete, who was putting in Mrs. O'Keith's storm windows, and Frank and Kenny, who were digging up my backyard. The place was littered with paper cups half full of cold coffee from a diner on the highway.

"Looking for something?" asked Bruce's brother Barry, coming up behind me. Barry always looked angry even though he got to hang around the office instead of going out with the crews to do real work.

"I told Bruce I'd stop by to see him."

"He never shows before eleven," Barry said, going back to a metal desk in the corner where he'd been reading a paper.

"I'm at the beach then."

"That so?" Barry said, not looking up.

"Bruce and I agreed I'd stop by around eight thirty," I told Barry, because he seemed the most official in his chair behind the desk.

"That's very funny."

"Why?"

"I told you, the bastard never shows up before eleven."

I didn't know what to do. I'd promised Bruce I'd come by, but Howie was counting on me too. I looked to Sam for his opinion, but he just wanted to scram.

"I'll wait a few minutes, if you don't mind," I said, looking around for a nice corner where Sam and I could sit.

"It's your time to waste. Just don't go expecting miracles," Barry shrugged, half smiling until we heard Bruce's car drive up.

THE day after the storm was very busy. The beach was full of leaves and trash and fallen branches. I worked so hard helping to clean up that Howie gave me his extra whistle and let me stay for the big kids' afternoon workout. It isn't easy keeping up with kids thirteen and fourteen, even when they're loafing. It took all my concentration not to get lapped.

"You tired?" asked Howie.

"Nope," I said, though when we finished I threw myself down on the dock and just lay there panting, not even caring if I got splinters in my back.

"You sure you're okay?" Howie asked, scrambling back over the catwalk to the dock with a towel.

"See those squirrels?" I said, pointing.

"Yeah," he said, tossing the towel over my shoulders. So we sat there awhile watching the trees on shore shake as black squirrels big as cats leaped from branch to branch.

"They say that all the black squirrels are in Princeton, but there's this yard in Boston full of 'em, Howie told me."

It was five thirty before I even thought to ask the time, threw on my sweats, and rushed over to Mrs. Baskin's to help Bruce.

I knocked on Mrs. Baskin's front door, then went inside where I heard voices. The cards were still out, but the other ladies had already gone and Mom looked real relieved to see me. Bruce seemed glad too. But I couldn't interrupt the story Mrs. Baskin was telling about a labrador named Henry who dragged his master two miles to shore when her boat went down. "Now that's devotion," Mrs. Baskin said, her eyes glistening.

"No, that's a retriever," said Mom. Still, both ladies paused to clear lumps from their throats.

It was so nice sitting with Mom and Bruce that even Mrs. Baskin being there couldn't spoil it. There was also home-made gingerbread. I offered Bruce a piece, then took two myself. I could have sat there forever, only Mom kept clearing her throat to remind me that I'd promised to rescue her. So I wiped the crumbs from my mouth and stood up.

"There's an emergency. Sam just fell off his bicycle. You have to come home quick," I announced.

"Christ, Allie! Why did you wait so long to tell me?" Mom said, leaping up to play her part.

"Doesn't Sam ride a tricycle?" said Mrs. Baskin.

"It's still a big fall if you're little," I explained.

"I'm sure he's not critically wounded. Still, I'd better go," Mom sighed. "God, I hope he hasn't dripped blood on the white carpet."

"I have to go too," Bruce said. So we all got up and thanked Mrs. Baskin for the refreshments and promised to see her again as soon as possible. As she walked us to the door, Mrs. Baskin's hand accidentally brushed against Bruce's arm. She glanced at me to see if I caught it. Bruce looked embarrassed.

"Bye, Kim dear," Mom said, kissing Mrs. Baskin's cheek to hide her smile. I tried to sneak out with Mom and Bruce because I could tell Mrs. Baskin was going to start in with her questions about what I made of the way Bruce looked at her, and I knew it would hurt Mrs. Baskin to hear that I thought Bruce looked at her as if he wished she'd disappear.

But there was no escaping Mrs. Baskin.

"Oh, Allie, could you help me clear the glasses a minute?" she called.

If it had been a kid who called, I could have pretended not to notice. But you can't be rude to grown-ups, so I marched back inside.

"Well, what do you think?" Mrs. Baskin asked, all excited.

"I have to think about it," I told her.

"What do you think he wants?" she insisted.

"I'll tell you tomorrow," I promised, rushing back out to the driveway, where Bruce was also talking about wanting something very badly as he and Mom stood close together, looking pained and flushed like when you're racing on a hurt foot. Then Mom looked up and stepped away.

"I loved running into you, too. But why start back down a road that goes nowhere—especially when it's such a dangerous road?" Mom said, all cold. She had a hundred different looks and voices, some that made you want to cry.

"What do you mean?" Bruce asked, not knowing Mom thought being clear sometimes spoiled the whole effect.

"Oh, Bruce," Mom laughed. But Bruce just stood there. "Cheer up," she said, smiling as she slipped into her car.

"Goodbye," Mom said. But Bruce didn't even smile back at her when she threw him one last glance.

"Hey, Bruce," I called, grabbing my bike and catching up with him as he walked off.

Mom drove past, waving like always.

"You want to put your bike in the back of the station wagon?" she asked, slowing a second as she passed. But I told her it would only scratch the paint.

"This was a bad idea. I'm sorry," I told Bruce as we watched Mom's brake lights flare at the corner before her car disappeared.

"It's not your fault," Bruce said. And I suppose he was right. The only thing wrong with the plan was that Mom didn't act nice.

Bruce had his car parked at the Walters place, so I went along with him, walking my bike. We might have made a new plan as we walked, only Bruce didn't say much. He mostly looked at the ground.

I could see why Bruce was down. But if you thought like Mrs. Baskin, you might also be encouraged, because

whatever Mom said one day, she would change her mind
the next. I told Bruce that, only he didn't laugh. He just
smiled sort of sad, like he already knew it. Then he asked
me if someone else was stopping by to visit Mom and I
told him no. Bruce didn't ask me if anyone was sending
letters.

"And who are you seeing?" Bruce asked, just kidding.

"Me?" I said. Just then some of Bruce's men drove by
and honked their horn. I bet they thought I had a desperate crush on Bruce—that's how stupid some guys are.

"Yes, what about you? Are you going to get married like
your mother?"

"I never want to get married," I told him.

"No one ever *wants* to get married, but everyone *gets*
married," Bruce said, smiling, a little more like his old self.

"You're not married, are you?"

"No, guess not," Bruce said as we reached the old
Walters place. "Well, goodbye," he said, stopping at the
end of the driveway.

"Bye," I said. We both just stood there a second. Then I
flipped up my kickstand, mounted my bike, and rode
home.

Poor Bruce. You might have thought he'd get discouraged, but maybe he wasn't so different from the boys who
showed up at the door minutes after I bit them, still asking
if I could come out to play.

I began swimming over to Mrs. Baskin's around four
thirty each day when Howie was busy with the big kids'
workout. Bruce and I had run into each other there once,
then Bruce had started stopping by the Baskin job that
same time each day for no real reason. Me, I went to cheer
Bruce up.

"Hi, Bruce," I'd say.

"Hey, Allie," he'd say. Then I'd sit on Mrs. Baskin's

dock dangling my feet in the water, and Bruce would pace around.

"I sort of regret the whole thing," Bruce said, while I regretted not bringing my fishing rod since tons of sunnies kept nibbling my toes.

Bruce's guys couldn't figure why he'd started dropping by the Baskins' backyard.

"Who's your new girl?" Barry asked when he ran into Bruce and me walking back from Mrs. Baskin's.

"My name is Allie."

"Isn't she a bit young?"

Bruce eyed me a moment. "Too young to wear stockings and too old for anklets," he laughed. It was the first time I remember feeling stupid about anklets.

"Allie? Allie Gardner? Why start that again?" Barry growled.

"I'm not sure I can," I heard Bruce say as I ran off. But he was wrong. Bruce had friends at our house. I liked him. Sam liked him. Ada liked Bruce too, and used to make a big production out of washing and pressing any T-shirts or jackets that he left around. Even Stormy liked him enough to let him scratch her head if I said it was okay. Only Tad refused to see that Bruce was special. Bruce ran with the grown-ups, but he didn't act like a real grown-up. I told Bruce I thought that he was secretly my age.

"You crazy? Here, look at this," Bruce said, touching the sandy waves at his left temple. "What color do you see mixed in there?"

"Blond," I said.

"Blond, my foot—it's white," Bruce said. "I bet none of your other playmates are gray."

I didn't dare tell Bruce that my mom put a rinse in her hair.

"Look at this gray!" she'd say, shaking the bottle of color

she'd get all over the bathroom so that Ada always said it looked like something had died.

"Do you know how old I am?" Mom would ask her reflection.

"You're not so old. You're just perfect," I'd tell her. I would have given anything to be Mom's age.

"But I look old!" Mom would insist.

"Anyone looks old when they frown like that!" I'd say, making my face all wrinkly too.

Mom was sitting at her vanity, staring into the mirror. But she was thinking, not looking. Dad had gone to Washington on business that morning and Mom was acting all edgy, like she was maybe up to mischief. Mom got so distracted with her thinking, she didn't even hear the water slurping in the bathroom. Lucky I was around to run in and turn the tap off just before the tub overflowed.

"I'd kill myself if it weren't for you," Mom said, settling into her bubble bath. It always scared me when she said that in the bathroom because a tub is where the movie ladies slit their wrists. That's why I wished Bruce were there. Not Bruce from that afternoon after cards, but the one from the summer before who had only to sneak up behind Mom to make her smile.

"Mind if I stay with you?" I asked, perching on the edge of the tub.

I needn't have worried about Mom. Just settling into the bath so cheered her she started telling me stories about her favorite aunt, Aunt Ruth, who lived for love, which Mom says is the best way not to get it. I always loved Mom's Aunt Ruth stories and could usually listen to them for hours, but today I had something to say.

"I want to talk to you about Bruce," I said, and Mom laughed. Still, I didn't let that deter me.

"Bruce makes me feel good," I told her.

Mom nodded. "Sometimes, for hours, it's heaven," she sighed, sinking down into the trembling bubbles so that just her toes peeked out.

"Then why don't you like Bruce?" I asked, since you have to be firm with Mom when she starts talking nonsense.

"I don't *dis*like him," Mom said, shrugging her shoulders crowned with bubbles. "Bruce is very nice. He's just not exactly what I had in mind. But there *is* someone almost perfect." Mom smiled, starting to talk of her old beaux.

Of course I didn't tell Bruce *that* when I met him over by Mrs. Baskin's just past four thirty. But I may have looked a little worried.

"What's up?" said Bruce.

"Nothing much."

"You sure?" he asked, cocking his head to study me.

"Sure," I answered, blushing.

"Okay," Bruce said, patting my shoulder.

We had a nice walk up the back path kicking pebbles, although Bruce looked a little sad, like he was also thinking of my mom.

Then I had to leave him to go and visit Mrs. Baskin to keep her from getting too suspicious.

"Why doesn't he ever come to the house?" Mrs. Baskin groaned, peeking out from behind the checked kitchen curtains as Bruce walked off. "Do you think he's afraid of Larry, or is he afraid of what might happen if we were to find ourselves alone?" she asked, offering me fudge.

"I don't think Bruce is afraid of Mr. Baskin," I said, taking the piece with the most nuts. No one was afraid of Mr. Baskin.

"Maybe if I went walking out back and you came with me..." Mrs. Baskin began, telling me everything that had ever passed between her and Bruce—a few words—practically nothing before last month when she hired him to put in a tennis court. Then Bruce showed her the plans, sent two men, and disappeared.

"And that was it—he barely checked their progress. Now, suddenly, he stops by almost every afternoon, walks around back a bit, then goes. You know, you see him. You're always here then," she said. She had to know if he was waiting for a sign. It was driving her mad, breaking her heart, she said. But Mrs. Baskin always talked that way because she was boy-crazy.

"Of course I'm upset. I'm a genuinely passionate person. Not like your mom, who only wants to be admired. Don't leave!" Mrs. Baskin cried, offering me a fudge. "I'm sorry. I don't know what came over me. Some people like your mother. But that's not important. What matters is that Bruce drops by here to see me almost every day. I mean, why else could he be coming? Do you think he'll make a pass at me soon?" Mrs. Baskin asked.

"A what?"

"You know," she giggled. "Will he?"

"I don't think so," I said, accidentally wiping my fudge-smeared hands on her white tablecloth.

WHEN I got home around seven Ada fed us hot dogs and gave me a note from Mom which said she had gone to New York to meet an old friend. I hoped it would be the nice lady who gave me the book on Cinderella, only I was disappointed, for later on Mom came back with a man. The second he walked in I guessed it was Erich. He was tall and blond and looked very handsome in his dark blue suit and crisp white shirt.

"Meet Tad and Allie." Mom was smiling, showing us off like prize poodles.

"And Sam," I said.

"And Sam," Mom said. For Sam was standing right there beside me and Erich might have thought Mom couldn't count.

We all shook hands. Erich said a few words with an accent I could notice—not like Dad's. Then the boys went back to the den to watch TV.

"So this is your little girl," Erich said, resting a hand on my shoulder as I stood there. "So tell me, Allie, what is it you like to do?"

"I just finished burying some dead birds," I told him. "First I put them in a shoebox and make twig crosses, then I bury them out back. Dad says they sometimes have diseases."

"That's very good of you," Erich said.

"Go wash your hands right now," Mom said. But I started asking Erich millions of questions about what Mom was really like at school.

"There was no one quite like her," he said, frowning as he remembered some funny stories Mom never told me, where she'd acted bad.

"That's not true," Mom said.

"Oh, yes," Erich insisted. "Your mom had a smile that made you willing to do anything for her, only she could never decide what it was she wanted you to do! It drove me mad," Erich said, looking straight at Mom while supposedly talking to me.

"You know I've changed," Mom said.

"So heartless . . . Remember that poor professor."

"I'm not like that anymore," Mom protested.

"I know," Erich said, laughing like Dad when he teased you for things like being skinny which you couldn't help.

"Tell me about the professor," I said, since Mom and

Erich were busy looking at each other that stupid way big kids sometimes look.

"Are you still here?" Mom sighed. "Why not go watch TV?"

"Tad's just watching a war movie."

"Then read one of the books on my night table."

"I've read them all."

"You can't have."

"I've read all the good ones."

"How can you know if you haven't bothered to read the others, sweetheart?" Mom said, her tight smile warning me to watch it.

"You can't tell a book by its cover," Erich told me.

"No, but you can tell everything by the first page," I explained.

"Young lady!" Mom snapped, finally ordering me out to find Stormy, which was like saying "Go play in traffic," because Stormy had bolted hours before.

"What a determined little chaperone! Is she her dad's favorite?" Erich asked as I lingered by the door.

"Mom," I began.

"Young lady, I'm warning you . . ."

"Till soon," Erich called, waving. I walked out feeling just as miserable as if I were letting Bruce down myself.

"Ha-ha!" Tad said as I trudged past.

"What's so funny?" I snapped. But Tad just kept dancing around me, making faces. "Just you wait till you fall in love!" I cried.

"Oh, who's in love?" he laughed.

IT isn't easy to be happy, but everyone is always trying. That's all the grown-ups talk about—about the cars and girls and dresses—about the ways in which they're always trying to be happy. That's what I liked about Bruce. He never bothered with all that. He'd just say, "How's it going, Mouse?"

"How's it going with you?" I'd ask. Then we'd both shrug.

"I'D like to have a word with you, young lady," Mom said, coming into my room the day after I met Erich. "Young lady" is Mom's name for me whenever she's especially disappointed. I thought Mom would scream, but she just told me Erich lived in Geneva where they spoke three different languages at once and that he was almost divorced.

I was glad that Mom was being nice. Still, it didn't seem fair to me that Mom should waste the one night of Dad's trip going out to dinner with a stranger when she might have spent the time talking with Bruce.

"He's not a stranger, darling. He's a dear, dear friend. Wouldn't you like to go to Geneva on a holiday?" Mom asked.

I told her I would rather go to the Grand Canyon with the Dietzes.

"Oh, come on," Mom said. "Switzerland has mountains and real castles and Geneva is built on a big lake." That lake business was supposed to excite me, but I knew she was lying.

"Is that where the letters with the funny stamps come from?"

"Look, I tried to explain things in a nice way. It's not *my* fault if *you* can't be adult," Mom said, stomping out.

"Don't go off shopping and forget your chorus practice," I called as Mom slammed the front door.

"Damn," Mom said, coming back inside a few minutes later. "Double damn!"

"What's the matter?" I asked, racing downstairs.

"Why can't anything ever be simple?" Mom asked,

throwing down her purse. She picked up the phone. "The car won't start," she said, dialing. "Today of all days."

The garage was in another town and very busy, but they promised to try to come by and look at the car sometime early the next day.

"Do you know what it means when a repairman says he'll come by 'sometime early tomorrow'? It means I'll be stuck here forever! This is just terrific," Mom muttered.

"You've still got chorus even if you can't go shopping."

"I don't care," Mom said, all depressed at getting stuck.

"Look, I'll take you," I told her.

"How will *you* take me?"

"In the sailboat," I said, since Mom's small chorus met in a house across the lake.

"I don't know..." Mom said. But you can get Mom to go along with almost anything when she's depressed.

"You sure this is safe?" Mom asked, crawling onto the Sailfish while still clutching the dock.

"Dad and I sail every weekend," I answered. But even as we pushed off I could already see there was a big difference between just doing what Dad said and actually being captain myself.

At first I couldn't catch the wind at all. Then I got a gust that sent the boat skidding along, half on its side, like a skipping stone.

"Are you doing this right?" Mom asked, suspicious.

"Isn't this fun?" I said, trying to reassure her. "Look how far we've gotten!"

We were halfway across the lake.

"You *sure* you know how to sail this?" Mom cried, fingers white from gripping the fiberglass.

"Don't worry," I said, not yet understanding that a Sailfish is really just a giant kickboard with a sail, so it flips over real fast. Once I finally did learn how to sail it, I'd flip the Sailfish over just for fun whenever Sam and I felt like a swim. You're skimming along like mad, then *plop!* over you go. I even thought it was fun the first time we tipped over, but Mom was scared.

"Help! Help!" she screamed. But we were way out behind the island where no one could see or hear us.

"It's okay," I said. There was no need for Mom to be worried. Howie taught a Red Cross lifesaving course Tuesday mornings, and I was almost a certified lifesaver. The only trouble with class was we never got to practice lifesaving holds on people who were really drowning. The kids playing victim in class would struggle at first, but then they always started to laugh.

"You lack practical experience," Howie told us. And it was true. The hard part of the course wasn't saving a giggling person, it was swimming forty laps in your soggy sweatclothes—whatever that's supposed to prove.

Luckily, Mom had a very serious attitude about drowning. From the second we flipped over, Mom proved an excellent victim. She cried and clawed and kicked and grabbed, trying to drag me under with her just like the drowning people in our lifesaving films.

"Help! Help!" Mom cried, wasting her breath.

"Just be calm. Relax. Try to float a little and I'll grab you under the chin," I told Mom, only wishing Howie could see.

"I can't float!" Mom cried, flailing her arms like she was trying to climb out of the water.

"I can't either," I confessed. Howie says you have to be drowned already or to have some body fat to float. So Mom had to be able to float, since she wasn't as skinny as me.

"Just lean back, relax, and I'll grab you under the chin," I told her.

"I can't float," Mom sobbed, still slapping the water. I had never seen her so active.

"I can't float either."

"But you can *swim!*" Mom screamed.

"Please, Mom. Swear you won't grab my neck and I'll save you," I said, treading water just beyond her reach.

"Sure," she promised. "Sure." But I just couldn't trust Mom until she got too tired to drag me under. Then I sneaked up underwater, grabbed her by the chin, and dragged her back to the boat. That neck hold is terrific because the victim can't reach you. I don't know why drowning people insist on trying to take you down with them, but all the way back to the boat that's what Mom struggled to do.

"Now quit fighting me and hold on to the centerboard," I told her when we finally reached the overturned boat.

"Don't talk to me like that."

"Just grab the boat and hang on," I said, disappointed Mom didn't need artificial respiration since that had been my second highest mark on the lifesaving final. Although, to be honest, I still wasn't a certified lifesaver, because for that you have to be twelve.

We'd flipped over midway between the beach and Mrs. Baskin's. There was a boat at Mrs. Baskin's and Bruce was there. The beach had all the lifesaving equipment, and, of course, Howie. But he got to save people all the time. I looked at Mom hanging on to the centerboard and I could see that she was dying to be rescued.

"Just hang on a little longer. I'll be right back," I called. Then I sprinted off free-style to get Bruce.

Chapter
Seven

*M*y plan worked better this time. When
Bruce and I showed up in the Baskins' boat
ten minutes later we found Mom still clinging to the Sailfish as tight as she clung to Bruce's neck once we fished her
out. The ride back home went fast because Bruce was a
strong rower.

"I think she's slightly hysterical," Bruce whispered. I
told him not to worry, Mom was always a little like that.

Bruce helped Mom out onto the dock, but she still clung
to him, weeping.

"It's all right," Bruce said, patting Mom's arm as he led
her up to the house.

When they got to the patio Bruce paused a moment,
then carried Mom up the steps, though she could have
climbed them herself.

"Why don't you go out front and look for Stormy?"

Bruce suggested. I guess Bruce hadn't noticed Stormy was already tied out back, going crazy watching the crows feast on grass seed from an open sack.

I was about to tell him when he carried Mom on inside and left me standing on the patio alone.

"Hey, Bruce," I said, starting in after them. The entrance hall was empty. They were already upstairs.

"You okay, Mom?" I cried, suddenly frightened. But they couldn't hear me. There was nothing to do but go, so I went back out and untied my dog. Stormy lunged for the crows, who scattered, cawing, their flapping wings loud as clapping hands.

"Stormy!" I called. But she was gone. You had to respect her single-minded determination. She was a hunter and, every chance she got, she hunted. You'd be walking the back path, look up, and there she'd be, crashing along, stalking some squirrel. Stormy was supposed to be a Labrador retriever, but she also killed. Mom said it was disgusting when Stormy brought me dead animals as presents, yet how could I yell when Stormy lay her mangled rabbits at my feet?

"Why, thank you, this is lovely," I would say, patting Stormy's head, though Mom was right. Stormy's presents were pretty gross.

"Ada! Come quick!" I'd yell the second Stormy got out of earshot, never before, because Stormy looked so proud, I thought it was important to encourage her. I didn't want her to give up and get depressed like all the neighbor ladies who sat around doing nothing.

"Stormy!" I called, walking back toward the house through the hedge roses, which smell best of all in August when they relax and spread their petals like a happy rabbit lets down its ears. Walking around the house I heard Mom laughing. The door to my balcony was open. If you didn't know better, you might have thought the noise was coming from my room.

"Hey, Stormy," I called one last time. Then I walked all the way down to the end of the driveway to play hopscotch after stopping in the garage for some chalk.

Bruce came downstairs whistling an hour later. I know, because I was just lying on the yellow living-room couch thinking, since the hopscotch wore me out. Bruce paused at the foot of the stairs.

"God Almighty," Bruce said, stretching both his arms above his head. Then he reached down to smooth his rumpled T-shirt. Bruce always had nice eyes, but when he came downstairs that day they glowed.

"I suppose I should take the Baskins' boat back," Bruce murmured, walking past the couch on his way to the door.

"I'll go with you," I offered, sitting up.

"You're the most wonderful little girl in the world," Bruce said, shaking his head. But he wasn't looking at me.

The day after Bruce and I saved Mom she went out shopping. Clothes were very important to Mom. That's why I thought she might have loved Bruce. Mom mostly went out shopping when she was hungry for life and full of hope. Sometimes she'd take me shopping with her and tell me where she'd wear each dress and who might see her. Then she'd buy another dress to wear to the special places these new people would invite her after that. Of course, even Mom knew it was all just a game that she was playing—especially since, in real life, she didn't even like going out all that much. Mom also shopped when she was angry, but then she made a point of showing Dad the bill.

When Mom went shopping the day after Bruce saved her she didn't show Dad the bill because she was happy. I was happy too. I don't know when I sensed this was different and could only end by changing everything, but I was very happy for a few days. Sam and I would get up early, have breakfast, then go out to look for Stormy until Dad drove off to work. When we came back Mom would be downstairs, dressed already, sipping coffee.

"Well, did you find her?" Mom would ask.

"No, but we saw her. At least she's in the neighborhood," I'd say, and Sam would nod like it was true.

"Why did I ever let you get that dog?" Mom would say as she stood by the glass doors watching Frank and Kenny cross the lawn to start back in on the job.

IT was a funny summer. When Bruce's men finished planting, Mom decided they should build a tennis court behind the new garden. "It's a present for you and Allie," she told Dad when he asked what the hell the guys were doing. That gave Dad a good laugh. Not that he was around much weekdays. Dad said he was too busy to take a vacation and often didn't get home much before eight. Sometimes he even stayed at work way past my bedtime. Yet once in a while he'd show up midday for a few hours, or would come all the way back from town just for lunch.

"I like to see the kids," Dad would say, only he never bothered to call us home when he dropped in.

Dad liked Kenny and Frank okay, but he always got mad when he saw Bruce. Dad never came right out and said that's why he was angry. But you could see that just running into Bruce set Dad off. Not that Dad came home early enough to see Bruce all that often. Still, it helped if I was there, so I started leaving the beach early, to drop by, just in case. Kenny said Bruce came by before noon. He was still there when I came home near four.

"Hey, Allie! Where's Sam?" Kenny asked, just to talk, since he knew I always dropped Sam off at Frankie's on my way home.

"Hey, Allie!" Kenny called, but I ignored him, racing on up across the lawn to bang in the back door, crying "I'm home!"

"Why don't you go look for your dog?" Mom would call downstairs, which was her way of asking me to go outside and watch for Dad.

I always hate waiting for people because it makes you think about them. If you love them and they're late, you start to worry that something might have happened. And if you don't love them, you still feel sorry, thinking how bad they must feel inside to act so mean.

It was very lonely at the end of the driveway. My head was too busy for me to jump rope or play jacks, and I couldn't just sit looking down the driveway or the red ants who lived there would crawl up my legs. Sometimes Tad and Dave came by. They were some company at least, but the second they rode off I couldn't help thinking of a time before when things were simpler and you knew for sure that ratting on people was bad and helping your mom was good. It made me feel better to remember those days. But the best thing was not to think at all and just to concentrate on scratching Stormy's stomach.

Stormy was very clear about her stomach. I'd be waiting at the end of the driveway when the shrubs would start to shake and out she'd pop. It was almost as if she'd sensed I was unhappy and had come to visit. I was glad to see her, but I couldn't just run and grab her. The key was not to move too quickly, like with a wild animal, which is what Bruce told me Stormy must think she was. Stormy would appear, tilt her head, and sniff, checking me out like she had to make sure of me all over again, right from the start.

The important thing was to stay quiet while she stood poised, sniffing. It was all right for me to smile and say "Hey, Stormy, how you doing?"—just so long as I didn't ruin things by calling her, and making her feel guilty for all the times she didn't come. You had to wait for Stormy to feel like seeing you, then never grab her choke chain.

If I sat still enough, Stormy would walk up to within five feet of me and roll on her back, which was her way of asking if I'd rub her stomach.

Stormy roamed the woods all day. Still, in the end, she liked to be fed Dash dog food and to have me rub her stomach, though she would bite anyone else who even tried to pat her head. Stormy couldn't stand sitting still, but if I rubbed her tummy just right, she would lie there in a trance while I talked to her for hours, trying to figure things out, the way I once would pray.

I sometimes suspect these frank talks gave Stormy her great contempt for people. At least Dad said she held them in contempt. Yet I don't think she disliked people. They just bored her. That's why I never really tried to find Stormy all the hours I spent out looking. Waiting out front was always better when Stormy showed, though I never could figure if she came because she loved me or because she knew that I loved her.

I used to leave the beach every afternoon no later than three thirty. "I'm home!" I'd call, banging in the kitchen door. Sometimes Ada would be standing there, all quiet, doing dishes. Other times Bruce's red jacket slung over a stool would be the only thing around.

"I'm home!" I'd cry. There was always a pause before they answered. I say "they," although they never answered me together. Sometimes Mom would mumble "Just a minute." Other times Bruce would walk in from the living room to say hi. It was funny about Mom and Bruce. They were both usually such good talkers, but for a while there the two of them would greet me almost shyly.

"Why don't you go out and look for your dog?" Mom

would say, touching my arm. And I would march back out front to watch the red ants dig the dirt out from under the asphalt, like they had plans for a great tunnel to let them cross beneath the driveway without getting crushed.

"You want to come to town with me, if you're doing nothin'?" Dave would ask whenever he biked past without Tad.

I might have liked going to town, although I wasn't sure Dave meant it. Besides, I wasn't doing "nothing"—it only looked it. I was busy watching. I'd become just like the grown-ups. In a way, my whole life had changed.

I still went to the beach mornings, but I gave up tennis lessons to keep watch. Hanging around out front wasn't much fun, but it was no worse than tennis, which is very boring if you're no good because you have to spend all your time running around picking up balls. I didn't mind skipping tennis lessons. I only worried that Dad might notice my game was getting worse. But Bruce said not to worry, my game couldn't get worse. That was one thing Dad and Bruce agreed on.

"Appalling," Dad said whenever we played.

Still, tennis was something Dad and I could do together, besides sailing. Saturday was okay because we always booked a tennis court, then later we sailed. Sometimes Dad and I would even go shopping for a power saw or tractor to store way back in the tool shed. Sundays the stores were closed and it was harder to keep Dad busy. If he started drinking early he'd already be in one of his bad moods by the time I got back from church.

"We did that yesterday," he'd say to everything I suggested, until finally I hit on something really dumb like bows and arrows, which we hadn't done in ages because we both hated it so much.

"Okay," he'd say, "that's it." Then off we'd go to the archery range and get bruised arms.

"If only he'd die!" Mom said when I went upstairs to show her the black-and-blue spot. "If only he'd die." But of course Dad didn't die. He wouldn't even work weekends. I was stuck.

You'd think Dad and I might be friends after I'd entertained him the whole weekend, but it was like nothing. I was nothing. I'd bring Dad home at the end of a long day of diving, tennis, and sailing and Mom would be so busy writing letters she wouldn't even bother to thank me. I'd go looking for a magazine feeling pretty rotten. Then I'd spy Sam in a corner playing quietly with his trucks, and knowing it was like he'd had a home where he was safe all afternoon was thanks enough.

Besides, it wasn't going to last forever.

"It can't go on much longer," Mom promised. Not that hanging around to keep an eye out was all work. Sometimes it was great, like the day Bruce stopped by with a shiny new silver-gray Ferrari. I'm personally not crazy about cars, but I could see how you might fall in love with Bruce's.

"Look! It's a car just like in the spy movies. I bet it can go over two hundred! What do you think?" I said to Mom, who'd come outside to ask how much it cost.

"A lot," Bruce told her.

"What's this?" Mom said, leaning over the dashboard and pointing to a dial.

"Revolutions per minute. Come feel some," Bruce said, looking right at Mom. I would have liked to ride with them, but the car had just two seats.

"I can't go for a ride," said Mom, who always refused when you first asked her.

"Come on," Bruce said.

"I can't go for a ride with you," Mom repeated.

"Oh?" said Bruce, like it was news to him. "Come on," he said. "Hop in."

"I can't!" said Mom.

"Why not?" Bruce asked, still not believing.

"It's a convertible. Someone might see me. Be reasonable," Mom answered, cross at having to explain.

"You don't like the car."

"It's just fine."

"Just fine! It's the greatest car since—" Bruce grinned. "Aw, come on. It's three o'clock. He's stuck in some windowless conference room forty miles away."

Mom smiled and shook her head.

"Not even a little ride, just to the highway? You've got to feel her," Bruce pleaded. But Mom still shook her head no, strict as a princess. "Okay, you win. I'll settle for a spin around the block," Bruce said, touching Mom's hand.

"*Especially* not around the block," Mom whispered. "Ever hear of neighborhood gossip?"

"Nobody knows a thing. I just come by to check the work."

"Which is why I can't go riding with you!" Mom insisted. "Why don't you give Allie the thrill of a lifetime," she added, since Bruce and I both looked so disappointed.

"That what you want?" Bruce said, still staring at Mom. "That what you want?" he asked again. "We could always go inside."

"We can always go inside," Mom said, "but you just bought this car. It deserves a ride. Off you go," Mom said, patting my rear. "Have a nice time."

"You guys work as a team or something?" Bruce asked, squinting into the sun as he looked our way.

Mom looked at Bruce and laughed so low I wondered if

she really liked Bruce, or was only kidding him to keep in practice.

"Don't get your hair all tangled, or I won't brush it out," she warned, turning back to me.

"What if her father comes home?" Mom called as I slipped into the low seat with real leather soft as Stormy's stomach.

"You'll think of something," Bruce said. He waved, then revved up and off we went. It was a tight fit inside Bruce's car, with the dashboard all full of dials like a cockpit. His side also had brakes, clutches, and a stick shift he kept changing as the engine growled.

We made the highway in no time.

"This is fun!" I said, nose tingling from excitement. "The most fun in the world!" I shouted, so Bruce could hear me above the wind, the engine, and the radio. And I really meant it for once. I wasn't just faking it like with Dad.

Bruce grinned, nodding, because there's nothing more exciting than tearing down the highway like the wind with the towns flipping by you like flash cards. We were having such a great time we forgot all about my hair tangling or ever going home. Everything was terrific until the radio started playing a song they played a lot back the summer before, when Bruce was doing the patio and Mom would drift out on her own to watch him work. I think Mom really liked Bruce then. I guess Bruce thought so too, because when the song came on he got sort of quiet. Mom was funny that way, how she could haunt you. I knew what Bruce was feeling, hearing that song, because sometimes just listening to the neighbor ladies talk about her made me rush home lonely for my lonely mother who couldn't see why I'd come.

"What do you say we head back? It's getting late," Bruce

said, although the song was just beginning and maybe if he waited till it was over that lonely feeling might disappear.

"Sure," I said, not even looking disappointed.

Still, I guess Bruce suspected I felt bad because we'd no sooner turned around than he said, "How about some ice cream?" and took me to a special dairy where they make their own from scratch. Bruce wanted raspberry sherbet and I wanted cherry vanilla. We got a scoop of each flavor on one cone, which I held so Bruce could eat and drive at the same time. Both flavors were good. The only trouble with ice cream is you can't save it. Between the melting and the eating it all disappeared so fast. Bruce ate the whole cone, so all I could save was just the napkin. I took it home and put it in *Victorian and Later English Poets* where Mom pressed roses, but it only made the pages stick together.

"Just four thirty-five," Bruce said, checking his watch as we pulled in the driveway.

"Should we tell Mom about the ice cream?" I asked.

"Huh?" Bruce said, looking back over his shoulder as he leaped from the car and rushed in the front door. The sun still seemed bright, yet it was too late to try to make the big kids' workout, so I went around back, untied my dog, and went out front to watch for Dad.

It was a busy afternoon. Overhead some jets were flying together, rolling around on their stomachs like frolicking seals. Tad and Dave passed by on their way to the movies. I know, because they said where they were going just to make me jealous. Tad and Dave could go anywhere. They weren't only older, they were also boys, which meant that wherever they weren't allowed to go, they could still sneak to.

"What you doing?" Tad asked, as if it was any of his business.

"Nothing."

"You sure?"

"Sure I'm sure. What do you see?"

The boys eyed me a minute while I sat perfectly still.

"She's doing nothing," Dave agreed.

"Whose car is that?" Tad asked.

"You see those jets?" I said, pointing, though by then they'd already flown way over to the far side of the sky.

"There's three of them!" said Dave.

"Aren't they doing skywriting or something?" I said.

"Do you think it's the army?" Dave asked.

"Whose car?" said Tad.

"I think Bruce is working out back."

"That isn't Bruce's car. You're lying."

"I'm not lying. It's new."

"It's a Ferrari!" cried Dave, running up the driveway.

"Ferraris stink," said Tad. "Let's go." So I watched them take off on their bikes. Dave told me they often rode all the way to the next town, which had a soda fountain where you could buy comics. But Dave said I had to keep their trips a secret. So many secrets! Every day brought new things I was supposed to forget about Mom and Bruce, who seemed very happy when Mom wasn't worrying about Dad coming home, or fighting with Bruce about his being so jealous of her taking calls.

"Do you want me to refuse to speak with an old friend when I'm sitting right here?" Mom asked when Ada sent me into the living room to tell Mom she had a long-distance call.

"Fine, talk to him!" Bruce said, rifling the raw-silk cushions of the couch for his navy sweatshirt.

"It's on the floor behind the couch," I told Bruce, pointing.

"You'll excuse me?" Mom said, smoothing her blouse as

she stood up, and Bruce stormed out, coming back inside a few minutes later to apologize.

No wonder Mom and Bruce fought. At least Mom and Dad used to go out to parties, but all Bruce and Mom ever did was stay inside. I would have gone stir-crazy always stuck indoors, although it didn't seem to bother Mom, who let her hair down in shining waves like Rapunzel, who spent a lot of time at home too. Afternoons, Mom mostly wore her satin robes, long, down to the floor, with flowing sleeves and fronts full of antique lace and dozens of tiny pearl buttons with delicate thread loops instead of buttonholes.

When Bruce came by and saw Mom like that, he wouldn't hang around out back with me but went right upstairs with her. The third floor got awfully hot since Dad hated air conditioning and refused to let Mom install it upstairs. Downstairs was like an icebox since no matter how often the grown-ups turned the air conditioning down, Tad would turn it way up. Both Mom and Bruce complained of the heat in Mom's room. Bruce was always sweating when he came downstairs, yet it was sometimes hours before Bruce would finally appear and come outside to watch me climb birches, which is tricky since you have to shinny up whole clumps, three at a time. Climbing birches skins your knees like crazy, but that's the challenge. Even babies can climb trees with branches strong enough to take your weight.

"That's very impressive," Bruce told me once, watching. Then, when I was sure I had his attention, I told him how worried I was.

"Your mom and I have fun," Bruce said. But he was only trying to reassure me. Bruce knew I worried that Mom was still unhappy. I know she was never real happy before. Yes, sometimes she was flirty and gay, but never around Dad. And, besides, that isn't happy. That's pretending. Mom got real good at just pretending. In fact, she finally got so good she began to lose track of what was make-believe and what was real.

Tad never lost track of anything.

"I'm going to tell Dad that I saw you with Bruce today," Tad said, popping out of the hedges with Dave just after Bruce left.

"There's nothing to tell."

"You're so fucking stupid it's embarrassing," Tad said, twisting my arm so hard I thought he'd break my elbow. "How could anyone be so stupid?" he asked, as I dug my teeth into his shoulder and hung on while he yelled to Dave for help.

"Oh, leave her alone. She's just a girl," said Dave, whom I could have kissed for just standing there.

"So fucking stupid! Grow up!" Tad screamed, backing off. Then he and Dave retreated to their secret treehouse.

Tad wasn't the only mean one. Bruce came by so much the neighbor ladies were full of questions.

"Why doesn't your mom ever visit? What's she up to? Have you seen Bruce? You know, he hasn't stopped by my house in over a week!" Mrs. Baskin complained, stopping me on the path as I raced home from the beach.

"I have to buy Allie some new jumpers," Mom told Mrs. O'Keith to change the subject when Mrs. O'Keith dropped by to warn Mom people were talking. Mrs. O'Keith did it to be nice, not mean, that first time, but Mom never had much to say to the neighbor ladies. She wasn't unfriendly to them, she'd just sit there thinking things that had nothing to do with coffee, canasta, and Spring Lakes. In fact, Mom hated polite conversation.

"It makes me feel dead to just stand there, smiling and nodding with the others at a tea or cocktails where nothing happens beyond those empty smiles and nods," Mom sighed, coming back from a party. "Words are just words and make pretty stories like colors make pretty paintings, but I want to *feel*," she'd say, running both hands through her hair like she might pull it herself from sheer frustration. Then she'd notice me and force a smile. I think Mom faked that smile because she hoped that I'd grow up to like parties. Yet I suspect that seeing people made Mom even more lonely. It wasn't just Dad's drinking. In a way, our isolation suited her. Mom had no patience for everyday living, but liked love and hate and playing make-believe on the phone with Erich and going upstairs with Bruce.

"Bruce doesn't pretend to have conversation," Mom once told me. "He has something else, and being with him I never feel alone."

What Mom was trying to say was that her being with Bruce was like me and Howie, where the point wasn't really talking, but just the way that being together made you feel.

But Bruce wasn't exactly like Howie, since just hearing Bruce's name could make Mom nervous. Sometimes Mom was anxious before Bruce came, edgy when he first showed up, then worried after he left. The part Mom always forgot was how good she felt most of the time that Bruce was with her. I think Mom liked Bruce a lot, she just didn't like to think about him. It was almost like Mom imagined Bruce was this big wrecking ball which threatened to come smashing down and ruin everything, destroying the house on the lake with Mom's closets full of clothes for her trips with Erich. Then other times it was like the house and clothes were one big headache and Bruce was Mom's relief.

"Bruce isn't like me, but at least he isn't like them either," Mom said, coming back from the Fourth of July party for Dad's law firm. Mom said going places full of people like that made her feel just like a Martian. She said that about a lot of different places, yet I never saw the world where she belonged.

"You have to go visit more," I told Mom, because it wasn't just the neighbor ladies who were talking. Kenny told me Bruce's brother Barry had told guys it was my fault that Bruce and Mom got together. Then he called me a little devil in Mrs. Baskin's hearing.

"Why would he say a thing like that?" Mrs. Baskin asked.

"He's just mean," I told her.

"Isn't there something more? Think, Allie. I'll give you a cookie if you can explain it. You all right?" she asked.

"Of course," I said, but I really didn't feel so good. Bruce wasn't feeling so good either. Some days when I came home early he was already down by the dock skipping stones and looking out at the water so hard I didn't need to ask how he was. We'd just walk up the path together saying nothing at the most magic time of day when the sky is on the edge of changing and there's a pause like the space in a dive after you soar up from your bounce. It's so peaceful when you just sort of hang above the board before you have to come down and start flipping around. The better diver you are, the longer that floating moment lasts, but everybody gets that soft space before sunset. Even the animals feel it. That's why they get so quiet and sit on their branches thinking about what they want to do that night.

"Who's Linda?" I asked Bruce as we were walking along the back path almost halfway to the cliffs, which are so far away they're in a whole different town.

"What are you talking about?" Bruce asked. So I took him still farther on to the tree where I'd found his name carved next to this girl's name way high up on the thick trunk.

"What's that?" I asked.

"That's ancient history," Bruce said. "It isn't even important."

"Then you should have put it in chalk. Aren't you going to fix it?"

"I can't put your mother's name up there!" Bruce said sounding as shocked as Mom.

"You can carve mine," I suggested, taking Bruce's Swiss Army knife out of his pocket and starting to open it up.

"Careful, Allie," Bruce said, taking it back. "That's one bitch of a blade."

"I'm not afraid of knives," I told him. And it was true. At least I wasn't when I held them. I wasn't even scared when Tad and Dave gutted bass with rusty pocketknives. I wasn't afraid for myself, that is, but Tad was such a pain about Bruce I thought he might do something awful like slash Bruce's tires.

Lucky thing Tad and Dave were always busy running some game all us kids had to play. I don't mind war, tag, or spud, but Tad's new favorite game was sending us out onto the Boulevard to play chicken with cars. That's a very bad game if you trip, and I wouldn't let Sam do it. Tad and Dave still got lots of the other kids to play by calling them babies if they were frightened. That was the trouble with Tad and Dave, they were only happy causing trouble. That's what I told Mrs. O'Keith when I stopped by for my usual visit after Brownies, and she agreed.

"Remind your mom about canasta tomorrow. Tell her I said it would keep her out of trouble," Mrs. O'Keith told me when I went to leave.

I promised Mrs. O'Keith I'd remind Mom, but I'm afraid that underneath Mom was a little like Tad and found trouble exciting.

"WHY doesn't Bruce check the work here anymore? Why is he always checking your backyard?" Mrs. Baskin groaned, offering me some fudge. I told her no, thank you. I was through with chocolate. The big girls at the beach wouldn't touch it because they said it gave them zits.

"But you don't have pimples," said Mrs. Baskin.

"I will soon," I said.

"Can't I get you anything?"

"No, nothing, thanks. I'm late for tennis lessons," I said, though I was going to skip again.

"WHY won't the club send your bills?" Dad asked, when Tad and I were playing him that weekend. "I haven't paid for a lesson in weeks. Are you so bad that Brad is embarrassed to bill me?"

"Allie hasn't been taking tennis lessons. She's been with Bruce," said Tad, the big rat.

"Is that true?"

"I've been helping the guys," I said, flashing my nails at Tad to remind him how he'd pay.

"Young lady, when I want you to become a laborer I'll let you know. Now get up to the net, Tad. Allie, you stay back," Dad said, starting to serve.

"There's more I could tell," Tad whispered, grinning.

"Just try it," I warned, throwing a pebble from my pocket at Tad's back.

"Christ, Allie! Pay attention!" Dad swore as his serve zipped past.

•   •   •

I WASN'T the only one distracted. Poor Bruce was getting all kinds of grief from Barry, so he practically stopped going to their office. One afternoon Barry got so mad at Bruce for avoiding him that he drove to our house and rushed around back screaming "Bruce!"

"How you doing?" Bruce said, like Barry always came to visit.

"You crazy or just a lazy shit?" Barry asked, while Kenny and Frank stood there looking as if they wanted to dive into the holes they'd just finished digging.

"That's enough," said Bruce.

"Why hang around here checking a few piddly jobs when you've got a whole development in Wayne you haven't so much as looked at? I had to go up and okay the foundations yesterday—me!—when all I know are the books."

"I'll get there eventually."

"Yeah, well, when you decide to come back to work I've got a whole list of places for you to visit—like just about every place we've got a major job. Why hang around here?" Barry said, steaming. "Or should I say, 'Why hang around *her?*'"

"That supposed to be a trick question?" Bruce shrugged, which only made the veins in Barry's forehead pop out. "Go on back to the office. I'll be there in a while," Bruce said, picking up Frank's beer and taking a sip to let Barry know he'd be taking his time.

"Don't give me that 'sit tight' crap you give Joyce and Linda. Then when they call *I'm* the one who has to make your excuses. Some hero!" Barry snorted, thrusting his face so close to Bruce's that if I hadn't known Barry was a coward, I'd have bet he was going to punch Bruce.

"Back off," Bruce said, real quiet.

Barry took two quick steps back, but couldn't stop talking. "Joyce and Linda are both nice girls," he said. "But you spend your nights cruising the streets waiting for this bitch to be thrown out."

"Maybe I got tired of the missionary position and have taken up missionary work."

"This missionary work too? How can you stand to have her tagging along?" Barry said, pointing to me. Frank and Kenny both stared.

"Allie's not tagging along, she's invited," Bruce said, making all the trouble seem almost worth it.

Still, the trouble wouldn't stop. People kept talking.

"Why you wanna go and spoil your fun, Bruce? You never call Linda. I never even see you around Spencer's bar anymore," Pete was saying when I slipped into the Walters place late one afternoon. There were maybe a dozen guys standing around the big empty downstairs, gathering up their stuff to go home. I just stood by the door real quiet. Pete stopped talking the second he saw me, but Barry jumped up from his desk to start in again at Bruce.

"Man, what's come over you with this bitch? You lost your mind?" he said.

"Hope not," said Bruce. "But it's none of your business."

"None of my business?" cried Barry. "Man, you're just running after her and forgetting *our* business."

"So I'm having a little fun. It's nothing serious."

"Nothing serious?" screamed Barry. "Look, her husband may not mind your day-tripping, but I've got things for you to do!"

"Shut up," said Bruce.

"If it's not serious, then why you shouting?"

"Get out," said Bruce.

"I work here," said Barry.

"Not for too much longer," Bruce muttered. The room was still while Barry looked at Bruce like he wished he could kill him. But I bet Barry had always wished he could kill Bruce. It must be hard having a bald spot.

"Bruce, I'm warning you," Barry said. Then he rushed out.

None of the guys knew what to say.

"Well, can you beat that?" said Bruce.

"How does he know her husband doesn't mind?" Pete asked. "It always looks like a smart husband don't mind till he sticks a knife in your ribs to show he does. You remember what happened to Tom Thatcher."

"What happened to Tom?" I asked.

"Nothing. When did you walk in?" Bruce said, turning around.

"Tom got caught. I mean hurt. I mean he had an accident and finally lost his eye," Kenny said.

"You finally lose everything," Bruce snapped, "and I'm losing my temper right now. Why scare a kid with stories like that?" Bruce said, raising his voice, which shut everyone up, since Bruce never yelled.

"I think he was trying to scare *you*, Bruce," said Clem, the old man who sold Bruce the business years ago. Clem didn't have to work for Bruce. He just liked to be with the guys and Bruce was glad to have him around.

"I've seen a lot of these things go down and, you know, it's funny, until it's not funny anymore, and then it's tragic," Clem said in his skinny old man's voice.

Everybody looked at Bruce.

Bruce didn't say a word. He just walked over to Clem real slow, while no one even dared breathe or sip his beer.

"Come on, Clem, you know this town ain't big enough for tragedy." Bruce grinned, putting a hand on Clem's shoulder. And they all laughed.

Chapter Eight

They say as you get older things start happening more quickly, but that summer things were already happening too fast. Bruce came by a lot to visit Mom, which was nice, I suppose, except for the way it made Mom anxious, so that Bruce no sooner left than she'd insist on going up to my room to tell me stories of magic evenings spent in Paris with Erich on her way home from visiting Grandma.

"People think July is bad in Paris, but it's heaven," Mom said, perched on the bed by the window. She was turned away from me, facing the garden. Still, I knew she was smiling. I could hear it in her voice.

"Are there things to do? Is there a lake?"

"No, but there's great theater," Mom said, describing a play she and Erich saw about a lady who liked her son-in-law so much it drove her mad.

"Racine understood the eloquent economy of passion. Six words to death and ruin. *'Je t'aime, je t'aime, ta bouche!'*" Mom sighed. "That's all Phèdre says."

"I hate visiting cities in the summer. Remember Cleveland?"

"Oh, no, sweetheart. Paris is cooler with parks all over, and romantic walks by the river, beautiful despite the dirt."

"Like the back path," I said, thinking how my heart thumped each time I raced home through the roots and trees and vines and poison ivy, hoping that when I rounded the last bend I would see Bruce.

"No, strolling along the Seine is *nothing* like walking the back path," Mom said, shaking her head in disgust.

"Did you see the Eiffel Tower?" I asked.

"You can't avoid it," Mom said, going on about how much she liked just being driven through the city in Erich's car.

"Oh, is your car broken?" I asked, wanting Mom to stop.

"Don't be an idiot," Mom answered. "Forget the car," she said. "In Paris even the cab drivers argue the relative merits of *ideas* or authors—not baseball teams. It's a different world," she said, going on for half an hour before sending me back out to look for Bruce.

"Oh, hi," she said, looking up from reading a letter, which she stuffed in my junk drawer when Bruce walked in. She'd changed into her pretty teal robe. "Sorry to be such a bother." Mom smiled, a little embarrassed at having sent for Bruce a second time in the same afternoon.

"It's no bother," Bruce said, touching her arm.

"It bothers me. Could there be anything more crazy?" She shuddered as Bruce kissed her shoulders.

"We could run away." He smiled, lifting his face to look at her.

"You're right," Mom laughed. *"That's* something more crazy."

It got so that Mom saw Bruce so much, they were always together, except for the times Mom lay out back in the hammock, sipping her iced tea.

"Where do you think he is?" Mom would say.

"Who? Bruce?"

"No."

"Dad, then?"

"No. Erich."

Erich! Sometimes Mom made me sick with her stupid old Erich.

"Where do you think he is now? What's he doing?" Mom wondered, while Bruce was right there working in Spring Lakes, so close I could usually find him in twenty minutes and bring him home still warm with sweat from the same sun we felt.

"We're back," I'd shout, bringing Bruce in through the kitchen.

"In here," Mom would call from the living room, where she'd be curled up on the pale yellow couch reading her book, always the same book full of poems we both knew backwards.

"Oh, hi," she'd say, unfolding her legs. Then Mom would smile at Bruce, and it was time for me to go.

"HEY, you guys," I called coming in after sitting out front for what seemed ages. "Hey, come on. It's almost five."

"Hay is for horses," Tad called from the kitchen, where he was fumbling around looking for matches in every drawer.

"Hey, Allie, what's up?" Dave asked, bored with watching Tad.

"Nothing," I said, wanting to kick Mom when she waltzed into the kitchen trailed by Bruce.

"What did you say?" Bruce asked her, ignoring the rest of us.

"'We look before and after, and pine for what is not,'" Mom sighed, reciting an old poem as she opened a cabinet to look for cookies.

"I found them!" Tad cried, slipping some matches in his pocket.

"Let's go," said Dave.

"What are you talking about?" Bruce asked Mom, who frowned.

"Jeanne," Bruce pleaded, touching Mom's shoulder as she opened a fresh box of Social Teas.

"It's just a poem," I told Bruce.

"Us," Mom said, arranging a plate of cookies. "I'm talking about us."

"YOU wouldn't be in this jam now if you'd been serious about canasta," Mrs. O'Keith told Mom the second time she stopped by to warn her. "I see Allie out front every evening. If she's in the way, you know, she's always welcome at my house," Mrs. O'Keith said, in that dry way grown-ups say nice things when they really mean "You'd better watch out."

"She can't come over because she's helping," Mom said.

"How on earth does Allie's sitting at the end of her driveway help anything?" asked Mrs. O'Keith.

"I like to know when her father is coming," Mom said.

"How could you make her sit out there?" Mrs. O'Keith insisted.

"I'm not making her do anything. She's been going out

front to wait for her father to come home ever since she could crawl."

"It's not the same," said Mrs. O'Keith.

"Nothing's the same," I said, because Mom couldn't slap me in front of Mrs. O'Keith.

"What's all this talk about your mom?" Mrs. Baskin whispered when I dropped by her house for lemonade so good even Tad and Dave came along to gulp some down.

"Such sweet boys," said Mrs. Baskin when they rode off on the new ten-speed racers they just bought with the two hundred dollars Dave said he found.

"Now, what's all this talk about your mom sneaking out?"

"Do you know where your no-good mother is?" Dad would say, glaring at me nights after Mom had left alone. Dad and Mom always fought when Dad drank. We'd had to run away some nights ever since I could remember, but Dad used to have to get pretty mean before Mom left. Only that summer it got so the minute Dad started in drinking Mom just fixed her makeup and walked out. I think she was wrong because you couldn't always tell with Dad. Sometimes when he started in drinking, I could still distract him. Besides, the rule was we didn't leave until we absolutely had to. The key thing was to keep pretending we were all still a family. Sometime that summer Mom forgot and started slipping out the glass doors, not even taking her car, so Dad wouldn't come out when he heard her start it up.

Mom never used to worry how she looked when we ran out. Always before we never even had time to grab a sweater, but waited till the very last minute, when it was leave or get killed. Then we all made a dash for the nearest door. Yet by late July, Mom was waltzing out like she was going to a party.

Once Mom left, Sam and I had to run too because Mom's leaving made Dad more crazy, only we had nowhere to go. Besides, we were frightened. The streets seemed darker without Mom, the cars more dangerous, their headlights whipping like roller coasters around the curves. Back when we all used to sneak out together, Mom would walk along singing every song Cole Porter ever wrote, which is why I know all the words. Mom would walk and sing, doing requests, like we were all just off on a stroll. Then when she finally ran out of rhymes, she'd start to cry.

That at least gave Sam and me something to do. We could work on cheering her up. It was lots harder without Mom. Sam never cried. I never cried. We both would have cried like babies had we imagined it might help things, but we knew it wouldn't. So after we sneaked out alone we'd just walk along kicking pebbles like you dribble a basketball. Still, kicking pebbles was better than talking. When Mom was along I could tell her it would be all right, because a lie was what she wanted. But I couldn't lie to Sam, and I couldn't say what I was thinking or we'd both cry. So we two just walked along in silence ducking headlights until we sneaked inside somebody's garage and found a corner where we could curl up. Then we would joke about it the next day to make it seem like nothing awful had happened. The worse it was, the more we joked. Even when we straggled in full of twigs, Mom never once asked "Where have you been?" the next morning, although by day she still forbade Sam even to cross the street alone.

The first time Mom just up and left without us, it was all so different. I watched her sit at the vanity plucking her eyebrows, but I didn't see what was going on.

"Hmm," Mom said, tilting her head straining to hear the cocktail shaker downstairs. "Martinis tonight," she sighed, smiling to check her teeth for lipstick one last time before she turned around. If you looked right at Mom in the mirror, you could see everything she saw except yourself.

"Well," Mom said, with the nervous smile that was her new way of saying goodbye. Then she picked up her purse and walked out.

Sam wondered how Mom could bear to leave us behind. Did we all just disappear inside her head? he asked.

The first time Mom just up and left, I was shocked too. In fact, I never could believe it. Each time it happened I was even slower than Dad to realize Mom hadn't just left the room, but was really gone for the night.

"Know where your no-good mother is?" Dad would say, as the night breeze set Mom's favorite chandelier swinging, specks of light dashing like fireflies across the dark entrance-hall walls.

"Know where she is?" he'd ask. But he never once mentioned Bruce.

MORNINGS after, Dad got up and left for work like any other morning. Then Mom would drift back and just sort of hang around the kitchen waiting, like Stormy, for someone to greet her without scolding her for having taken off.

"Don't go away and leave us," I'd say.

"I'll never leave you," she'd answer, going upstairs to brush her teeth. My parents may not have been wonderful, but I didn't want to be sent to a foster home. Foster homes were awful. The week after Marilyn Monroe killed herself I sat on the floor and read all about them in *Life*. Marilyn Monroe had died the summer before, but the magazines still ran whole pages of pictures on the anniversary of her death. In some shots she looked young and hopeful. Other times she seemed more tired that Mom after a bad phone call from Erich. Marilyn Monroe was dead, but Christine Keeler was still alive and smiling, only now the story was mostly about her friend Dr. Stephen Ward, "society osteopath."

"What's an osteopath?" I asked Mom.

"A bone doctor," she said, not looking up. But she must have been wrong, since that didn't make sense.

"What's an osteopath?" I asked Mrs. Baskin when I dropped by to tell her Mom couldn't come for cards.

"You mom thinks what she does is invisible and that people can't see. People can see."

"See what?" I said.

"Come on now, Allie. Don't play games with me. I'm your friend."

"No, you're not," I said. Then I watched Mrs. Baskin pale under her makeup and felt awful because that's when it struck me that poor Mrs. Baskin talked to me so much because she had no other friends.

"What's an osteopath?" I asked to change the subject.

"A bone doctor," Mrs. Baskin said, blinking back tears as she groped for a Kleenex. But it still didn't make sense.

"What's an osteopath?" I asked Mom trying to show her the article in *Life*, to help her see what I wanted to know.

Mom was perched on the bench in front of her vanity, smudging the liner on her eyes.

"I'm late," she said, eyes still fixed on the mirror.

"Look," I said. "There." I pointed at the page. Christine Keeler had long dark hair teased into a flip, a white mini-skirt, and unbelievably big eyes.

"She's wearing false eyelashes," Mom said, examining the picture.

"What's an osteopath?" I asked.

"A bone doctor," Mom said, handing back the magazine.

"But that doesn't fit," I said, trying to find the piece again. "Read it and tell me."

"What makes you go on about that tart?" Mom snapped, taking the magazine and hiding it before she left.

"What's a tart?" I asked Howie first thing next day at the beach.

"What kind?"

"I don't know."

"Good," he said. "Then we'll start at the beginning. It's a French word meaning pie. When you go out to a French restaurant you'll see that there are apple tarts and cherry tarts and *tarte de jour*, which is just a fancy way of saying whatever kind they baked that day."

That didn't seem right either, but I knew that Howie would never lie to me on purpose, so we talked instead about my disappointment in God and Howie told me, "When you become a big girl and go to college, you'll read Wittgenstein and see that it doesn't matter so much if God really exists—everything is still a religious question." And I told Howie that all Mom talked about was buying us new clothes for school, although class didn't start for weeks.

Mom was funny about time. She got all worked up about school coming, time going by, and her getting older even though I kept telling her nobody cares how old you are. Then one day I walked into the living room and nearly fainted when I heard Bruce actually ask my mom her age.

"How old am I?" Mom repeated as I stood there dying because I really should have warned Bruce never to mention that. I thought Bruce could see me shake my head, to help him, but he just looked at Mom and blundered on.

"I don't know. Twenty-nine?" Bruce guessed.

"Tad is twelve," Mom said.

"You're thirty-two."

"Guess again," Mom said, real quiet.

"Thirty-three?"

Mom laughed. She always laughed like a young girl. But this was not her young girl's laugh.

"Now what's the matter? Thirty-five? Older?" Bruce asked, surprised.

"You can leave," Mom told him, making my heart stop.

"I don't care how old you are. It doesn't matter," Bruce said, pulling Mom close.

"By the way, how old are you?" he asked, after they kissed.

"It doesn't matter," Mom said, smiling.

I was already in the hall when she cried out, "Oh, my God! Five thirty. Out you go. Time to clean up."

That was a summer full of baths and showers. Everyone was always washing up. Mom was the champion, but even Sam and I were supposed to take a shower every time we came home from the beach. Of course we didn't. Ada always grumbled that we must like to track in sand, but the truth is I had nothing against showers, I just forgot. Mom used to take showers in the morning and long baths after Bruce left.

"Allie!" she'd call from her upstairs bathroom. Then she'd laugh and tell me stories until it was time to fetch Sam at Frankie's. I could take my time walking over and Mom would still be soaking half an hour later when we got back. Mom soaked so long Ada started making dinner. Soon Mom gave up cooking dinner entirely, which made everybody very happy since Ada was a far better cook. But while dinner was better, Tad kept getting worse.

Tad never listened to Mom anymore and only laughed when he frightened people. His two favorite games besides chicken were to throw Sam into a big plastic garbage pail and roll him down the lawn into the lake, and to threaten us with one of Dad's guns.

"Mom! Tad took the gun off Dad's dresser and is pointing it at me!" I'd scream, because sometimes you have to tell.

"You sissy! It's not even loaded," he'd say.

"How do you know?" I'd ask.

"I looked."

"Mom! Make him stop!"

"Come on, Tad, stop," Mom would call upstairs, but she was usually busy on the phone.

"Your father shouldn't leave guns lying around, and your mother shouldn't . . ." Ada would mutter. But I never could make out half of what Ada said.

Ada made dinner early as a special favor to us kids so we could be back out playing before Dad got home, only it didn't always work.

"Not you, young lady," Dad would say as we all tried to scramble off. Then I'd have to sit there with Dad for hours while he talked instead of cleaning his plate. Mom used to sit listening too, but things were changing. Dad wasn't real comfortable with Mom anymore. Sometimes he'd be as charming with her as he was with strangers. In fact, Dad got so polite that if you weren't smart you almost might think things were getting better, when it was just that Dad knew Mom was desperate to get out, so he wouldn't fight to spoil her excuse for leaving. It got so Mom would finally walk away from the table when Dad was talking, yet the new Dad never lost his temper. He'd just smile watching her go.

"Not you, young lady," Dad would say, grabbing my arm when I tried to follow Mom out. Then Dad made me sit and listen to a thousand dumb complaining stories about the office. Every so often Ada would come in to clear the plates or fool with the silver and look sideways at me like she knew some secret.

"What's the matter?" I'd ask, but she'd just shake her head. Even later, when we were alone, "You'd best be careful," was all she'd say.

Things were changing. Mom never brought this up, of course. We talked for hours each day about lots of things, but I was afraid to mention others, like Christine Keeler, or why Mom should care so much about Erich writing and calling, or even to ask Mom what she was finally planning to do with Bruce. Mom promised me she wouldn't leave, but Sam said he didn't believe her and Ada said it might be for the best if Mom went.

"Then your father should get a new wife right away," Ada said, because she didn't know any better, and that's the way they do it back in Trinidad.

"Has the mail come yet?" Mom asked, rushing out to the box. If there was still no letter from Erich, she would march me up to my room and start again with her stories of Erich and Paris and all his clever opinions.

I couldn't see why Mom bothered with anyone but Bruce, and I said that.

"You don't understand about Bruce. Bruce is not from a very good family," Mom said, staring off into the garden.

"You call *this* a good family?"

Mom looked ready to slap me, but all she said was "Don't be fresh." And so we sat there a minute as poor Mom struggled with her waiting. But Mom was born without patience.

"You want to make a little trip?" Mom said at last, which was her way of hinting that I should go find Bruce.

Mom saw Bruce more and more each day, which was

nice, I suppose, only one afternoon around four the phone rang and it was Dad.

"Why aren't you at the beach?" he asked, sounding as cross as if he knew the real reason.

"I'm washing the dog," I said, dropping the phone.

"You sound awful."

"I'm going to die from the smell," I told him, because one wet dog close up smells worse than an entire barn. Then Dad said that he'd just called to tell Mom he'd be working late.

"You want to talk to her?" I asked him.

"Why?" he said.

I suppose I should have asked what was up, just to be friendly, but it's hard to have a serious conversation when you're wrestling with a soapy dog and trying to hold the phone. It was only after I hung up that something in Dad's call struck me as funny. So I let Stormy go and ran out the kitchen door, past the geraniums red as Mom's lipstick, the dandelion-yellow mums, and the shocking-pink phlox.

"You stay!" I told Stormy, but she rushed on past me all soapy to dive into the lake.

I found Mom and Bruce out in the garden for cut flowers, walking arm in arm very slowly, like a couple trying a new dance. They looked just right for each other. Bruce in his blue jeans and T-shirt. Mom in her diamond earrings and lilac sundress with practically no back.

Mom leaned over to smell a hedge heavy with roses and started sneezing.

"All you can smell is the insecticide," she sputtered.

Bruce grinned. "Let me take you away from all this— just as soon as we finish re-landscaping."

"Only if you take me to a garden where the roses don't smell of bug spray!" Mom laughed, then paused, suddenly sad as she stood thinking. "You know, sometimes I feel as if I've spent my whole life trying to get out of New Jersey," she sighed, taking his arm again.

"What's wrong with New Jersey?" Bruce asked.

Mom stopped strolling and looked at him like he was crazy a moment, then shrugged.

"Oh, look, here's Allie! What can we do for you, little girl?" she asked. Then she smiled and Bruce smiled too, happy again, now that Mom squeezed his arm.

"Dad called to say he wouldn't be home from the office before nine," I said.

"She didn't tell him that I was here?" Bruce asked.

"Allie's not stupid!" Mom told Bruce. "You'd better go."

"But it's only..."

"A trap. He never calls, even if he's stuck past midnight." Mom was frowning and turned back to the house.

"Just remember what I said about us taking off," Bruce said, softly touching Mom's shoulder.

"Okay. And you remember what I said about the garden."

"What about the garden?"

"What about eloping?" Mom laughed, running away.

Dad came home just twenty minutes later. He was very angry to have come all the way home and found no one, though of course he didn't say that. He didn't say a word about being early or having lied to me on the phone. He didn't even go upstairs to talk to Mom once I told him where she was. He just said, "Let's see the dog," as if he didn't believe that I'd really come home to wash her.

"She went swimming," I said. Stormy hated smelling clean and always jumped into the lake after her bath. So Dad went out in the back yard and called. But, of course, Stormy didn't come.

"Where's the bitch?" Dad shouted, racing back into the

kitchen all crazy. "You lied to me! You lied!" he screamed, grabbing me by the shoulders and shaking me so hard I couldn't think.

"I wasn't lying!" I cried. But Dad wasn't listening because he smelled like gin.

"You don't believe her, then *you* clean the sink," Ada shouted, storming in angry because the kitchen was full of dog hair. "Look at the sink!" Ada fussed. The drain really was a mess, which made Dad feel a little better once he noticed. But there was still something eating him.

Dad went upstairs without a word, taking the front stairs up to his study while Mom came down the back stairs.

"So what's for dinner?" she asked Ada, who was still muttering to herself about the mess. "What are you doing?" Mom asked me, as I just stood there.

"She's peeling peaches," said Ada, pointing to a big white bowl full of wet fruit. Then she reached up to the magnetic knife rack and passed me a paring knife. I peeled and cut what felt like fifty peaches before the first bowl was empty and its twin filled with sticky yellow-red slices.

"Time to fetch Sam," I announced, washing my hands and fleeing the kitchen before Ada could find some new chore.

I took off up the path and walked straight to the beach which was empty but for a few teenagers from the next town who sneaked in after the guards had gone. It was almost dark. I left my shoes on the steps by the clubhouse and walked along the shore way past the swings. The guys who didn't belong grew quiet when I came near where they were pushing each other off the dock.

"Hi," I said when I passed them, because I knew everyone on the beach.

The still warm sand had turned cold before I collected

my shoes and cut back down the path to Frankie's.

"Where were you?" said Sam, who was sitting alone outside.

"Why?"

"You're late," he said in a small voice. "They're already eating."

"There's a firefly by your shoulder. I just saw it," I said, pointing, wishing I'd stopped by for Sam first.

Sam got up and took a step back, not quite believing, since most fireflies come in June. Still, we both watched the spot of empty air a second, then two, when, sure enough, the spot began to glow.

When we got back home Mom wanted me to go up and call Dad down to dinner, but I wasn't crazy. Finally Tad went. At dinner Mom and Dad both sat at their ends of the table, not eating, while us kids were supposed to keep squabbling and passing the salt like everything was fine. We did our best, because Dave was eating over, only no one was very hungry. When Ada brought in her great peach cobbler, Dad told Mom he was firing Bruce and hiring a regular gardener to replace him.

"He's very good," Dad said, "but I don't know if he's your type."

Chapter Nine

I don't remember a time when things were ever
good between my parents, but that was the
summer everything sort of fell apart. Once Dad fired
Bruce, there was no reason for Bruce to stop by the house,
so he and Mom had to find other places to meet.

"We have to think ahead," Bruce insisted, trying to get
Mom to agree on where they'd meet again the next day.

"I don't have a schedule," said Mom.

"Come on," said Bruce. Then he would suggest one
place and Mom would say no. So he would mention another, which she would say was too far, and a third she
thought might be too public, finding excuse after excuse
until Bruce finally gave up.

"All right, *you* think of something," he'd say.

"I don't know why I need to do this. It feels dirty,"
Mom would say, getting into her car as Bruce just stared.

"That's it," she'd say as we drove off. "It's finished."

It would have been okay if that was it. Sad for a while, but still okay. Only that was never it.

"I don't know what to do. I feel awful," she'd say, stoping by the beach to find me late the next morning. "I don't know where he is," she'd sigh, like it was suddenly some big tragedy, which was silly of her, considering she wasn't the one who'd have to get on her bike and look for Bruce.

It wasn't easy to find Bruce since he worked a lot of different places, which meant that Mom would have had to call half a dozen neighbor ladies like Mrs. Baskin to ask if Bruce was around—which would never do. That's why I sometimes spent the whole morning racing from job to job. But the best way to look was just to go to the old Walters place and stay, which was like sticking by the information booth when you get lost at the circus. Eventually your friends have to show up. Sometimes I'd end up waiting outside the Walters place for hours with nothing to do but sit and watch Corky the crow tear some poor bird's nest apart.

"Thank God," Mom would say, hugging me with relief when I finally came back with word of where Bruce would be waiting. Mom might even sing happy songs driving out to the very place she'd called "too far" the day before. Once Bruce and I drove all the way to a Carvel so far off I'd never even been there before and Bruce bought me a flying saucer to eat while we watched for Mom. Then we took off and Mom followed our car until we got to a state park, where we stopped and Mom pulled up three cars away. The park was like a forest, only with signs for the different flowers on paths made of pine chips.

"Well," Mom said, locking the station wagon and walking toward us.

"Yeah?" said Bruce. Then they both looked at me the very same second.

"Here, Allie," Bruce said, giving me his watch. Then he walked me over to the start of the wildflower trail and made me promise to be back at the parking lot by one o'clock.

That was one of the most fun times, though Mom and Bruce went off the marked trail and got poison ivy. The only trouble with that plan was it took all morning and I couldn't tell Sam about getting ice cream or he would have felt left out.

Sam wasn't the only one we couldn't tell. Days she met Bruce, Mom had to go visit one of the neighbor ladies before we went off, so she could say that was where she'd been in case Dad asked. We mostly dropped in on Mrs. O'Keith, but one day we went to visit Frankie's mother.

I always liked Frankie's mother. I like all grown-ups who don't try to make you feel as if the world ended last Tuesday and you just haven't gotten word. I especially liked Frankie's mother since she was peppy and divorced and had gone to graduate school like Mom. She also worked in the city like a man. That's why Frankie usually had a housekeeper instead of a mother and hung out all day with Sam. Frankie's mother stayed home only one week in the summer and another around Christmas, although sometimes when she was sick, she would stay home in bed just like us kids.

Every year Frankie's mother and mine were friends during Frankie's mom's summer vacation, when they would sit out back, their long silver spoons gaily tinkling against the tall glasses as they stirred their iced tea.

Frankie's house was one of the smallest in town; still, the neighbor ladies agreed that Frankie's mother was lucky to have it. I thought she was lucky too, because there was a nice little birch grove in back with eight or nine pieces of slate laid in a circle just big enough for our three chairs.

"So tell me," Mom said, leaning forward. And Frankie's mother told her about this dreamy man she'd just started seeing in the city, only Frankie's mother had her doubts.

"Keep them," said Mom.

"Keep what?"

"Your doubts about love. Love, Christ! How long can it last? A month? A year? And even then, the whole thing's so stupid, trivial, and exhausting," Mom sighed, sipping her iced tea.

Frankie's mother nodded. "So many things can go wrong. But nothing's better when it's right. It's right with you, isn't it?"

"I'm not so sure," said Mom. But she was never sure.

"Is something the matter?" asked Frankie's mother.

But Mom was already saying "Thank you. We must be going," very politely. It's hard to stay friends with someone who hasn't got time to keep up with the neighborhood.

"Why don't you tell Frankie's mother?" I asked, trailing Mom out to the car.

"Hmm?" Mom said, far away, thinking.

"Why don't you tell Frankie's mother?" I repeated, since it's hard to feel relaxed with people if you never tell them anything when you've got all these things going on.

"Tell her what? That I feel trapped?" Mom asked, slipping into the car.

"Why don't we all run away?" I said, because that's what I'd always most wanted to ask her.

"But if we left, where would we go?" she asked, starting the car and backing out.

"We could go anywhere," I said, which made Mom laugh.

"Oh, honey, I'm not laughing at you. It's just you sound so much like . . ." She didn't finish the sentence. "Baby, it's cold outside. You don't know the things you take for granted," Mom said, reaching over to pat my shoulder without taking her eyes off the road.

"We should run away."

"Sweetheart, I just told you . . ."

"What would we miss?" I insisted.

"Not everyone has azaleas like this," Mom said, pointing to some phlox as we pulled into our drive.

"I can live without flowers," I told her.

"It's more than the flowers."

"You're just making excuses."

"You're just little. Men and children are so impractical," Mom sighed.

Bruce wasn't impractical. He was just jealous. And I could see why.

"Of course I'm jealous," he told Mom as we walked along after meeting in a big furniture warehouse nine whole miles from my house.

"Yes, but why?" Mom asked, calmly pretending to shop.

"Why!" Bruce said.

"Yes, why?" Mom whispered, smiling at a clerk busy changing price tags for a sale the next day. Nothing could upset Mom on days when she'd gotten a letter from Erich that morning.

"Why?" Bruce said again, real loud. But no one paid much attention since a couple down the aisle was arguing still more loudly over which bedroom set to choose. Furniture stores were good places for Mom and Bruce to meet because the clerks left you alone since it was hard to shoplift a couch. Bruce and Mom used to walk a path in the woods on the far side of town, but I warned them against taking it since Dave told me Tad had a girlfriend named Joanie who lived across from those woods and that he and Tad spent hours there smoking cigarettes waiting for her to come by.

"Bruce," I said, but he wasn't listening. So I turned to Mom, who saw that I was asking her to be nice to Bruce, but she just shrugged and told him, "You're crazy to be jealous."

"Why?" Bruce asked again, and even I could see that the right answer was for Mom to take his arm and say "Because I love you." But she didn't.

"Hey, remember me?" Bruce said, grabbing Mom's arm. "I used to see you two or three times a day. We were always together. That's all we did, all the time," he said, eyes all over Mom.

"Apparently that's what people think..."

"Christ, we spent half of most nights..." Bruce said, looking at Mom hard, as if the strength of his stare might change things.

"Shut up," Mom snapped, not wanting him to look at her like that.

"I don't know why you're so jealous. I'm not sleeping with him," Mom said at last, like she was doing Bruce a favor.

"Cheaters always say that," Bruce said.

"It's not on account of you. Do they always say that too? How does it go between you and your other cheaters?" Mom said, half ready to slap him. And I saw Bruce was almost relieved that Mom still cared enough to get mad. That's how it always went between them. Sometimes I thought Mom loved him, then it would seem she hated Bruce.

"Send my husband the final bill for your work," Mom

told Bruce as we walked through a whole room of wrought-iron tables.

"I don't need his money. I want his wife."

"Bill him for your work, or you'll confirm what he already suspects," Mom said, after suggesting that I might want to go visit the next room, which was full of love seats.

"I don't need any furniture," I told her.

"You're both such a pleasure!" Mom said, like she'd just about had it. I couldn't hear Bruce's answer because the loudspeaker was announcing a special on hide-a-beds. But Mom heard it and she frowned. "Just bill him," she said.

"I wouldn't if I were starving. And I've got thirty guys on payroll," Bruce said, as insulted as if Mom had insisted on paying for her own meal.

"But he owes it. It's no favor. You're a builder," Mom said.

"That's right, an enterprising builder—at least I was before we met."

"Don't blame me," Mom said, stopping to finger a stereo cabinet. "Like this for the basement, baby?" Mom asked, meaning me. Bruce stopped by Mom's side.

"Baby," he said, meaning Mom. Somehow, when Bruce said it, "baby" sounded like a whole different word. "Baby," Bruce repeated, taking Mom's hand. But she was only joking about the cabinet, so she wanted to move on.

"Dammit, Jeannie, why can't you ever make up your mind?" Bruce said, so softly even the swearing sounded nice. He looked at Mom and you could see he was just dying to stand close and talk a moment, but Mom just walked on because she'd skipped lunch and that makes her cross.

"Why can't we meet somewhere else?" Bruce said, grabbing Mom's arm as he caught up. "Somewhere we can really talk."

"I don't know of any hotels in the neighborhood, but I do know a lot of gossips. Next thing I know, you'll be suggesting we meet at a Howard Johnson's on the turn-pike."

"I don't care where we meet," Bruce said, getting angry. "I'll do anything to see *you*, but sometimes I think you only get off on showing your legs."

Mom shot me a glance. "You, next door, to love seats," she said. Then she turned back to Bruce. "So you don't like my legs?"

"Sure, you know they're great. That's not the point."

"The point is you're an adult who drives around looking like a teenager."

"It's not my fault your old man can't wear jeans to the office."

"There's more to life than just driving around pretend-ing to be somebody," Mom said, giving me a little push to remind me to get lost.

"Who's pretending?" he said. "I'm Bruce."

But we were pretending. Mom and I kept pretending we were going to go shopping for school, only we never went anywhere except those awful furniture showrooms. Mom finally got so embarrassed about always showing up at one that she bought a fake French Provincial dresser for the attic.

"I don't know what to do," Mom told Mrs. O'Keith, the only lady Mom almost trusted.

"Why don't you do what I'd do if it weren't for the Church?" said Mrs. O'Keith. "How can you believe in nothing, yet be afraid of everything?"

"Simple," Mom sighed, studying her fingernails. "I think too much."

"Surely not about others," said Mrs. O'Keith.

Mom frowned. "Come on."

"No, really, I thought you were an atheist."

"An Episcopalian."

"Atheist, Episcopalian—same difference. Imagine committing adultery outside the Church and not enjoying it," scolded Mrs. O'Keith. "Now *that's* my definition of mortal sin."

"Howie says that everything is a religious question," I said.

"Oh, God," said Mrs. O'Keith, turning red as her freckles. "I forgot she was here!"

But I was always there. Mom and Bruce needed lots of help. Sometimes I'd spend three hours looking for Bruce to tell him when it was safe to sneak over. Then he'd slip out the back so soon it hardly seemed worth all the trouble of trying to find him. But Bruce always told me I was wrong.

"It's okay," Bruce said. Still, being careful was driving everybody crazy. Mom and Bruce couldn't even go for a walk without first driving miles. One day we drove Route 46 all the way to where you finally pick up the Garden State Parkway. Then we drove on that awhile before turning into a Howard Johnson's where we met Bruce.

The trip was not Mom's idea.

"This is absolutely asinine," she said as we pulled up.

"What's the matter?" Bruce asked, face flushed from waiting in the sun.

"You smell like sweat," Mom said.

"It bother you?" Bruce asked.

Mom shook her head, then they both looked at me.

"We can't just leave her in the car," Mom said, checking her face in the rearview mirror.

"I never said to. Why even bring her along?"

"For company," Mom said. "Ever try driving a station

wagon with a broken radio for nearly two hours all alone?"

"There are probably worst things—us just standing here, for instance, when I haven't touched you in nearly..."

"Now then, Allie, would you like a nice ice cream?" Mom asked, getting out of the car to whisper a word to Bruce. So Bruce walked me into the restaurant and got me a corner booth and a double cone.

Bruce smiled. "Stay put. I'll be right back," he promised, avoiding my eyes. Then he paid, gave the waitress an extra five, and left. Howard Johnson's makes the world's best chocolate chip mint ice cream, but eating a big double cone all alone can make you sick. Mom had given me a pack of sandy cards from the glove compartment, so I spread them out on the table and started playing solitaire.

I'd just laid out the third game when Mom popped her head inside the door and signaled me to come out. Mom was already in her car, Bruce leaning against it, neither one of them talking, when I reached the parking lot.

"Hey, Allie," Bruce said, but his heart wasn't in it.

"Is your door really shut? Then lock it," Mom told me as I got in.

"Come on, Jeannie," Bruce said.

"It's just so sordid and depressing. I don't know what to do," Mom said, near tears.

"Don't leave this way," Bruce pleaded, reaching in the front window.

"I've got to," Mom cried, then cringed, though Bruce had only tried to touch her cheek.

IT was very hard to arrange for Bruce and Mom to get together, then when they got together, they fought because they couldn't get together more.

"I don't know what to do," Mom would say when Bruce sneaked over. Sometimes she did nothing, and would just sit on the far side of the living room still as a painting we were supposed to admire. Other times she and Bruce sat on the yellow silk couch so close they almost seemed to breathe the same breath. The only trouble was their visits never stayed nice because they both knew they'd have to say goodbye soon.

"It's nearly six," Mom would sigh.

"I just want to swallow you," Bruce would say, grabbing her, suddenly desperate.

Other times it was Mom who acted like it killed her to see him. "Why did you come?" she'd cry when Bruce walked in.

"Because I had to," he'd say, so sad that I believe he had no choice.

I guess that's just how it is—grown-ups get into these things, and bang, they're stuck. But I must have missed the nice part, because there had to have been a nice part, or why bother?

"Come here!" Mom would cry. Then they'd just stand there on the stairs eyeing each other.

"This is torture," Mom said.

"Death, just death," said Bruce.

I KNOW Mom and Bruce didn't mean to fight, they were just both very tense, especially Bruce when he couldn't see Mom. Some days Bruce would get so desperate he'd just show up down by the boat docks or even out in front of our house, which drove Mom crazy since someone might see.

"What the hell do you think you're doing?" Mom snapped, smiling hello at Bruce like she just happened to bump into him while walking me down the street.

"I just had to see you," Bruce said.

Mom cased the street for cars. "You're wonderfully brave when it's my neck."

"What's wrong with me wanting to see you? I *need* to see you," Bruce said, happy just to be near Mom, though I wasn't so sure what good it did since seeing each other in public always wound up making Mom and Bruce more nervous, like scratching poison ivy, which feels great at first, yet makes things worse.

"I wake up missing you," Bruce said, starting to walk with us, but Mom just brushed his hand from her arm.

"I never see you. I want to be with you all the time, and I can never even see you," Bruce said, real quiet.

"That's not true," said Mom.

"This can't go on," said Bruce, but Mom just kept walking until we reached the intersection.

"I saw you yesterday," Mom said. Then she turned around and headed back.

"For about three minutes!" Bruce snorted.

"You always say I never give you enough time," Mom said, stopping by our hedges.

"Because you never do. Don't you love me anymore?" Bruce burst out, all upset, though I'd never heard Mom say she loved him to begin with.

"Look, this is crazy. You can't just pop up here. What will people think?" Mom asked, looking around.

Bruce met her gaze and smiled. "You say you hate being nervous, but it excites you."

"No, it drives me to distraction."

"That's all I am for you, a distraction."

"No, sometimes you're a pain in the ass," Mom said, then smiled. "Maybe if you came in the house like a civilized person..."

"Is what we're doing all that civilized?" Bruce asked, stopping by our mailbox.

"Quintessentially."

"What does that mean?"

"For the fate of Western civilization?" Mom asked, looking back over her shoulder as she walked up the drive.

"No, I mean the word."

Mom shrugged. "It doesn't matter. You coming, Allie?" she asked, turning at the door as Bruce stood there staring after Mom so hard even she could feel it. "Come on, Allie," Mom said. Then she disappeared inside.

"Want to go for a walk?" I asked, taking Bruce's hand. But he still stood there, looking after Mom, amazed.

"What am I, the idiot of the century or just the decade?" Bruce asked his friend Pete a few minutes later when Pete met us walking the back path.

"Don't laugh. Something awful will happen," Pete warned him.

"I'm not laughing," Bruce said. "Sometimes I think that, from where I stand, it already has."

"What's that?" Pete asked as Stormy trotted up to drop a dead rabbit in front of me, then ran off.

"Oh, gross!" I said, once Stormy was out of earshot. Pete thought we should just kick the carcass back into the woods, but Bruce took out his Swiss Army knife.

"Want to get lucky?" he asked me.

"Sure," I told him. So he cut off a rabbit's foot each for Sam and me. Boy, was I ever sorry. They were drenched in blood.

I LIKE summer because you're free of school and "Be home before dark" means you can stay out playing almost past bedtime, only I wasn't playing a fun game. I was neglecting everybody, leaving Sam at Frankie's so much I was afraid he'd think I'd stopped liking him.

I worried Howie might think that too. The few times I went back to the beach now I felt funny. I couldn't go sit with Howie anymore because I'd let telling him go so long I felt like a liar for hiding everything. I *was* a liar, too. I had to run around telling stories to Tad and Dad and all the neighbor ladies. And while I told the lies, the secrets weren't mine to tell.

At least Bruce and I still got to go for walks down the back path, where I almost stepped on what looked like a busted bike tire, but was really a dead old black snake. I know you're supposed to be afraid of snakes, but what can a black snake do to you, especially if it's dead? Water moccasins are the ones to watch out for, but they don't bother with the back path since they'd rather swim. Water snakes are very beautiful and so proud of their poison that they glide along on top of the water, arching their necks like swans.

"What's going on?" Pete asked, catching up to us on the path as Bruce grabbed a stick to turn over the dead black snake.

"Allie almost stepped on this," Bruce answered. The snake's insides were full of ants.

"That's not what I mean," said Pete.

"Oh, that. Beats me," Bruce said. "What does a man do when he's in love, yet he feels he's being suckered?"

"If he's in love, he can only hang around," Pete said as Bruce flipped the dead snake off the path with his stick.

"Even if she won't see him?"

"She sees you."

"She sees me and she won't see me."

"Look, she's a woman and she sees you. The whole

town sees it, so it's sort of funny you can't figure it out yourself."

"That's not what I mean," Bruce said.

"Isn't that what we're talking about?"

"No, that isn't. I just told you I'm in love. What do you say?"

"I'd say you've got about as much sense as this little girl, but I don't dare insult your friend."

I *was* Bruce's friend. I hung around to try to help him even during the day when we weren't expecting Dad because I was afraid Mom would treat Bruce so mean that he would leave. Then one day she did. They were sitting together on the hammock and Mom said something funny and cutting the way she likes to, just to test if you really love her, but Bruce didn't go. So Mom walked inside. And I walked over to our big bottle-green hammock and sat right down next to Bruce.

"Why don't you leave now?" I said, not even thinking how rude it sounded, for I was sure Bruce knew I was saying it because I liked him. Poor Mom was very unhappy and had to say things to hurt people. It was like she was under a magic spell and couldn't help it. At first I'd thought Bruce's love might help her, and it had for a while. But it's very hard to make real changes.

"I'm warning you," I said, afraid I wouldn't have the strength to say it later.

"Thanks, kid, but don't sweat it," Bruce said, not wanting to see that our house was really a very dangerous house.

"*No joke*," I repeated. But Bruce just patted my head.

MOM was terrible to Bruce. I know she was busy, with lots of shopping to do and old school friends like Erich to meet in New York before she caught a show with Dad. Still, it wasn't fair of Mom to send me racing off to tell Bruce she'd meet him in the parking lot of a carpet store on Route 46, then not be there. No wonder Bruce complained when he finally did see Mom. But Mom avoids people who do that.

"Allie and I spent nearly an hour waiting at the showroom. Where were you yesterday?" Bruce demanded, showing up in the garden without even being asked.

"Wednesday?" Mom said, vague as if it hadn't just happened, while Ada decided it was time to take the flowers Mom just cut into the house.

"Look, the main thing is we're both here now."

"Right," Bruce said, "with Allie, and it's already past five."

"Allie was just leaving," Mom said, giving me a push. "And her father is never home before six.

"Terrific, twenty minutes and counting. Cheat and run, eh?"

"What's that?" Mom asked, rushing inside to catch the phone.

"I'm sick of this," Bruce muttered as he watched Mom race off across the lawn, her copper waves bouncing like a cocker spaniel's ears.

I'd never seen Bruce so mad. He looked ready to throw a rock through a window, which he couldn't do of course, because Mom was special. She could just reach over and slap you and you wouldn't even think of slapping her back. Bruce watched Mom go like he was losing something and I felt sorry for him because I knew all about how Mom could read you poems and tuck you in, and every moment you shared would be magic. Then she'd pretend to forget.

"Let's run away," I told Bruce, feeling more flushed than the night my hair caught fire.

"You know you couldn't leave the kids," Bruce laughed,

playing his part. So I went back to playing mine.

"You can go inside," I said. "It's all right. I'll watch out front." So Bruce left me on the patio and slid through the glass doors Mom always forgot to close. I watched Bruce go in, then walked around the house through the hedge roses beneath my balcony just like on that first day, only this time I didn't hear Mom laughing.

What I like most about summer besides the beach is picking tomatoes and eating them right there in the garden, still all warm from the sun, without even salt. Picking peaches from one of the three peach trees in front isn't half as good; in fact, it can be torture if you're allergic to peach fuzz. But if you don't do it, you can't eat Ada's peach cobbler later. When I walked around front I saw that the peaches looked about ready to pick, with some on the ground already rotten. So instead of just sitting at the end of the driveway I ran over to Frankie's and brought Sam back home to help.

"Look," Sam said when I was up the tree tossing down peaches he was supposed to catch.

"What?" I said, trying to reach just a few more big ones before the itching drove me crazy.

"Look."

"Yeah. Catch these," I said, scrambling down, not paying attention, itching all over from the peach fuzz.

"Look!" Sam said, grabbing my face in both his hands like he did whenever he had to talk to Mom.

I looked up and saw Dad's car practically in the driveway. "Go tell Bruce," I said, giving Sam a shove that sent him running to the house as I went out to greet Dad.

"What's the matter?" Dad asked, pulling up.

"I'm dying from peach fuzz," I said, and it was true. Peach fuzz itches worse than poison ivy or chicken pox, only no one feels sorry for you since they can't see any spots.

"Why don't you go dive in the lake?" Dad said, getting out of his blue sedan that looked like every father's car. "Maybe I'll come swimming with you."

There was nothing in the world I wanted more than to dive into the water that very second, but I figured we'd better take our time going in.

"Don't you think the peach trees look sick?" I asked. So Dad stopped to examine their leaves for bugs.

The house seemed empty when we walked in. Still I changed into my swimsuit in seconds.

"Going for a record?" Dad asked when I came running downstairs panting. Dad had a meeting in town later, so he didn't bother changing after all, and just walked down to the lake to watch. I dove in a couple of times and Dad stood on the dock talking with the new gardener. Everything looked okay, but I still didn't like it and ran back up to the house all spooked for no reason like the ladies in "Alfred Hitchcock Presents."

"Mom!" I cried, racing upstairs.

"What's your trouble?" she asked, sitting on the bed painting her toenails so calmly I didn't even have to ask if Bruce had gotten away.

"It's like Dad came home for no reason," I told Mom. "He never even asked where you were."

"Because he came to see you, baby," Mom said, which only made me more nervous.

"Please come be nice to him," I begged, practically dragging her down to the dock with just one coat of polish on, when you should use at least three with red.

"I was just doing my nails," Mom called as she walked down toward the dock, waving at Dad like a homecoming queen greets the crowd. Dad, Mom, and the new gardener talked a few minutes before the three of us walked back to the car, past the rhododendron, peach trees, and dwarf apples.

Mom smiled. "How pretty the dogwood looks."

"They're not dogwood, dammit," Dad said, less mad than sad, like his whole life had been a waste.

Chapter Ten

You'd think a few close calls would have made them more careful, but it's like playing chicken. Get away with it once, and you want that thrill again. Mom and Bruce wasted whole days driving halfway around the state being careful. Then, suddenly, in August they started acting as if they didn't care anymore about getting caught.

It was Mom who set the pace, like always.

"What are you doing?" I'd ask when she first started calling around to Bruce's jobs—exactly what she said one mustn't do.

"Come over," she'd say when she finally found him.

There'd be a pause when, I guess, Bruce asked, "Are you sure it's safe?"

"*Come over,*" Mom always answered. "Come over *now.*"

So Bruce started stopping by to visit without even the excuse of working out back.

"Come on, be careful," I said, when Bruce walked into the living room all sweaty one evening.

"Why bother?" Mom asked, depressed at not having heard from Erich.

"Mom!" I said. "It's nearly seven!"

"Go find your dog," she murmured, losing herself in Bruce's arms.

Mom wasn't the easiest person to help. Nor, when it came to Mom, was Bruce.

It was crazy, I know, but Mom only got reckless after the night Dad nearly shot her. She was terrified that night, then I guess she got mad and wanted to show Dad, or maybe she was just in shock.

I WASN'T the one who told Bruce about the gunshot.

I told Bruce to come home with me quick, but I didn't tell him about the gunshot because I knew the second he heard what had happened, he and Mom would just have their "Why don't you leave?" fight all over again.

That's what I wanted to do the morning after.

"Come on, Mom, let's pack," I said, rushing into her room just as soon as Dad drove off to work.

"Later," Mom said, pulling the covers back up around her. Mom always got up early, so it was weird to find her still in bed.

"Mom," I said, sitting down on the bed beside her. "It's bad luck to pull a blanket over your face." I guess Mom wasn't listening, because she didn't pull back the blanket.

"Mom, are you okay?" I asked, hugging the blanket.

"Go away," said a muffled voice.

"Where?" I asked, almost crying.

"Just go," said the voice.

I would have asked "Where?" again, only she started laughing sort of crazy. "Mom," I said. But she wouldn't pull back the blanket. That's when I figured that her telling me to go away really meant "Go get Bruce."

"Hey, Sam," I called, racing back downstairs. Sam was sitting in front of a bowl of soggy Rice Krispies.

"Why didn't you eat?" I asked.

"They started out soggy," Sam said. It was so humid the towels we hung outside the night before still smelled dank.

"Come on."

"Where are we going?" Sam asked.

We were walking along the Boulevard on our way to the old Walters place when the cops pulled up and stopped us.

"Are you the kids playing chicken?" the big redhead asked, hanging out the window so far I hoped he'd break the door.

"First thing in the morning? Nobody plays chicken in the morning," I said, amazed a grown man could be so dumb he didn't know you only play chicken at dusk.

"Where's the nice policeman?" I asked.

"I'm nice," said the nasty old redhead.

"No, there's another one."

"She means Tony," said Jim, the young cop.

"Maybe."

"You mean a young guy—tall, dark-haired, sort of skinny?" the redhead asked.

"No, Tony's got a pretty good build," said Jim.

"I mean the nice policeman who took me to the hospital once two summers ago. He even went back to look for some of my teeth that got knocked out."

"Tony for sure," said Jim.

"Oh, he's a detective," said the redhead. "He's got a different job than us. We cruise around to head off trouble. He shows up after it happens."

"Never before?" I asked.

"Why? You got an accident waiting to happen?"

"Never mind," I said, grabbing Sam. And we just walked off.

Bruce wasn't at the Walters place yet when we arrived. Eight thirty was really too early to expect him. I just wanted to be there the second he showed up.

"Here comes the daughter of the Bride of Frankenstein," Barry said when he saw me coming.

"You'll be sorry when I'm bigger," I warned him.

"Oh, yeah," Barry said. "You've got me real frightened."

"Planning to grow up soon?" Frank asked.

"Why do kids always think where they're going will be any better than where they've been?" Pete laughed, showing off for the guys standing around before work.

But Barry wasn't laughing. "I don't want you here," he said, glaring.

So Sam and I sat out front watching the guys go off to their jobs except for the few who stayed to fix the Walters place. Most left by nine. Then Dave rode by, looking real sneaky. "You know the O'Keiths' dog?" he said, stopping his bike but not getting off.

"Yeah, sure. So what?"

"So what?" Dave smiled. "So what? It's missing!"

"So what?" I said.

"What's eating you?" Dave asked, shaking his head as he rode off.

The sun burned off the morning fog, but Bruce still didn't come. I'm usually very good at following my rule about staying put when I'm looking for someone, but I couldn't just sit there quietly the morning after Dad shot at Mom.

"Please, it's an emergency," I said, going back inside trying to get someone to help me find Bruce.

"Out!" screamed Barry. But what was he going to do? Call the cops?

"Better run. We're blasting," Kenny explained, pushing me out of Barry's reach. But that was just an excuse.

"Let's just go to the beach," Sam said, near crying.

"It's not that they don't like you," I told him.

"It's that they don't like *us*," he said, tugging at my arm. Sam was getting a little nervous about starting kindergarten, even though I kept telling him it was a snap.

"Why don't you go on to the beach? Go straight to Howie and say that I asked him to watch you special, okay?" I told Sam, and off he went. It was such a good idea I only wondered why I hadn't thought of it before. Maybe because I missed Sam once he left.

The sun moved past noon. The guys stopped work and came out to the porch with their beer and sandwiches. Bruce still hadn't showed. Ken offered me a sip of his warm beer, as I sat there wondering if the night before had really happened. Sometimes when it got crazy at home I thought I must be dreaming. Other times I knew the danger was real, and the beach a dream.

At last I heard Bruce's car. A hundred cars might pass, but I always recognized the sound of his. It wasn't that his engine sounded so much smoother than anyone else's. It had as many sounds as Mom had moods, and I knew each by heart.

"Hey, babe, how's tricks?" Bruce said, pulling himself out of the car to pick me up and twirl me around his special way.

"That girl wouldn't leave when we were blasting," said Barry.

Bruce grinned. "You guys never had a woman you could tell 'Meet me at the corner' and the wreckers could come and trash the building, but when you showed, she'd still be there?"

"Right," Barry said. "Enjoy the pup's devotion now, before she grows up to be another bitch."

"Want your wise ass kicked in?" Bruce asked, putting me down.

"Bruce, Barry, forget it," Pete said, jumping in to stop their fighting.

"I'm your best friend," Pete told Bruce, holding him back as Barry stalked off. "That's why it kills me to see you jump whenever that Gardner woman snaps her fingers. Sure, she makes you feel like God when she needs you—still, you're nothing but a lark to her. And you know, in a way, she's right. *You are nothing, because you let her make you nothing.*"

When Pete finished talking it was quiet. Barry had stomped back into the house and all the guys outside were busy pretending not to hear.

"Bruce," I said.

"Haven't you caused enough trouble?" Pete asked. So I just stood there as Bruce and Pete stared at each other over my head.

BRUCE drove me home from the Walters place and even parked his car in our driveway since I said there was no way Dad would feel like coming back early that day.

"Hey, Mom," I cried, banging in the front door, Bruce right behind me.

"Jeannie," Bruce called. But no one answered, so we ran

upstairs and found Mom still lying beneath the covers breathing hard. "Jesus Christ," she swore, hair tangled, eyes bright as she stared out from under the blanket.

"Here, take this," I said, handing Mom a comb and lipstick. There was nothing in the world that calmed her more than making up.

I didn't tell Bruce about the gunshot because I didn't have to. Bruce wasn't in the bedroom a minute before he saw the bullet hole in the wall behind me and went beserk.

"How can you let these things happen?" cried Bruce.

"It just happened," said Mom.

And she was sort of right. There was noise and there was trouble, but it didn't start out such a special evening. Dad had been drinking since he came home, but no worse than usual—not to say we weren't scared, since we always figured the night Dad finally ended up killing us wouldn't start out all that different from an ordinary bad night.

Dad had been drinking through dinner, refusing to eat, screaming at Mom because she had Ada serve hot soup in summer when Dad said any idiot would have known to choose something cold.

"It doesn't bother me," I said, trying to help.

"You see," Dad yelled at Mom. "She's growing up just as ignorant as you!"

"Dad," I said, since he sometimes grew ashamed of himself and stopped if you talked real quiet.

"Hot soup in August!" Dad screamed, slamming the table and stalking off, while Mom looked to the doors. But Dad was watching them all from the entrance hall.

"Well, don't just sit there!" Dad said, lurching back through the dining room where we all sat staring at the soup, afraid to move.

"Want something to eat?" I asked Sam as we scattered.

"I'm not hungry," he said, trailing me into the kitchen

where I grabbed a package of Fig Newtons off the counter. Then we took the back stairs up to my room where we sat still as rabbits listening on the lawn. On bad nights Sam and I spent hours like that, waiting. Some nights when Dad drank he would scream for hours about nothing. Other nights he just drank, saying nothing. I don't know which scared us more.

Sometimes the door would fly open.

"What do you think you're doing?" Dad would ask. Then we had to pretend that we were up to something useful. That's why Sam and I always kept a couple of shirts on the bed with hangers nearby so we could say "We're just cleaning up." Tad would sit in his room watching TV. But we couldn't just pretend nothing was happening, because sometimes we had to run and other times we had to help.

Dad stayed on the third floor that night. He was yelling at Mom, talking so loud you could still hear him through the army of crickets chirping outside. Only we couldn't make out his words. We guessed the danger from the voices. He'd been at it since the soup. Nine had turned to ten, and ten to eleven without him stopping. Still, it really didn't sound so bad until we heard the gunshot. Kids are always saying "Was that a gun?" at the drop of a firecracker, but a pistol sounds different. It's sharper than a tire blowout and louder than the pinging of a rifle. Sam looked at me. I couldn't believe what I'd just heard.

"Get under the bed," I said. And Sam crawled under the bed, into the dust. I wanted to crawl in after him. I didn't want to go upstairs and look. I figured if Dad had shot Mom he wouldn't stop there, but I couldn't just leave Mom alone to bleed to death. You can be afraid and afraid, then one day you can't be afraid anymore. At least that's what I think.

"Allie?" Sam whispered, reaching out from under the bed. And the only thing I wanted to do more than to stay and hide with Sam was grab his hand and run.

I crept out into the hall. There wasn't a sound from upstairs, still I kept going. I had no choice. Mom was my friend.

I raced up the front stairs. "He's *not* going to kill me," I told myself, stopping just outside Mom's door to take a deep breath, like you do to seem poised when you walk out onto the board in a diving meet. Looking relaxed makes the judges think you know what you're doing. I tried to look calm, but I have never been so scared as I was walking in that door.

Mom was still alive when I walked in. Dad was over by the dresser with the pistol and Mom was frozen like a deer caught in headlights near the door.

Dad didn't say hi, but he looked over like he'd been expecting me, because, of course, he knew I had to come.

"Well?" Dad said, looking at Mom, and I prayed she'd keep her mouth shut because I knew that if Dad shot Mom he couldn't have faced me afterward and would have had to kill us both.

"The next one goes through your head," Dad said. I stopped three feet inside the door. I didn't know whose head he meant. I'm not sure that even he did, 'cause Dad kept looking at me like I was supposed to help him. That's when I saw it was all a mistake. Dad had probably just picked up the gun and pulled the trigger on impulse. Now there he was, stuck. Murder wasn't what he wanted, but he was drunk, upset and frightened, so the least embarrassing thing for him just then might be to kill us all, and then himself.

Dad looked from Mom to me, then back to Mom, and I could see he didn't want to have to shoot us. He was secretly hoping for some way out, only he couldn't hand me the gun since that looked like a surrender. So we all three just stood there sweating, Dad rocking back and forth on his heels, grinding his teeth, which made me so scared I couldn't breathe, let alone think.

Then I figured it out.

"Tad," I called, and Dad just stood there.

"Tad," I yelled again, and, for once, Tad was almost decent. He'd been listening, of course. After that shot even Tad couldn't help but listen. So I called his name once more and then he came.

"Okay, Dad, give me the gun," Tad said, walking toward Dad very quietly, one arm already outstretched to avoid making any sudden moves up close.

We watched Tad walk across the room very slowly, Mom not moving, me scarcely breathing since you never knew what Dad might do when he was drunk.

"Okay, Dad. Give me the gun," Tad repeated when he reached Dad, as matter-of-fact as a cop on TV. Dad turned the revolver around. For a moment I thought he might solve everything and shoot himself. But he had just turned the gun around to hand it to Tad. Tad took the gun, clicked open the cylinder, and flipped it around to empty out the five remaining bullets, which he dropped into the silver dish full of change on Dad's dresser. Nobody said a word. Mom had been crying like mad the whole time, only you couldn't hear her, you could just see the tears streaming down her face.

"That's enough, Dad," Tad said. Then Tad put the empty gun back on the dresser to show he trusted Dad not to shoot anyone, which was smart since Dad had other guns, was tons stronger than Tad, and could have killed us all any time.

Tad walked over to the door and looked at me.

"Well," he said. And it was over, like nothing had happened. Mom looked at us. It wouldn't have been smart to look back at Dad, so Tad and I just walked out.

"SOMEONE'S going to get killed around here," Bruce muttered.

"What can I do?" Mom moaned, still lying in bed brushing her hair.

"You've got to leave right away," Bruce said, touching the bullet hole as if he almost couldn't believe it.

"Jesus," Mom sighed, still undecided. I only wished Mom could be more like Stormy. Stormy didn't waste time whining. When she felt like going, Stormy bit right through leather, undid knots with her teeth, and was even smart enough to know that not pulling was the way to slip her choke chain.

"Come on, Jeannie," Bruce said, grasping Mom's shoulders.

"Go away," she said, shrinking back under the quilt.

"Jeannie, you can't just ignore this."

"It was no big deal. No one was hurt. No one is going to be hurt," Mom announced, like it was up to her to decide.

"You're joking," Bruce said, looking from Mom to the bullet hole in disbelief.

"It's no big deal," Mom repeated. Bruce closed his eyes like he was hoping that maybe when he opened them, the bullet hole, or even the whole house, would be gone.

"We can't go on like this—it's death," Bruce said.

"How can I leave, when Sam starts kindergarten in two weeks?" Mom asked.

Bruce and I just looked at each other. It was that bad.

"Why don't you call the police?" I suggested.

"And tell them what—arrest my husband? Then where would I be?" Mom asked.

Mom always had an answer for everything, and that answer was "No way."

"Your mother is a genius—at doing nothing," Dad used to say. I don't know why Dad hated Mom so much when all the rest of us forgave her, any more than I know why Bruce didn't just walk out.

"Don't worry," I said, but Bruce ignored me.

"Why don't you leave?" he yelled at Mom.

"I have no family to go home to," she said.

"Who am I? Huh?" Bruce said, taking everything so personal like always. "This is your big chance—who can blame you for leaving now? Think about it. You've got options," Bruce insisted, pacing back and forth in front of Mom's bed. Then he paused like he was waiting for an answer. I knew just what Bruce was thinking, but Mom looked as blank as if she'd forgotten Bruce once suggested she move in with him.

"What a scandal that'd be!" Mom had laughed, shaking her head. I hadn't encouraged it because Bruce lived nearby and I thought they should go all the way out to California since Bruce had his St. Christopher's medal to protect him while traveling, but nothing to keep Dad from hurting them if they stayed close to home.

"Well?" Bruce said, taking Mom's hand.

But she just looked at him.

"What are you going to do?" he cried, wanting to shake her. "Someone's going to get killed around here," he repeated.

"Death, the end of all our second chances." Mom smiled, sounding almost relieved.

MOM told Bruce it was no big deal, but after the gunshot she stopped eating. Mom never ate much before, but that August her neck seemed long as a swan's and the bones at the base of her throat stood out, making her seem even more like a princess from some story. And the crying. Mom hadn't been much of a crier before, but after the bullet she started breaking into tears each night just before dinner, so it was lucky Ada did the cooking. We'd all sit down and the boys would eat while Mom just sat on the edge of her chair and stared at her food like there were snakes on her plate. Sometimes she'd push the plate away and cry. Other times she'd jump up and say "Is that the phone?" But it wasn't, since everybody knows it's rude to call at dinner time.

"I have to take you shopping. You've outgrown your pretty jumpers," Mom would say as she paced from the table to the hall, then back again to the dining room.

"You should get some new sundresses," I told her. Mom was so thin the straps of her sundress kept slipping off her shoulders even when Bruce wasn't around.

"Your Mom looks skinny as a girl," Mrs. O'Keith said, the last time she dropped in to try to talk sense to Mom.

"Where do you think I should go for the best jumpers?" asked Mom, who always talked about shopping when she was afraid someone might mention Dad or Bruce. I guess it made Mom nervous to have Mrs. O'Keith recall how Mom once said that having a good lawyer was even more important than having a husband with a good heart.

"Did I say that?" Mom asked, frowning, like Mrs. O'Keith must be pulling her leg.

"You should get a good lawyer," Mrs. O'Keith repeated, reminding Mom of Dave's parents' divorce where his Mom went off and lost her children. She was stuck in Florida on vacation with a man for the rest of her life. She had a pretty pink house with a swimming pool, only she always wrote Dave these crying letters and he wasn't allowed to go see her.

"Really, think about calling someone," Mrs. O'Keith said, putting her hand on Mom's arm as she left.

"First I'll get Allie some new jumpers."

"No, let me get a pocketbook first. I want a pocket-book."

"You have a nice black patent leather one for church."

"I want a big one for school."

"You don't need a pocketbook for school. You need a lunchbox," said Mom. We planned to go shopping that afternoon, only Mom had to wait for a call.

"We should go away," I told her as we sat on the yellow couch waiting.

"Uh-huh," she said, but Mom was only listening for the phone. Sometimes she'd spend hours stretched out just staring at the ceiling as she waited.

"Go away? What are you talking about?" Tad said, walking by on his way upstairs to steal some movie money. "We're not going anywhere," said Tad, who had never been so happy as he was now with Joanie, even thought I thought she was a little fat.

"Maybe you're right. Maybe we should go far away," Mom told me, coming back from taking her call upstairs.

"Yes," I said.

"All right," Mom answered, all dreamy. Still she did nothing.

"You just don't understand the complications," Mom said when I complained. I don't know why grown-ups always insist on being so particular. Kids live life straight-forward, like checkers, but grown-ups think they're play-ing chess, so they wait around trying to find a move so smart it sets them up for an even better move six turns later. Only none of Mom's plans would matter if she stalled so long that Dad killed someone.

I don't know how Mom could go on acting as if what

had happened was just over. But she couldn't pretend inside, so she began to tell me crazy things, like her idea that she never really loved anyone. But we can say things, and they're not true. I'm not talking about lies here, just mistakes, like when you think you're very tired but for some reason you can't sleep. The truth about Mom was that she was confused. She wanted everything and nothing. She'd gotten lost in what she was hoping and fearing, so that even quiet times in the garden she just couldn't think.

"Mom, act right," I said, joining her in the garden with the rose clippers.

"What am I doing wrong?" she asked, interrupting my answer to shift in the hammock, sighing, "It's summer."

"So what?" I said.

"Well, summer is different," Mom said, explaining how when things were hot you got lazy and careless and maybe even started doing stuff you never would have dreamed of doing at other times.

"Bruce and I met in the summer. This all started last summer when Bruce came to check the work on the patio —you remember last summer?" Mom asked, stretching out on the hammock to watch me cut some roses for the house.

Mom loved roses.

"Even weeds are pretty in the summer," said Mom. She was right in what she said, only she didn't really believe it because she'd toss out the cornflowers Sam brought her, calling them weeds. Mom even hated mums because they smell as green as dandelions. Dad liked what stayed the same from year to year, so he liked tulips, crocuses, and just about any plant that grew from a bulb. But he especially liked tulips of every description, where naming all the different kinds which really aren't so different is half the fun.

I don't like tulips much myself because you always know just what they'll look like. I like sitting under cherry trees where there are so many blossoms you can't count them and the whole world smells like heaven as you look up at the flower clouds. Dad liked tulips of every description. Mom liked roses, only roses, and big red roses were the best.

Picking roses can be painful if you grab them wrong or hold on too tight. So just as soon as I clipped the flowers, I'd drop them on the ground.

"Why don't you clip some from that branch on the left, sweetheart," Mom suggested.

"Why don't you like Bruce more?" I asked, since it seemed the more she saw him the worse she acted. Tad never could see why Mom liked Bruce. I couldn't figure why she didn't like him better.

Mom looked at me as if I'd just pestered her about Christine Keeler. Then she shrugged and said, "He fits into my life, not my dreams."

"Should I cut these?" I asked, getting back to business. "Or are there too many buds?"

"No. Over there," Mom said, pointing. But the clump was too high up. "Erich has a lovely garden," she said.

"How do you know?" I asked, bending to gather up the roses.

"Erich told me," Mom said, slipping off the hammock to help collect the flowers.

"Bruce has one too," I said.

"What do you mean?"

"Bruce might move into the old Walters place himself."

"Ouch!" said Mom, dropping her roses. "Who said that?"

"Bruce said."

"Quiet, honey. Is that the phone?" Mom asked, grabbing my arm, poised, like Stormy pointing. "I guess not," she said, relaxing her grip on my arm.

"Erich said he'd be back in New York this week. Do you think he'll call?" Mom asked, sounding so much like Mrs. Baskin I could have cried. But why waste tears when it was still summer and you could roll down the lawn all the way to the lake.

"You want to go looking for night crawlers with us?" Dave asked, as the boys strolled by. Then Ted dangled one close to my face. Only a toad was more disgusting. But it was all part of summer, just like the whirring sprinklers and the smell of new-mown grass. I didn't get to the beach much anymore; still, every evening when I heard the sprinklers start whirring, I thought of my friend Howie and of vespers, whatever they are.

MOM was very busy shopping, otherwise she stayed indoors waiting for the phone. She never bothered with bridge or chorus or canasta anymore, or even with slipping off to meet Bruce. Now when Mom went shopping, she didn't go to the furniture warehouse, but instead came home with all sorts of fancy clothes she'd try on for me when she opened the packages. She kept talking about buying jumpers, but we couldn't both leave at once because of phone calls, and anyway I hated even thinking about the start of school.

"Did anyone call?" Mom would say first thing when she came back, so I'd tell her about the calls from Bruce and Mrs. O'Keith and Mrs. Baskin and all the other ladies she made so mad.

"So no one called," said Mom. "You want to see a fashion show?" Then we'd go up to the third floor and Mom would unwrap the clothes and I would cut the little tags off after she twirled around in each outfit once. It was better than having a Barbie doll, except when Mom got tired of looking all pretty for no one and sent me after Bruce.

"I just don't know. Life is such a disappointment," Mom sighed, when we came back to find her writing a letter downstairs.

"You shouldn't say that," said Bruce.

"No, I shouldn't feel it. After I think it, it doesn't much matter if I say it," Mom said, leaving Bruce to stand there feeling helpless as she folded the note.

"Maybe it matters for other people," I said, although it wasn't my part to talk. But I just couldn't stand there and watch Mom make Bruce feel like nothing. It wasn't that I was any smarter than Bruce. It's just I knew the scene by heart.

Bruce didn't know what to do when Mom talked about killing herself. The right thing was just to listen and quietly pat her like you might a sick animal. You have to say "It's all right" and pretend you're sure. But poor Bruce acted as mad as if Mom had talked of killing him.

"Don't say that! How can you say that! Do I count for nothing then?" he cried, kicking a chair, but at least not slamming Sam or me like Dad did.

"It's not that you're nothing," said Mom, who was always polite.

"So why can't I make you happy?" Bruce asked, sinking back down into the chair he'd kicked.

"Sometimes you do. It's just that I'm tired, very tired," she said, like an actress making each word count.

"There's nothing wrong that I can't fix. Give me a chance," Bruce said, leaping up again.

"You don't understand."

"Of course I don't understand. You say you want out. I offer you an out. Then you say 'No, thank you. I just want to die.' Now who would understand that?" Bruce asked, grabbing a beer.

"I knew you wouldn't understand."

"Shit," Bruce said, slamming his hands down on the table. "I try and try, and what do I get?"

"All I get is older," Mom sighed.

"You forgot about varicose veins," Bruce said, and Mom began to cry. So Bruce took her in his arms. That's why it was sometimes almost better that Mom cried. Because at least then Bruce could take Mom upstairs where they made up.

"Let's just get out of here!" Bruce pleaded. But instead of letting Bruce wrap his arms around her like usual, Mom broke away and ran across the room.

"If he'd only die," she sobbed, throwing herself down on the couch. Bruce looked at her like he was going to be sick. Then he turned and left.

"Go take care of your mom," Bruce told me when I started through the dining room after him.

"Don't look at me like that—like him," Mom said, walking in to straighten her dress and hair in the dining room mirror.

"Look, it's crazy of me to see him—he doesn't do a thing but make me happy. I mean, make me feel happy for just that moment," Mom said, taking a napkin from the sideboard to wipe the liner smudged beneath her eyes.

"Once you grow up, you'll see that love loses its present once it no longer has a future," Mom said, but it sure didn't look that way to me, for Mom had barely finished fixing her face before she sent me back out after Bruce.

"I would hate to be without you," Mom cried, leaping up from the yellow couch when I dragged Bruce home an hour later. "I would hate it," she said, smiling as she reached to touch his cheek, but he just stood there, numb.

"Why did you send for me?" he asked, eyeing her, exhausted.

"I missed you."

"What does that mean?"

"Why does everything have to *mean?*" Mom asked, stepping back, all flustered. "The simple fact is that, despite myself, I missed you. Missed you!" Mom cried, as if just saying that hurt her.

"Yeah, sure," Bruce muttered.

"Christ, can't you see that I'm giving you something— it's even the truth!" Mom cried, grabbing Bruce's arm. "Why is it that whatever I offer you is never enough?"

"Because I want *you.* I want your love. Why can't I ever be enough?" Bruce asked, coming alive. Mom said nothing, though I was scared to death of all the things she might say.

"Well, if I can't have love, I'd like a little information," Bruce said, settling into the cool grin he gave most ladies.

"Who says you can't have love?" Mom asked, standing before him still as a ghost, her thin dress dancing in the draft from the hall.

"Bruce, I'm scared, real scared," Mom whispered, so low that Bruce leaned forward.

"What—of him? Or of falling for me? I'm sorry, Jeannie." He headed for the door.

"God, Bruce, don't leave me," Mom said, stricken.

"I love you so much. So much," Bruce cried, burying himself in her, all his stiffness melting. "So very much," he confessed, sounding more miserable than Dad.

"Christ, this is crazy," Mom sighed. Yet she seemed happy. I left the room before she ever remembered to send me out after my dog.

I sat out front until I heard Bruce slip out the back door, whistling, like always, as a signal to me that he was gone and I was free to go inside to talk with Mom. Not bursting in, of course, but once I heard her start the bath I'd race up to perch on the rim of her tub.

"Well, well," she'd say, slipping from her teal robe into the bath with a glow on her face I almost shared.

Mom always ran her bath right after seeing Bruce, but the day he told her how much he loved her I waited a whole twenty minutes, yet heard nothing, so I slipped upstairs to check.

"Mom!" I said, for there she was, not fixing her nails, not reading poems, not even playing solitaire, but just lying in bed without even her robe on, thinking.

"You know, Allie, you're right. We've got to get away from here. Far, far away," Mom said. Somehow, I didn't feel relieved.

THE next night Bruce walked into the kitchen in a great mood because Dad said he'd be working late. That was for sure, since Mom had me call Dad's office to say hi and talk with him about the registration for a father-daughter race we were going to sail in soon.

"Hey, Alice!" Bruce said, grabbing me up off my feet and tossing me in the air till I was dizzy with laughing.

"The place for roughhousing is outside," said Mom.

Bruce smiled. "Hi, baby," he said to Mom.

Mom frowned, distracted. "Isn't it time you went to bed?" Mom asked me.

"No," I said, trying to tickle Bruce.

"Yes, it is. Go change into your pajamas."

"Already?"

"It's past nine."

"That isn't late! Last week you let even Sam stay up past—"

"Don't argue," said Mom, reaching over and slapping me.

"Stop that," said Bruce, grabbing her hand.

"Don't touch me!" she screamed.

"I don't often get the chance," Bruce laughed. But it was not his usual laugh.

"Don't you have any homework?" Bruce asked Tad, who'd just walked in.

"I don't have homework in summer," Tad said, as Mom shook off Bruce's arm.

"I understand your people prefer to entertain in the kitchen, but you know this house has other rooms," Mom said, marching off with Tad.

"Would you tell your smart mother that even men like me have brains they're not too eager to have her crazy husband blow out? The kitchen has a door. And I like to stay near an exit. Can you remember to tell her that?" Bruce asked.

"Mom just acts like that sometimes. She doesn't mean it," I explained.

"Oh, yeah? Tell me about it," Bruce muttered, but he didn't seem to want to hear. "I'm going to take a walk," he said, getting up, as I sat there hoping Mom would come back to stop him from leaving.

"What are you staring at?" Mom snapped, walking back into the kitchen a few seconds after the door swung shut.

"He didn't apologize," Mom said, seeing my gaze follow Bruce's trek across the lawn as I sat there wishing Mom hadn't gotten a telegram from Erich that morning.

Funny how Mom never remembered to say "I'm sorry" herself, only "He didn't apologize." But I didn't dare say that, so instead I only asked, "How long before I grow up?"

"It apparently takes several lifetimes," Mom said. But I just gave her a look and kept watching Bruce walking away.

"All right, all right, go bring him back," she sighed, since she could see I was steaming.

I ran out the door and sprinted halfway across the lawn, then slowed down to a walk when I spied Bruce slouched against the birches by the dock.

"Hey, Bruce," I said.

"Should I just go?" he asked, looking back at the gray house ringed with roses.

"Gee whiz," I said, sitting down next to him, and remembering all the times when I used to sit alone on the dock waiting to wish on the night's first star. Most of my wishes were for him. That was before I understood how tricky it can get making wishes. I still can't stop myself from making wishes, but now I always wish "Please make everything all right," since that's by far the safest one.

"Please hold my hand," I said, another one of my wishes. Then I told him that Mom was sorry, which didn't seem such a bad fib. So we walked together back to the house and found Mom curled up sipping her iced tea on the living room couch.

"Darling, it's August," Mom told me. "Dogs and people get snappy. The heat sits right on top of you like a gargoyle on a roof and won't let go. Know what I mean?" Mom said, after she'd explained to me all about gargoyles.

"No, I don't understand," said Bruce, who was still angry. "I love you. I try to make us happy. What more can you want? If it's money, I've got money, even if I don't bother to spend it, but you can spend it. Allie can spend it. That shitty son of yours, Tad, can spend it, for all I care."

"It isn't money," Mom said, her voice dead. No one in

the world could make you feel more happy, and nobody I knew had made more people feel so sad. I guess it wasn't her fault, but I wished Mom would sometimes just pretend to be nice. Why, when Bruce asked "Don't I ever make you happy?" couldn't Mom say "You do"? Instead, she sighed.

The next morning when I was sitting on the dock dangling my feet in the water Bruce came up and sat down beside me. "Is she crazy or something?" he asked.

But Mom could still be wonderful sometimes, like that very afternoon when she and I were sitting in my bedroom talking.

"Oh, look," I said, pointing, when I spied Bruce cutting across the back lawn. Mom went to my balcony and waved, looking prettier than Cinderella in her cross-backed sundress. Bruce looked up and waved back. We went downstairs. Bruce had already let himself in and was at the foot of the stairs in a bound.

"Hey, Allie," he said, picking me up, that happy crinkle around his eyes.

"I wonder if you'd take a look at the hammock. One side seems shaky," Mom said, hair glowing as she led us outside. The phone rang just as we stepped off the patio.

"Tell him that sweet story you just told me about the bird," Mom called back over her shoulder, rushing back inside.

I guess Mom hadn't been listening too carefully because I hadn't really been talking about a bird. What I'd said was that seeing her fluttering around going crazy not leaving reminded me of when a bird gets stuck in a room and you try to help it back out the open window, only it keeps flying away until it finally kills itself smashing into the glass.

"Well?" Bruce asked, but he was trying to pick up Mom's phone conversation, so he didn't much care when I said nothing.

Mom was gone maybe five minutes.

"Want me to go?" Bruce asked when Mom came back with her faraway smile.

"Oh, no, let's retire to the kitchen where you feel comfortable," Mom smirked.

I thought from the look on his face Bruce would kill Mom, but all he did was drag her upstairs.

"You don't respect me!" screamed Bruce.

"You always say that."

"Maybe because it's true."

"Maybe because you don't respect yourself," Mom said.

"You think you're too good for me. You're ashamed because you've got more degrees than a black belt and I never went to college. Well, I went to the war, I didn't have to go to college."

"You didn't go, you were drafted."

"I was drafted and I went," Bruce sighed, giving up. I know because I sat listening on the stairs by the big window that stretched halfway to the attic.

"Why don't we split?" Bruce asked.

"If he'd only die," Mom said, her answer to everything.

"Sometimes you make me sick," Bruce muttered. Then things got real quiet. I guess Bruce was trying to convince Mom to leave. "You're only young once," he said, when I finally could hear them again.

"Yes, but I'm not young anymore. I'm a married woman with three children and I'm already thirty-six—thirty-six and no one loves me," Mom said. Not quite the problem as I saw it.

"Thirty-six," Mom said again, like it was death.

I looked out the window and saw Dad's car just up the road.

"Mom!" I screamed, running for the door. It was locked, so I started banging.

"What is it?" Bruce called.

"Dad!" I cried.

"*What?*" Bruce said, opening the door a crack with just his blue jeans on.

"Look!" I pulled Bruce out into the hall where he could see.

"Guess who's in the driveway?" Bruce called.

"But he never comes home for lunch. If he drops in, he comes later," Mom said, though she had eyes and a window to see.

"Well, take a look," Bruce said, ducking into his T-shirt.

"He'll kill me," Mom said, slipping into the hall in her teal robe.

"Kill you? Here *I* am stuck on the third fucking floor!" Bruce said. Then he looked at me.

"But it just can't be," Mom muttered, racing back into the bedroom to check Dad's top drawer to see if he was wearing a gun.

"I can't remember how many he has!" she cried, sinking down on the bed next to her crumpled sundress.

"Mom," I said, since someone had to go take care of Dad.

Mom hid her face in the pillow.

"She can't do it," Bruce said. And, of course, he was right. Mom just couldn't do it anymore. I had no choice. Soon I'd grow up, get out, and take Sam with me—a heartbreaker at twelve, she'd promised. I could hardly wait to grow up, but I wasn't so sure about the heartbreaker business anymore.

"Okay, I'll handle Dad. Go to my room and drop from the ledge off my balcony. Tad sneaks out that way all the time," I told Bruce, handing him his watch before I raced downstairs.

"Hi, Dad!"

"Where's your mother?" Dad asked, walking in the front door with his briefcase.

"Upstairs with a migraine. Want me to go tell her you're here?"

"No, don't bother. I just want a sandwich. You'll probably do just as bad a job of making it as she would with more of an excuse."

Dad smiled, looking around a little nervous, like he half expected an ambush.

Ada was in the kitchen and made Dad a roast turkey sandwich with lots of mayonnaise and a big fuss. Sam and Frankie stopped by, wanting to eat, which made me nervous since you couldn't trust Frankie not to mention things he didn't know might get us killed. I wondered how I could get rid of the kids, but they only wanted potato chips. So I gave them a whole big cellophane bag and they went back out.

"What's up?" Dad asked, trying so hard to be cheery that if I didn't know better, I would have said he was more scared than me.

"Have you seen the paper yet?" I asked, and so he mentioned a couple of stories as I sat keeping him company, joking a little like always, feeling more grown up every minute. Not nervous at all, even while wondering if Dad would have killed us had he found out.

"Hmm," Dad said, looking over toward the stairs when he finished lunch.

"Have you seen what they're doing to your roses?" I asked, jumping up to make for the back door.

"Japanese beetles again?" Dad asked, rising as we exchanged grave nods. So I walked Dad outside to see what the bugs were up to, hoping he'd leave without going back inside. We talked awhile about the insects and I promised to hand the new man the note Dad gave me about the right brand of bug spray.

"You're the only one who cares," Dad said, giving me a hug that felt like nothing. I guess it was the best he could do.

We walked out to the end of the driveway together. Mrs. Baskin honked as she drove by. We both waved. "Who was that?" Dad asked, getting into his car as Sam and Frankie came up to ask if I would play.

"Damn, I forgot my briefcase."

"I'll fetch it," I said, flying off to the house and racing back with it in seconds.

"Thanks," Dad said, taking the briefcase. "Well, look after the roses and things," he said, starting the car.

"Goodbye, Dad," I said, feeling awful.

"Come play monster," Sam said, grabbing my arm.

"Not now," I said, standing on the end of the drive waving until Dad disappeared. But I couldn't wave the thing away.

Chapter
Eleven

*I*t was very odd about Mom's disappearing. Mom and Dad were there, together, fighting, my whole lifetime and I kept saying "Mom, leave," but she'd only go shopping. Then one day Sam and I came home and Mom was gone.

That was the day Frankie's mom had promised to take Sam, Frankie, and me all the way to the shore. We drove along in traffic for hours and hours. Still, Frankie's mother wasn't upset, so we weren't either. When we got to Asbury Park we banged around in bump cars and ate salt-water taffy and ice cream and lost all our dimes shooting at metal ducks to try to win pink stuffed dogs we would have lost on the roller coaster anyway. Sam loved the roller coaster, but I wasn't so crazy about it because that's where the cotton candy I was eating got stuck in my hair.

"Let's try the funhouse," said Frankie's mom, but that's

a slow ride, so we took the flying saucers instead. I could have stayed on that ride forever, all the spinning was like being twirled through the air by Bruce, but Sam kept wanting to go back on the roller coaster, and you couldn't say no to Sam because he hardly ever asked.

We rode the roller coaster till Frankie's mom said she got whiplash. Then we piled into her small car, so sticky from all the cotton candy, taffy, and ice cream that Frankie's mom said she doubted that anyone would ever be able to separate us again. The highway back was packed with people sore from sunburn honking their horns, but we were so stuffed we didn't worry about not getting home till hours past dinner time, which was when Dad told us Mom had gone.

Dad said Mom left because her mom had died and she had to go take care of things.

"I don't believe it," Sam said when I tucked him in that night. But you just don't lie about people dying. Still, it did seem sort of strange that Mom had never even mentioned Grandma's being sick.

I don't know if it was because nobody believed Grandma had really died, or because Grandma was so old that it was bound to happen anyway; but no one seemed too upset about her dying, not even Tad, despite all the presents she had given him, but least of all Sam, who was so smart he ignored everyone who ignored him. I wasn't upset at first either. Funerals are nice and quiet, and Mom needed a rest.

You may think us kids were all heartless, but Grandma's dying wasn't sad like the death of Donna, my beautiful dark-eyed cousin, who was always laughing on the phone long distance, and who once even set my hair for me. My hair didn't turn out that hot, but Donna's always looked terrific. She was all grown up, taller than my mom, went out on dates, and wore high heels. November she got sick and had to spend Thanksgiving in the hospital. But they let her come home for Christmas, because it was hopeless, and she died Christmas Eve when everyone was so busy wrapping presents that they kept saying "Just a minute" when she called them till she finally stopped calling.

Donna was my favorite cousin, yet they didn't tell me she was dying. They didn't even tell me she was dead until after the holidays.

"Oh, Donna passed away," Mom said one day, which made me furious because if they'd told me Donna was sick I would have gone to visit.

"But I heard she looked awful at the end," said Mom, not understanding that Donna was beautiful and did makeup better than anyone and had the world's prettiest clothes and never could have looked bad.

"What do you think it's like dying?" I asked Ada once Mom left, but that only flustered Ada so much she dropped the wash she was carrying up the back stairs.

"What do you think dying's like?" I insisted, till Ada ordered me out.

Grandma died and no one cried. Still, I suppose it was too bad for Grandma, although she had seemed to be looking forward to it from the way she always loved to say that she might never see us again. Dad told us Mom's note said that Grandma had a stroke when she was asleep and was found by the cleaning lady. Grandma didn't even know what happened to her, which Dad said was par for the course.

"But you know what happened, don't you?" he said, coming into my room without even knocking, late on the night Mom left.

"Know what?" I asked, pulling the thin summer covers up to my chin.

"Did your mom talk to you?" Dad asked, standing by the open French doors, fingering my pretty white curtains.

"All the time," I said.

"Allie," Dad said in a voice that meant "Watch it." "I mean about her leaving today. Do you know where she went?"

"It's a mystery to me," I said. I mean, we weren't at the shore that long, but when we came back Mom had vanished even though I couldn't imagine her packing to go anywhere in under three days.

"You know what happens to wise guys," Dad warned, walking over to sit on the bed.

It was too dark to check his expression. I could smell the Scotch, but it didn't knock me out.

"Come on," Dad said, leaning forward. Then he flicked on the lamp and saw I'd been crying.

"Okay," he said, eyeing the crumpled Kleenex strewn around me. "Okay."

"WHY doesn't Mom call?" I asked Ada the day after Mom left.

"Don't get me started," she said.

Ada was glad Mom left because she thought Mom just got in the way, which is the very same thing that Mom thought about her. Tad was glad Mom left because she used to like to keep the line free. Now Tad could hang on the phone with Joanie all day long. Sam never mentioned Mom, so I guess he wasn't heartbroken. I wasn't even too sorry at first, since Mom had sided with the nasty red-headed cop who said Stormy should be put away for biting.

I don't know what made Mom agree that Stormy should be destroyed. Mom and Stormy had never been close, but

Stormy was one of my best friends and Mom of all people should have known that everyone misbehaves sometimes. Besides, the biting wasn't even Stormy's fault. She never roamed the town attacking children. They came into our yard to tease her. That was the thing about Stormy, she only bit when she was chained.

"I can understand that," Dad said, when I explained it. So he told the police that Stormy was a watchdog whose duty was to discourage trespassers and that she'd only been doing her job. That was the end of it, of course, for the police couldn't contradict a grown-up father. I thought it was very fine of Dad to save my dog for me, even though he only did it to spite Mom. The one good thing about parents who can't agree on anything is that you get to choose whose final word counts.

"Weren't you here when Mom left?" I asked, trailing Ada from the pantry to the kitchen. "I bet you were," I said.

Still Ada ignored me.

"What did she take with her? Did someone call? Did she seem sad?" I asked, until Ada ordered me out of the kitchen and I went upstairs to question Tad.

"Don't spill that grape juice on my comics!" he warned, sitting on the floor sorting stacks of comics so old some of the superheroes were discontinued.

"Remember what happened to Mom's Aunt Ruth?"

"What Aunt Ruth?" Tad said, cursing when one of the frayed covers he was holding ripped.

"Mom's Aunt Ruth," I said.

"I never met an Aunt Ruth," Tad said, intent on the ragged collection he swore would be worth millions by the time he grew up.

"Of course you didn't, that's because—"

"Don't you know that grape juice stains!" Tad screamed, afraid I might drop some on his precious *Captain Americas*.

"Don't you even care where Mom is?" I yelled through the door he slammed in my face. "Don't you even care?" I screamed, putting my drink down to bang with both hands on the door.

Suddenly it opened and Tad stood before me.

"Mom went to Ohio. Now you dry up," Tad said, so smug I would have splashed some of my grape juice on his comics just to show him, only Tad looked like he'd grown six inches since we last squared off.

"Ada," I hollered, coming back downstairs. "Did Mom say anything special? What was the last thing she said to you?"

"Hello!" called Mrs. Baskin, who'd let herself in.

"What are you doing here?" I asked, though anyone could see she was busy snooping.

"I just dropped by to see if you or your dad needed anything."

"Why?" I asked.

Mrs. Baskin smiled. "Oh, come on, Allie. You needn't keep secrets from me. Your mom is almost a missing person. Don't deny it. Your dad called to ask me what I knew, poor man. Oh, I brought you some brownies. Shall we eat them and talk?"

"There's nothing to talk about," I said pretending to be late for workouts. Still, after Mrs. Baskin left I couldn't help thinking of Mom easing into her bubble bath telling sad, funny stories like the one about Mom's Aunt Ruth and her poor lawyer husband who kept saying "Now, babe," and ducking whenever Aunt Ruth got mad and sent her china crashing into the wall. Mom says it was always exciting to see Aunt Ruth since she was a real flapper with long strings of beads, bobbed hair, a short temper, and a big heart.

Aunt Ruth had a shiny white car, but no children of her own. That's why she dropped by Mom's school once, to bring Mom and her sister goodbye presents. That day Aunt Ruth also had a handsome young man waiting in her car. Aunt Ruth kissed Mom and her sister goodbye and said she was going away on vacation. When Mom and her sister brought their presents home and told their parents about Aunt Ruth's visit, Mom's parents called Aunt Ruth's husband, Uncle Max.

"She'll come back," he said, since disappearing was one of Aunt Ruth's habits. But she never did return. And she never sent anything to the girls for Christmas, even though she'd already told them what she'd bought. Aunt Ruth never even wrote to ask for money, which Mom said flowed like water through her hands. Still, Uncle Max waited, then instead of divorcing Ruth, he died.

It was only when Ruth still didn't show to collect her inheritance that Mom's family finally called the police. Alice-Marie had died by then too, so Mom was the only witness. The police pressed Mom for details, but all she could tell them was that the young man waiting in Aunt Ruth's car outside the school that day had looked nice. Mom told me that the young men who'd waited for her aunt always looked nice, but that Ruth had seemed especially happy that last day because she was going to Florida, and Florida back then was like California now.

"COME on, think! Was there anything odd about your mother's behavior?" Dad said, calling me into the library the night after Mom left. "What could have prompted this?" Dad asked, straight-faced, although Mom left just five days after the gunshot.

Those last few days Mom seemed to be listening for the phone even more than usual. But maybe she already knew Grandma was sick and was secretly worried. Whatever it was, those last few days Mom and Bruce fought like crazy. I was walking along the back path with them once as they argued, when Mom just reached over and smacked me across the face. Bruce stopped, so I ducked behind him while Mom and he stood there glaring.

"There are rules, you know," said Bruce. "You don't hit people who are smaller than you."

"Oh?" said Mom.

"Yes, ma'am," Bruce said. "That's why I don't slug you now."

But I couldn't help wondering if maybe that's what Mom wanted, for Bruce to hit her so she could say good-bye, or maybe she just wanted him to straighten her out. Mom needed straightening out. She was still so wrapped up in her crackly phone calls that I didn't even bother telling her how great I thought Bruce was anymore. Maybe I should have told Bruce to leave again, but I didn't. Instead, when he got discouraged I told him how you might like someone at first because they're cute or funny but that love is a gift you give to someone because you give it. Sometimes bad things happen and you don't understand them, but you don't know everything God knows, and besides, the gift is what counts. If you're in love, then someone with a better car can come along and it shouldn't matter.

"It's like whether you believe in God," I told him. You can give reasons for love but there's finally no reason. "It's you do or you don't."

"She talks like an atheist," Bruce grumbled.

"An agnostic," Mom corrected. Thank God she didn't explain the difference.

"I'LL drive you to school whenever it rains," said Mrs. Baskin, who came by again trying to be nice, only she acted like it was Mom and not Grandma who'd died. "Have you talked to your mom?" she asked.

We'd tried calling Grandma's, only no one answered. Mom must have been staying with one of her friends not on the list Dad called.

"Can you think where she'd stay?" Dad asked all the friends he called, when Mom didn't phone the day after she left or the next day either.

"There's got to be a number or address here some-where," Dad muttered, pelting me with questions as he dug through the wads of sales slips in Mom's drawers. Where did Mom go? Did she have callers? Was there any-thing about her those last few days that struck me as strange?

"Nope," I said, not telling Dad that something about Mom had started to scare me. In fact, once when she came home from shopping and started her fashion show by put-ting on a long black cloak I got so scared I ran clear out of the house.

"What's the matter?" Mom called. "Have you lost your mind?"

But I hadn't, it was just that the cloak made Mom look like the killer in the scariest "Alfred Hitchcock Presents" of all, where the strangler is really a man who pretends to be a lady nurse. The big black cloak is what keeps you from seeing.

"Come back inside," Mom said, approaching me, still in

the cloak, as I kept backing away, feeling like a total jerk for running.

"Don't you dare go another step," Mom said, so I told her about the TV show, still standing twenty feet away.

"You're joking!" she laughed, which only made her seem more scary.

"All right," Mom said, taking off the cloak. "You win." But I was still scared and wouldn't go back inside until I made sure that Ada was there too.

Ada was shocked. "Now you've gone crazy too," she muttered, which scared me even more. Mom put the black cloak away to humor me, then two days later she was gone.

BUT once she left I couldn't escape her. There were evenings Mom appeared looking as ghostly as she did when she used to come read me "My Last Duchess." It was only a dream, of course. In the dream I called out "Mom, I'm thirsty!" like when I was little, and Mom would walk into the room with a glass of water like she'd never been away. "Mom, I'm thirsty," I'd say, but she never moved any closer than just inside the door, so I had to get up to reach her. Only, when I did, my hand went through her and she started laughing, leaving me feeling as empty as the glass beside my bed. The lights were still burning upstairs and I could hear Dad pacing. If I cried out in my dream, he'd come down and ask "Are you all right?" "Sure," I'd say.

One night I woke to find Dad looming over my bed.

"What's that?" Dad asked, pointing to the corner of an envelope sticking out of my desk.

"I dunno. A letter from Donna."

"Don't lie to me!" Dad said, putting down his drink to

fling open the top of the tiny white French Provincial writing desk. "It's a letter from Donna," Dad said, shaking his head as he surveyed the drawers jammed with lifesaving manuals, three-ring notebooks, and old report cards.

"What's this?" Dad asked, picking up the diary he bought me for my last birthday—a stupid question since it said DIARY in gold letters right on the cover.

"It's my diary."

"But there's no writing here!" Dad said, flipping through the pages.

"I'm sorry, Dad. I got too busy."

"Doing what?" Dad asked, starting to sift through the other desk drawers.

"What are you looking for? Mom didn't keep a diary either."

"No, but she kept this!" Dad said, flashing the kind of small white card that comes with store-bought flowers. On the card the words Happy Birthday were scrawled in the same stringy hand that addressed the air mail envelopes.

"Do you recognize that signature? It says Erich. Did he used to come here afternoons?"

"Who?" I asked.

"Erich!" Dad screamed, going on with a thousand questions about Erich, Erich, always stupid old Erich, while I thought about the important things—not just where Mom might have gone. Back when Bruce and Mom used to take their walks they would talk around the sort of things that I was thinking, never really getting into them, the way they walked around the lake but never dove in. Sometimes Mom wanted to talk about life. Other times it was Bruce. But they were scared to dream together, so they just walked and fought.

"I hear your mom kept very busy. Are you sure a man

named Erich didn't stop by here?" Dad asked, still digging through my dresser.

"Sure, I'm sure. Hey! That's my underwear drawer," I cried, leaping up. "You can't go in there! Even Tad doesn't go in there!"

"Jesus Christ!" Dad muttered. But he left my junk drawer alone.

SOMETIMES when Dad's questions kept me up half the night, I wouldn't get up until after ten the next morning. Then I'd take some magazines out to the hammock wreathed with roses to dream and swing, listening to the doves moaning like lovers once you left the room. Sam used to come by and ask me to go to the beach with him, but I told him he was big enough to go all by himself now. Dad wanted me to take more tennis lessons, but I was through with excuses, so I just told him I hated the game. Besides, I liked to lie in the hammock sneaking looks at the new boys Dad hired, watching them perspire, thinking how Bruce used to smell of sweat, but I liked it. And how Dad smelled of gin.

"You can't smell gin or vodka," Tad insisted. But I sure could. Bruce used to drink beer he brought, and take the empties with him. Dad mostly drank gin or Scotch and tossed the bottles in the trash. Tad didn't miss Mom, but he and Dave missed stealing the beers Bruce left in our refrigerator when he walked out mad.

I THOUGHT about Bruce all the time, wondering if he spent his days half expecting me like I waited for him. I missed being with him and Mom and all the walks we took and the things we did together, even if I was only invited along for appearance's sake. I even missed the bad times when Mom was on the phone and left us in the kitchen. I thought we always had a good time then, but I guess Bruce didn't because one day when I'd just gotten us a bowl of ice cream he turned to me and said, "Look, you're a terrific kid, but I didn't come here looking to have some eleven-year-old baby-sit me."

I didn't know what to say, so I just looked at Bruce ready to pretend he'd never said that.

"You want some chocolate sauce on this?" I asked, handing him his spoon, but he just moved his chair closer and kept talking.

"'You know, this is a nuthouse, and I'm no kind of social worker. I've had it here up to here with this place," Bruce said, pushing back his chair. Then he got up and left.

"Hey, no offense meant, Mouse," Bruce told me when he dropped by the beach the next day.

"I'm not mad at you," I said. Then we walked and talked some more like always, but all our walking only took us round in circles. Bruce and Mom were also going round in circles. Those last two days before she left we walked the back path more than three stray dogs. Bruce kept asking Mom to leave with him and she kept saying she thought "it" would all "work out," like she was half expecting someone else to fix things for her, only she wouldn't even let Bruce try to help.

"It's just I keep thinking it will end. Only it never ends," Mom said.

"Because you never end it," Bruce said.

"I can't end anything," Mom sighed, honest for once as she stopped walking and turned to face Bruce. I was walking a little behind, so busy thinking that I bumped smack into Bruce, who stood there staring at Mom.

"Do you want to end this?" Bruce asked. Bruce and I leaned forward to hear Mom's answer.

"Well?" Bruce said, for we could hardly stand it. But Mom just smiled her faraway smile.

WHEN Bruce didn't come by after Mom left, I tried to pretend that Mom and Bruce had run off together, but I knew it was only pretending because they fought so bad those last few days.

"I can't stand it. Sometimes I even think I can't stand you," Bruce said, slamming out the back door after he and Mom had almost the exact same fight they'd had the day before.

I started to run after Bruce, but Mom shook her head no and went on clearing away some glasses like nothing had happened. There was still time to call him back and make it up, but that was the night before Mom left and her mind was already off somewhere else.

"Mom," I began.

"Hush, darling," she murmured. "You were a good baby," she said to me. "You never cried."

I wish there were magic words for remembering and forgetting so that you could put whole summers out of your mind like letters tucked in the back of a junk drawer. So many bad things had to happen. I would give almost anything to never again feel the hurt everyone was feeling that August Bruce loved Mom.

I'd tried to help, but I began to wonder if maybe all my helping had only gotten us in worse trouble. All I wanted was for us to get out safely and for everybody to be happy, though try as I might everyone was miserable and we were all still there.

"People say that childhood is the happiest time, but I hope these aren't your happy days," Bruce told me once when we were waiting for Mom to meet us in some parking lot. I used to think all the running back and forth was a big pain, though once Mom left I kept remembering the three of us walking the back path and hoping that if you stuck all those walks together, back to back, they might lead somewhere.

I knew Bruce was sore at Mom, but I also thought he might know something about where she'd gone, so the fifth day after Mom left I got up early and started walking over to the old Walters place. As I walked, I thought of all the times I'd gone there with messages and how mean Pete, Barry, Frank and the rest of the guys could be when Bruce wasn't there. I walked halfway there, then turned around and walked back home.

Grandma died. Mom left for a few days which became several more, but things seemed better, except I lost a tooth biting into a frozen Milky Way at the beach. I bit down, then pulled to break off the piece, but my left canine stuck in the candy so that I yanked the tooth clean out. At first I was happy thinking of the tooth fairy money, then I started worrying what Bruce would think of the hole in my mouth. Of course, I knew another tooth would eventually grow in to replace it, but if I hadn't bought that frozen Milky Way the baby tooth would have stayed in until the big tooth pushed it out.

"It won't stop bleeding," I complained.

"It will if you take your fingers out of your mouth and stop poking it," Ada said.

"But it won't stop hurting."

"It will if you stop fussing," Ada insisted, which may have been true but I couldn't stop because stuff got stuck there and I had to poke around in the bloody gum with the end of my toothbrush. Besides, the hole not only hurt, it itched.

"Where do you think Mom has gone?" I asked at lunch.

Sam, Tad, and Ada were all busy eating and no one would answer. The hole in my mouth kept me from eating anything except Jell-O and soup. "Do you think Mom is on her way back by now?" Tad was reading his *Spider Man* comics and Sam was busy telling Ada why she couldn't take the den where he kept his toy trucks and turn it into her new room.

"Eat your Jell-O," said Ada. But you get sick of Jell-O as a steady diet. After a while all three different red flavors begin to taste alike.

"I hate this Jell-O," I told Ada.

"Come on, Allie," Sam said. "Be nice.

A WEEK went by. Mom didn't call from Ohio. "What about Bruce?" Dad finally asked one night after dinner.

"Bruce did the backyard."

"What else?"

"What do you mean?" I asked, but Dad just glared.

I thought about Bruce all the time. I figured maybe I should go see him so that the two of us could at least miss Mom together.

"I wake up missing you," Bruce used to say, stroking Mom's hand, but he couldn't begin to know what missing her was like! Even when Mom was home, she was far away. You could sit softly patting her shoulder and handing her Kleenex as she sat crying for hours and never even know what she was crying about.

"What does she want?" Bruce would ask, as if he thought I was some kind of expert. But I never understood Mom, because she never felt the same as I did. She was waiting for something that was nothing. For it's love that makes you lonely—it's loving something more than you could ever love yourself.

Mom and Bruce went up and down, but Bruce and I

were always pals. I was pals with Howie too, but that was different. You could fall asleep on Howie's shoulder and never wake up with a nightmare. I never felt all weird and shy sitting beside him like I sometimes did with Bruce. Howie had the world's best personality, but Bruce knew the story. He could see.

"Howie belongs to another world," I explained once when Bruce asked me about the difference.

"Don't tell me you're a snob like your mother," Bruce said, sounding hurt.

"No, I mean that he belongs to a different world from you and me."

The day after Mom left I went up to her room and spent a long time looking through the closets full of clothes that smelled like her. Some of my favorite dresses were gone, but the teal robe was still hanging there soft as a dream. So I tried it on.

"Don't you go crazy," Ada warned, when she walked in on me dancing around crying in Mom's robe. But missing Mom was only natural. Taking care of her had been my life.

"Let's go to the beach," Sam said, coming upstairs to find out what was keeping me. "Come on," he said, pulling at my hand. But later that afternoon I sneaked back into Mom's dressing room to try on some more of her pretty clothes. It was fun swirling around before the mirror, looking almost glamorous, holding the long skirts up. Sam liked to watch me do most things, but he hated to see me playing dress-up. "It makes you look like Mom," he said, because Mom used to dress and undress all the time.

"Why do Cathy and Heathcliff go walking on the moors at night when Cathy is sick and they know they're bound to get in trouble?" I'd asked Mom when we were upstairs checking out her latest dresses the day after Dad almost ran into Bruce.

"Who gave you that?" Mom said, grabbing the book from my hands.

"You did," I said, and Mom didn't deny it. She just kept looking at herself in the mirror as she tried on a black cashmere suit with a mink collar.

"How do you like the hem?" she asked, tilting her head as she approached the mirror. "Is it about right, mid-knee?"

"Why do they go out on the moors at night when Cathy's sick?"

"Maybe I should change into the heels I'd wear," Mom said, still eyeing her reflection.

"Why does Heathcliff throw himself on Cathy when she's just little and nearly dying?" I insisted.

"It's just a bad idea," Mom said, slipping out of her flats.

"It's more than that!" I cried, grabbing her skirt.

"Young lady, what's your problem?" Mom snapped.

"Do you think Mom will be back before school starts?" I asked Ada, who had to turn the vacuum cleaner off to hear me. Once she did, she turned the vacuum right back on, she was so bored with the question.

Mom hated questions too, and why ask where Mom had gone when things were more normal at our house once she'd left. Ada managed everything and on Tuesday Mrs. O'Keith was going to take us shopping for school.

Once Mom disappeared, I was free to go to the beach again, which was nice, but not as nice as it had been before Fluff got lost and Howie and Christine became engaged. I was sitting next to Howie on the guard stand my first day back when he told me they were going to be married. It was like someone just blew cigar smoke in my face.

"Isn't that nice?" Howie said. Christine was sitting on the other side of him looking at me so hard I knew that if I said one word she'd cut my tongue out.

Howie smiled. "Well?"

"Oh, gee," I said. What could I say?

"WHERE do you think your mom really is?" asked Mrs. Baskin, who was full of advice on how Dad should change the rooms and how Ada might improve her brownies.

"She should have left a long time ago," Dad said, confessing that Mom had asked for a divorce when I was just little, and he'd agreed, saying she could take me, but that Mom hadn't wanted to leave Tad! Poor Mom. I couldn't believe she'd been that stupid. In fact, I couldn't believe much of anything Dad said about her. He even blamed Mom for his drinking. But then Dad blamed Mom for everything. It was even her fault if the lawnmower didn't start.

Dad was all confused. One minute Mom ruined his life. Then the next minute he was worried something might have happened to her.

"You mean like with Mom's Aunt Ruth?"

"I never met an Aunt Ruth," Dad said. "Do you think I should call the police?"

"Why?" I asked, since no one was getting hurt for once. Still, someone might have gotten hurt if Bruce came by when Dad was home. That's why I got so nervous the night I heard Bruce's car. I recognized the sound of that engine. I didn't know what Dad would do if Bruce stopped in.

"There's a small crack in the sailboat's rudder. You've got to check it," I told Dad the second time in ten minutes that I heard Bruce drive past. So I took Dad's hand and

walked him across the lawn, out past all the improve-
ments, back through the old birch grove where I'd buried
all the animals Stormy brought me under two feet of dirt
so that she couldn't dig them back up.

"Isn't it a little dark to look at the boat tonight?" Dad
asked, when we almost bumped into the birdbath.

"No, it's lighter by the water."

"You're a funny kid," Dad murmured, off in his own
world.

"You're funny, all right. Funny-looking!" whispered
Tad, who was trailing along behind. It was twilight and
the bushes kept moving, which meant that Stormy was
trailing us too.

"Look, she's got something in her mouth again. What a
stupid dog," Tad said, forgetting all dogs are stupid. "Dad
should put her out of her misery."

"Why waste a bullet on a half-dead bird?" I asked. I
think Stormy tried to be a good retriever and not kill
things. Dave said all Stormy's animals died because she
accidentally squished their insides holding them in her
mouth. I suspect they died of fright.

"No, I mean the dog. Someone should kill your killer
dog," Tad said, trying to make me cry. But I just
shrugged. "You know, Dave can shoot his father's rifle.
Maybe I should ask him to shoot your dog."

"He'd have to shoot me first, and we both know Dave
would shoot you before he'd even pull my hair," I told
Tad, who shut up right away 'cause I was right.

"What has Stormy got in her mouth?" Dad asked.

It looked like a bunny to me.

"I won't touch it," Tad said.

"Nobody asked you to," I told him, thinking how Mom
used to say she felt as trapped as the hare leading the
hounds.

"So?" Tad asked as Stormy came over and dropped a limp rabbit at my feet.

"It's just little," I told them, "about the size of my foot."

"It's dead," Dad said, walking over and bending down to look. Then all of a sudden he started to cry. I mean, it was too bad and all that, but Stormy dragged in so many dead animals even I gave up looking for shoeboxes to bury them all in.

"It's okay," I said, gently patting Dad's back. Dad cried a lot when he was drunk, but that night he looked scared.

"I'm going to Joanie's," Tad said, ignoring Dad's tears. Tad could always shut things out, like Mom.

"Well, go to Joanie's," I said.

"I'm not going to touch that thing. It's probably poison. Do you realize that when Stormy licks you, you probably get more germs than there are people in China? I bet they'll kill you!" Tad laughed. Tad thought everything was funny.

"Go on to Joanie's!" I screamed, feeling bad Dad was still crying. Then I grabbed the rabbit by its hind leg.

"Oh, gross! I can't believe you're actually holding it!" said Tad. I couldn't either. Still, it was better to chuck the thing before it got all stiff.

"Get lost!" I cried.

"Do you know where your mother is?" Dad asked, still weeping as I tossed the rabbit's body into the lake.

"I'M going to go visit Bruce," I announced first thing the next morning at breakfast with Ada, Tad, and Sam.

"Why do that, when you don't have to anymore?" asked Sam.

"Because Allie's in love!" Tad hooted.

"Joanie's fat!" I sang right back.

"You'd better watch it," Tad said, chasing me around

the table so that my screams started Stormy barking outside.

"I won't let you go," said Ada.

"You aren't my mom," I said, and that shut her up. But Sam followed me out to the end of the drive to embarrass me for being so stupid. I didn't want to insult him by saying he was too young to see that I was only being adult, so I said, "Everything looks crazy now, but it won't always," just to reassure him. Then I rode off on my bike, cutting in from the street to ride down by the water along the path. The water level was so low I could see a dead tree that was usually underwater. From a distance its branches almost seemed to wave for help. I made the trip in just minutes and reached the Walters place by nine. I didn't have to go in, since the guys were out front.

"I've come to see Bruce," I said.

"Spare us," said Pete.

"He's gone away," said Barry.

"Where to?"

"He's away on a trip. I don't know," said Pete.

"He's off drinking," said Barry.

"He's out of town on a job," Kenny said.

"Your mom drove him out of town," said nasty old Frank.

"Where's your mom?" asked Pete. "She sure did quite a job on Bruce."

"Yeah, she's a real piece of work," said Frank.

"Yeah," Barry said, "a real piece."

"Can I wait for Bruce out front?"

"The man just told you he's not coming," said a curly-headed guy I didn't even know.

"Thank you, I still think I'll wait."

"Aren't we the polite young lady? But don't worry, fellas, she'll be a royal bitch like her mom in no time,

won't you, baby? That's what Bruce calls her, 'baby'!"
Barry laughed. Then everybody hooted. There were
maybe ten guys hanging around out front with their coffee, all of them acting worse than Tad.

"Come on," said Kenny, who knew I wasn't so bad.

"Your skirt's a little short, there. Starting young?"

"Give the kid a break."

"Look, she can't help it if she's a tramp like her mother.
So what do you want to be when you grow up?" Barry
asked, pinching my cheek.

"Grown up," I said.

Chapter
Twelve

I was busy taking a bubble bath and wondering where Bruce might have gone when I heard a car drive up and ran to look out the window with just the bubbles on instead of a towel. I could see a taxi from the city in the driveway, but a tree blocked my view of the lady with a suitcase who got out. I stopped a minute to listen for the doorbell, then I brushed off the bubbles and grabbed a robe from the back of the door.

"Mom!" I cried, slipping down the stairs on my soapy feet, tripping over the too long robe.

"Hello, baby. Slow down. Teal isn't your color—it's mine." Mom smiled, fingering the silky robe.

I hadn't known if I'd ever see her again, but there she was, dropping her suitcase and calling for Ada to bring iced tea.

"Hi, there," she said to Sam, who stared at Mom like

she might be a ghost. Tad had heard me screaming "Mom!" and came in from the back with Dave to look. "Hello, boys," said Mom.

"Oh, hi," said Tad. Then he and Dave went back out to finish their basketball game.

"Do you know there's just a week till school? So much to do getting ready," Mom sighed, still smiling. It had been over a week since she went to Ohio for three days.

"I came back because I was worried about your clothes," Mom said, slipping off her shoes and stretching out on the couch. What Mom really meant was that she was worried about my jumpers. School was going to start next week and all Mom could think of was did I have enough jumpers. You'd think all the stores in the world were going to close forever once we started school!

"Tell me about Ohio."

"Ohio is very flat. I don't mean the people, but the land, though I suppose the people are too. Didn't I ever make you read Thurber's 'The Night the Bed Fell'? Well, that's Ohio," Mom said, deftly peeling two Air France stickers off her bag.

"What about Dad?" I asked, but Mom was singing some song to herself.

"Should we go up to your closet and check what still fits?" she asked.

Sam looked at me. He hadn't said a word.

"Go visit Frankie," I told Sam, for I could see Mom wanted to talk a little in private. Sam looked at me, wondering if I'd forgotten that he wasn't allowed to walk to Frankie's alone, especially when it was almost dark.

"It's okay this time," I said, so Sam started off and I walked upstairs with Mom.

"Well, now, let's see what still fits," Mom said, stretching out on my bed.

"Nothing fits," I said, sitting down beside her, trying to feel we were still best pals.

"Is something wrong?" Mom said.

"Nothing fits," I repeated.

"Ada let your white curtains get a little dingy," Mom said, her gaze drifting out the open French doors.

"Where did you go?" I asked.

"Didn't Dad tell you about Grandma?"

"You were gone a long time," I said, but Mom didn't answer. I was trying hard to be patient, but learning about Mom's trip was even more difficult than discovering where Cinderella really lived.

"What about your red plaid?" Mom said, eyeing my closet.

"I tried on all my old dresses last week. They're way too short. Ada put them all in boxes to give away," I said, getting up to show Mom my empty closet.

"Oh, she did?" Mom said, not pleased at all, so I didn't tell her about Mrs. O'Keith's plans to take me shopping.

"Look what I lost," I said, smiling for the first time since she came.

"Not another tooth! What's the point of buying you clothes if you insist on losing your teeth? How did it happen?" Mom said, so stricken I didn't dare admit it was all my fault.

"Was Grandma very sad?" I asked, changing the subject.

"Grandma died," Mom said, folding her hands across her stomach. She had long hands which might have been real pretty, but for the veins.

"When?" I asked, sitting back down on the bed.

"Don't be fresh."

"Mom. Hey, Mom," I said, sort of loud since she was almost drifting off.

"Uh-huh," she said, propping herself up on one elbow.

"Where did you go?" I asked straight out, not wanting to waste this chance to talk when any minute Dad might show.

"Listen, baby," Mom said, leaning on both elbows, her shoulders peeking out of the beige linen traveling dress we'd bought together just weeks before.

"Your dress looks pretty," I told her, but Mom looked tired. Her eyes were circled with more than liner. The glow was gone.

"Listen to all the birds," Mom said, closing her eyes.

"Those aren't birds, they're crickets. Have you seen Bruce? Is he okay?" I asked.

"How would I know?" Mom asked, opening her eyes to look straight at me so I could see she wasn't lying, although by then I knew she always lied.

"Then where did he go?"

"Nowhere. Bruce is going nowhere." Mom smiled, settling back on the bed.

"But he's gone."

"What do you mean?"

"He went away just like you did."

"Don't be silly. Go fetch him."

"I can't. He's gone."

"Impossible," Mom said, springing up. "Want to go for a drive?"

I wouldn't go back to the old Walters place for her after what the guys had said to me that morning, so we just drove around.

"Fuck it," Mom said. "Fuck everything." She was in the weirdest mood, all happy-seeming, but not happy. "Where could he be?" she asked, shifting gears. We drove to several places where Bruce had crews working, only it made no sense, since we got there past quitting time.

"Where could he be?" Mom said. Then, after a while, she calmed down and it was like we were just out driving. You know how it is when you lose something and you're frantic. Then, after a while, just looking for it calms you, so you start thinking that maybe you weren't really meant to have it after all, and besides, you've done all you could do.

"Shouldn't we go back and talk to Dad?"

"I called him from the airport. He said he'd be home late. Come on, Allie, think. You know where Bruce hangs out."

"Then you *do* care about Bruce."

"Oh, sweetheart, when you grow up you'll have all sorts of strange feelings, and you'll see that all strong feelings aren't love. And even love—there it is like a torment or a gift, but so what? I mean, love doesn't come with instructions."

"Go away with Bruce!"

Mom looked at me a moment. "Love isn't the miracle you imagine, and it takes a miracle to change things. I'd better go unpack," Mom said.

"Let me tell you a little about Erich," she said, after we drove a ways in silence.

"Why?" I asked, just daring her to tell me straight.

Mom looked over at me as we pulled up to a stop sign. "Come on," she said, like I was hurting her on purpose. "Maybe you're just too young to understand the value of old friends."

That was supposed to melt my heart and make me feel like a baby if I wouldn't listen, but I just turned my head and pretended to be checking the intersection for cars. "It's all clear," I said, so Mom went on down the road and I kept pretending to be interested in all the pretty houses we'd only passed a million times.

"What will you do when Dad gets home?" I asked as we pulled into the driveway.

"Nothing. Why?" Mom said, turning off the engine. There was no one like her. But already everything was changing and I knew the day would come when my love for her no longer made me lonely and I could finally tell the truth.

Dad didn't get home before I fell asleep.

THE next morning Mom and I went shopping and she bought me everything she could possibly think of, including lots of clothes for herself. Driving to the store Mom told me about her talk with Dad, which was no talk really.

"He didn't ask a single question," she said. Then she smiled, forgetting that she always used to say nothing was more threatening than Dad's silence.

"What about Bruce?" I said.

"Oh, you were there," she answered, meaning that last afternoon when I guess you'd say they broke up, only Mom and Bruce said "Get out" and "I'm leaving" to each other so much that August, it was just their way of saying "Until soon."

"What are you going to do?" I asked.

"Do?" said Mom, whose new favorite subject was Erich and how much I'd like him. So I gave up on asking her where she was planning to go and where she'd been. When we finally got home from shopping after three, Sam told me the crackly phone calls had started again.

Mom was home listening for phone calls. Sam and I were at the dock getting ready to sail to the beach. Tad and Dave stood there snickering as they watched us struggling to untie the boat. Life was back to normal again, so I don't know why I still felt as if everything was changing.

"Look at that—it's a bad omen," I told Sam as a whole

flock of crows rose from the lawn as one black cloud.

"Oh, get off it," said Tad. "That just means your stupid dog is around."

"See that?" Dave asked, pointing to Corky the crow, perched nearby clutching a shiny spent cartridge he'd picked up in the woods. "Frank says Corky was tame once," Dave explained. "That's why he's so smart."

"You don't get smart from being tame," Tad said, lobbing some pebbles at Sam and me as we pushed off.

Sam and I sailed across the lake. Then we met Tad at the beach, gave him the boat, and I swam back. Halfway across the lake I spied Bruce walking by our dock.

"Bruce!" I called. But he couldn't hear me. He was looking up at my house, then he disappeared as I swam toward the dock.

"Bruce!" I yelled, pulling myself out of the water. "Bruce!" I hollered, sprinting past where his men once worked. No one answered, but I saw Bruce sitting on the weathered picnic table lost in thought.

"Didn't you hear?" I called panting as I ran up. I was so happy to see him I couldn't believe he looked so sad.

"Hey, Allie," Bruce said. "Hear what?"

"Oh, nothing. Just me calling." It was shady there beneath the trees. I was soaking wet, with goosebumps all over.

"I swam all the way from the beach to see you," I said, waiting for Bruce to pick me up and twirl me around.

"No..." He frowned, still thinking.

"I did too. I'll swim back again to prove that I can do it if you'll watch."

"It's okay, I believe you," Bruce said, so I crawled up beside him on the redwood picnic table and we both just sat there, Bruce thinking, me shivering, until Bruce gave me the denim jacket he'd been carrying and rubbed my shoulders to warm me up. It was so still there in the shade for a moment I dreamed anything could happen. I wanted to tell Bruce, "Don't you ever go away, but if you do go, take me with you." But, instead, we heard Sam screaming, so we both jumped up and ran like fire down to the water. Sam looked so happy to see me I peeled off Bruce's jacket and wrapped it around him after Bruce hauled him out of the lake.

"Tad said you drowned," Sam sputtered. Then he looked at Bruce sort of funny, the way he sometimes looked at Mom.

"Don't worry. Nothing ever happens to me," I told him. "Go get a sweatshirt from the house."

Sam ran off. Bruce and I followed.

"Hey, Mom," I said, banging in the back door. Mom was bending over a broken vase telling Ada to be more careful. Then she looked up and saw Bruce.

Mom didn't tell Bruce the truth, of course. She told him what she'd told my father, going on about selecting the coffin, worrying if she picked out the right sort of headstone, and describing how pretty all the flowers were except for some big wreaths.

"I hate wreaths, don't you?" Mom said. "Makes you start looking for the horses." Bruce listened very patiently while Mom told us what people had said after the service and went on about how hot it was that day as she fanned herself.

"Then where did you go after Ohio?" Bruce said, right out, while Dad had only said it with a look.

It got pretty quiet for a moment.

"I'd better go," Bruce said, getting up.

"But it's only four o'clock," Mom answered.

"It sure feels later," Bruce said, heading for the door.

Mom looked at Bruce then, almost frightened. I knew by now she didn't love him, but she still needed him for something. I think Mom thought she was going to leave with Erich, only he kept her guessing. I don't believe Mom trusted Erich. Maybe he was too much like her, or still only almost divorced.

Mom flashed across the kitchen.

"Are you trying to make me feel guilty?" she said, reaching out to touch Bruce's arm.

"I love you with all my heart, Jeannie. But it's clear I can't make you feel much of anything," Bruce said, pausing a moment in the door.

If Bruce only knew how Mom hated being called Jeannie, I thought. But maybe it was better he didn't know.

"Goodbye," Bruce said, looking down at Mom. He should have left then, but he didn't. He just kept standing in the doorway looking down at the top of her head.

"So who's the lucky man?" he said at last. He must have hated himself for loving Mom so much he had to stay and make that crack.

"You're mistaken," Mom said.

"Before, not now," Bruce answered. "Did you think you could just jerk me around forever?" Bruce asked with a smile almost as mean as Dad's. Then Bruce opened the door, and as far as I could see, he was serious. But he had always been serious as far as I could see.

"You don't understand," Mom said, still fibbing, when she should have said "I'm sorry."

"Stop trying to make this out to be some kind of mystery. How could you go off with another man and think I'd still be around when you got back?"

"Because I thought you loved me," Mom said.

"Not enough, I guess. I don't want to be here anymore,"

Bruce announced, less to Mom than to himself.

That hurt, because Mom died a little if lots of people didn't love her.

"Please don't go. There's no one else," Mom said, near crying.

That stopped Bruce a minute, that and Mom clutching his arm.

"By whatever feeling you may still have," Mom started to say.

"I'm sorry. That's the way the cookie crumbles and crumbles until there's finally nothing left. Goodbye," Bruce said, removing Mom's hand from his arm. And this time when he opened the door, he walked out.

Mom turned to me. I thought she'd forgotten I was even in the kitchen. Besides, I'd only stayed to make Bruce go if he lost courage. But I guess Mom thought I'd stayed, like always, to help her.

"I don't know what to do," she said, pronouncing each word very slowly. Then she sank into the nearest cushioned chair and started crying very quietly, like she didn't want me to notice. Mom was just like Tad—a bully who couldn't take it. Sometimes I almost hated Mom and whatever she had that always made you fall in love with her again.

"What do you want me to do?" I asked.

Still Mom just sat there like the kid who was "it" counting one, two, three . . . to let the others run off in a game of hide-and-seek. Four, five, six . . . Maybe Mom knew what she was doing but it seemed to me she was giving Bruce too much time to get away. His car was parked just around the corner from the beach and he took long steps. Seven, eight . . . Could I even catch him if I ran? Nine, ten . . . "All right, go after him," she said.

"Bruce!" I called, tearing out the back door, racing

across the lawn and right on down past the dock where Tad and Dave were casting, even though I'm scared to death of being snagged by a fish hook.

"Bruce!" I shouted, running up the back path calling the whole way until I finally spied his back. Still he kept walking. "Bruce," I said, catching up and grabbing his hand.

"Why are you doing this?" Bruce asked, and I couldn't answer. Still, I held on to his hand as he pulled me along.

"Hey, Bruce!" I said, 'cause my arm felt like it was being yanked out of the socket. It was worse than being dragged along by Stormy when she wasn't in the mood for being walked.

"Hey, Bruce," I said. "I never hurt *you.*"

That stopped him dead in the middle of the path. He looked at me.

"Oh, you're just great," Bruce said, "the two of you."

Chapter
Thirteen

*I*t was my fault really. I went to the beach for the Labor Day races and stayed on through the exhibition diving. I even stole back a dollar from Tad's drawer before I left that morning to buy Sam and me each a hamburger so we didn't have to go home for lunch. Maybe I should have checked in at home just to see how things were going, but Dad had waked up with a stomach-ache and was feeling too sick to make much trouble. Besides, he had a tennis committee meeting that morning, so he couldn't afford to get that drunk.

Labor Day is the last day of summer, so you hate it. But it's still summer, so you try to hold on to it too. I don't know how some kids can just walk off right after the races, acting like summer is all finished even before the guards haul out the boats and put away the lanes. Sam and I hit the beach early, then I spent most of the day with Howie, hanging around long after the sun had faded and the big girls went home to get their dresses ready for school.

School started the next day. Christine had already left for college, so I sent Sam home to tell Mom I'd be back late. Then Howie and I raked the beach together one last time.

"Can you believe it?" I said. There were more leaves than litter on the beach.

"It's that time of year," Howie answered smiling, philosophical as always. "We're getting rid of everything in the shack. Want a soda? Anything you want is free."

I didn't want a soda, but I took two bags of M&Ms that melt in your mouth and don't yank out your teeth. Then Howie and I put the rakes, buoys, ropes, and things in the shed, and the rest of the lifeguards came up to joke and say "Goodbye. See you next year" before drifting off. When time came for Howie to go, I went and hid in the trees near the parking lot because I didn't want him to see me cry. It was so stupid to be crying. I kept trying to stop, but I couldn't. I could see Howie looking around. He walked the beach twice calling my name, but I'm sure he knew why I'd disappeared because when he came back to the parking lot he smiled.

"Goodbye. I'll miss you," he called. Then I watched him get in his old banged-up car and drive off. There was so much I could never tell Howie, I was almost relieved to see him go.

"Goodbye," I said, watching him drive off.

Then I left the birch grove by the parking lot to walk the beach, saying goodbye to summer and the sun strong enough to make the waves dance like diamonds and the days when you raked burning sand covered with candy wrappers instead of leaves. I hate it when the leaves change. Some leaves had already fallen back on the sand

Howie and I'd just finished raking, and others floated down onto the water like fairy skiffs. You could rake the beach, but you couldn't do anything to protect the water. Soon leaves would pile up and cover the whole lake like ugly brown lily pads changing the water from crystal clear to moldy green-brown before the ice made it sparkle again.

It was so lonely on the beach without the piles of people you could recognize even sleeping face down on their towels. The wind blew and made the birches seem to shiver. I know seasons change, but it's still amazing how, when the sun goes down on Labor Day, summer goes with it. I was the only one still there, but I wanted to stay walking the beach forever, or at least until the sky became a bunch of stars. I guess I should have gone home to make sure Dad went to his meeting on time instead of making some excuse to stay home drinking, but I just didn't care. The truth is I finally saw you have to be crazy to go on caring in my house.

It was just three days since Mom had sent me after Bruce, yet it seemed like a whole lifetime since I caught up with him on the back path and we walked around for a couple of hours. We didn't do anything. We didn't say anything. We didn't even have fun. We just walked around the lake together, the whole way for the very first time. We walked all the way around the lake and he said nothing and I said nothing.

When I came home Dad was already standing at the top of the stairs saying, "Do you know where your no-good daughter is?" That's when I screwed up. I just walked on up to my room and closed the door instead of going into the living room to entertain him. It was stupid of me, I know. But I was thinking very hard about Bruce and what just happened and all the things we didn't say. I guess I was getting careless. Still, I thought it was time Mom took her turn entertaining Dad for a change.

I went right upstairs to my room and lay down on the bed so close to the window the white lace curtains tickled my nose. I closed my eyes to dream of Bruce, but I kept hearing Dad screaming downstairs. It was barely dark, and he was already drunk.

"What's your no-good daughter up to?" Dad yelled, until it made me so mad I jumped up and went racing down to stop him. When I came into the living room Mom was curled up on the yellow silk sofa and Dad was leaning against the far archway with his drink. I just stood in the doorway a minute. Mom looked relieved to see me, but her relief vanished when she saw I hadn't come to soothe Dad's feelings. I was fed up. I was finished. I was so mad I couldn't see straight.

I stood at one end of the living room and Dad kept leaning on the archway at the other. I could hear the ice crack in his glass as we eyed each other so hard it's a wonder neither one of us dropped dead. Then Dad looked at his Scotch and said, "I see your no-good. daughter has finally honored us with her presence." I suppose Dad felt neglected, and all he wanted was attention. But I didn't see that. I just heard the words, and I got madder than I'd ever been at Tad.

"You have no right to say that," I told him.

What a mistake! The minute I said it I saw I should have known better, because something snapped in Dad. He was looking my way, but he wasn't seeing me anymore. Suddenly, I was just this thing that made him mad. His eyes looked crazy. He *was* crazy. I screamed and ran for my room.

I'd just reached the second-floor landing when he caught up with me and grabbed my throat.

"I can say whatever I want to say, and you can say 'I'm sorry,'" he hissed, sounding almost like he was the one choking, not me. I tried to kick and scratch, but it wasn't anything like fighting Tad. Dad was so strong, I could hardly move.

"Dad," I gasped. But he couldn't hear me. He had me smushed up against the railing, hands locked on my neck. Dad was strangling me in earnest. It was nothing like being strangled in the movies, where people get time to think about their lives and reach around for something heavy. You could never do that in real life because you get all weak, your chest burns, your head starts swimming, and you finally know how awful it must be for kids who drown.

"Apologize!" Sam screamed, sounding way far off, like he was yelling underwater, making me think of a time Dad beat Sam so bad I thought each blow might break his neck. I was scared crazy then over Sam, screaming for Tad and Mom, who were always someplace else when there was trouble, though you could have been deaf and still heard Sam crying and me screaming, until Dad finally got tired and left.

I guess Dad felt bad when he saw Sam's bandages, but Dad couldn't help himself. It was like a magic spell. Sometimes he just got locked on automatic. Yet even as his hands kept closing tighter it took a while for me to understand that this time I wouldn't even make it to the emergency room. That stairway would be the last thing I'd see—the stairway and his crazy face breathing on mine when I hadn't even the breath left to cry "Help!"

Sam was going crazy, pulling at Dad's leg and screaming, scared to death of being left alone. If I didn't apologize, Dad would have to kill me as a point of honor. He would probably be sorry later, but right then my head felt ready to explode. Stars sprayed the rafters and Dad's face pressed close. A waste of air to cry for help. Sam cried for both of us.

I didn't want to apologize. I'd been right. Dad was wrong. I couldn't live with myself if I apologized, but if I didn't, Dad would kill me, and I'd never get to grow up.

"I'm sorry," I gasped, and I was very sorry indeed.

MOM was so funny. Later she came into my room, where I was just sitting on the bed crying.

"What's the matter?" she asked, like she'd been on the moon or something. "Your toes are swollen," she said, turning on the light to look at me.

"I guess he stepped on my toes," I sniffed. "Look at my neck."

"If your neck were broken you'd be dead. Those are just bad bruises. But we should get someone to look at those toes."

"You're wrong," I said. "If they were broken they'd hurt more, and anyway, there's nothing you can do for a broken toe." I knew, since I'd broken my big toe tripping on the dock the year before.

"I'm sure you've got a broken toe!"

"Mom..."

"Why won't you let me help?" she cried, shaking my shoulders until I agreed to let her take me to the emergency room. It was crazy, but that figured. Everyone was going crazy. What a night.

"But your toe might be broken," Mom kept saying, as if it mattered.

"What can I say about the bruises?" I asked as we walked to the car. I was wearing a hooded sweatshirt pulled up around my neck.

At the hospital, as usual, they asked no questions. The nurses there knew us, and there was a cute young doctor just back from vacation in Italy who joked with me and swore the hooded sweatshirt made me look like a madonna.

"Please, she's only eleven!" Mom said, forgetting I was old for my age.

The doctor looked at me and asked if my toes had been trampled by elephants.

"Why are you crying? You're supposed to laugh," he said, so I smiled for him.

The emergency room really wasn't so bad. It was a pain waiting around while Mom filled out the forms eight times with her Blue Cross number, but at least seeing them carry in kids mashed on motorcycles kept you from feeling sorry for yourself. One time when I was there waiting for Sam I saw what happened to a boy who got run over by a speedboat when he was waterskiing, and that's the saddest thing I ever saw.

Going to the hospital was just a waste of time, since the doctor said he could have my toes X-rayed but why bother when the only thing to do if they were broken was to be more careful of them, same as if they were just bruised.

"I told you," I said to Mom as we walked back out into the crowded parking lot.

"At least we know that you're all right," she said. "Now if I can only find the car . . ."

"Right by the ambulances, remember?"

"Oh, God, that's 'No Parking'!" she said, starting to run.

"Now where are the keys?" Mom asked, fumbling in her purse once we reached the car.

I pushed back my hood to study my neck in the rear-view mirror.

"Don't screw up the mirror. It takes forever to readjust. Did I give you the keys?" Mom asked. We both searched the car seat. "Look," I said, pointing.

"I don't believe I left the key in the ignition! How stupid," Mom clucked.

"What can we say about this?"

"About what?" Mom asked, turning the key and shifting to back out.

"About this," I said, pointing to my neck. "It doesn't look like I banged into a bookcase or tripped and fell."

Mom studied the bruise a minute. The two hand prints had run together so it was just one purple band.

"You know, it looks like the neck ribbons they wore in the movie *Little Women* with Katharine Hepburn, you remember?"

"Swell," I said. "Just swell."

"It's not fair to be mad at me. I didn't hit you."

"I need a story."

Mom considered that a moment as she watched the cars pass, waiting for her chance roll out onto Main Street. "Just say that . . . just say . . . Why tell a story? You don't need to explain that bruise. No one will even notice. Nobody ever notices anyone besides himself," Mom said, repeating the story of how she went to school with mumps for a whole week and no one said a thing.

But I didn't care. The story wasn't just for other people. I didn't want to think about what really happened. "I need a story," I said. "You're good at making things up."

"Don't make a big deal of nothing. You want another puppy or something?"

"You owe me a story!"

"You don't need a story, just a hooded sweatshirt," Mom

said, flooring it to cross before a truck in the near lane.

Ada left early the next morning. She only took one medium-sized suitcase. She didn't say goodbye or even tell me to be careful. She just said, "I'm not going to wait around to watch it happen." But she had always been meaning to go to London to stay with a married daughter. She used to tell me that all the time.

I was a little down after that night and sneaked out to watch the sunrise on the beach because the way it looks makes you think each day starts fresh from scratch. I would have liked things to start fresh. I wanted the whole summer to start over and I'd just stay there at the beach and steer clear of trouble, only now I had to leave before the other kids showed up since I didn't want them to see my neck. Some of the neighbor ladies called to ask why I hadn't come by to visit. Mom told them we were busy shopping for school, although I barely left the house.

Mom did most of the shopping herself. Sometimes Erich called when Mom was out, but he never called enough to reassure her.

Once, when I answered the phone, I stayed to listen.

"I've been waiting forever—all summer!" Mom cried into the receiver. I hated waiting too, but it didn't seem right for her to cry over the time we'd spent with Bruce.

"Are things okay?" I asked.

"Leave me alone!" Mom screamed when she saw I was listening, only Erich thought she meant him, got hurt, and hung up.

"Are you going off to marry Erich?" I asked when Mom's crying grew quiet.

"Who knows?" she said, looking up from her Kleenex.

"Has he asked you to marry him?" I demanded.

"They all ask you to marry them. The asking is cheap. The marrying is something else."

"Is that what you want?" I cried. "To go away and leave us?"

"Allie, really!" Mom said, grabbing my arm to stop me fooling with the sore spot in my mouth. "If you'd leave it alone, it would get better."

Still, my tongue kept slipping into the bloody hole. Each night when Mom came to tuck me in I'd fluff up my pillow to make sure she saw the tooth knotted in Dad's handkerchief tucked underneath.

"Oh, right, of course," she'd say, getting the hint. Each morning I'd look under my pillow, but Mom kept forgetting the tooth fairy money and a lot of other things.

LABOR Day is always tough. I was walking along the water thinking of Mom and Dad and Bruce and Erich and school starting the next day when Sam came by the beach to get me around seven o'clock. I was thinking so hard I didn't see Sam at first. I just heard Stormy growl.

"Hey, Stormy," I called. She didn't even wag her tail when she came up, she was so mad at being leashed.

"Mom made me bring her," Sam said.

"Give her to me," I said, since Stormy was snapping and tugging. Sam is a great kid, but he doesn't know animals. Dogs hate it when you think of them as dogs. They can tell right away.

"Mom wants you to come right home. No one made dinner," Sam said, trailing me.

"Go on back home and tell Mom I'm coming."

"No. Come now," Sam said, pleading.

"School starts tomorrow. Nothing can happen," I told him, thinking Dad had to be out of the house for his tennis committee meeting by eight.

"I'll wait for you," Sam said, still frightened.

"You go on back. I'll come real soon," I promised.

"Good. Then I'll wait."

I gave Sam a look.

"Okay," he said, and ran on off up the back path. Then I walked the shore with Stormy, watching the sun set purple as a bruise. I waited and waited, but instead of dropping down the sun just hung there on the horizon like it was sad to go home too.

"Hey, Allie, what are you doing here all alone in the dark?" Dave asked, coming up out of nowhere. Then he reached into his pocket to offer me a cigarette. Dave was a little lost now that Tad was always over at Joanie's.

"These are the best—Camels king size," Dave said, extending the pack.

"They make me cough."

"Don't worry. Everyone coughs the first time."

"My dad smokes Camels."

"I know," Dave said. "I stole them from your house."

"We're going hunting for night crawlers later," he said, like it was an invitation.

"Tad will never let me come."

"Tad isn't the boss. Want me to walk you home?"

"It's still light," I said. I began to think the sun had stopped.

"You've just been outside the whole time it got darker. If you go inside even a minute, you'll see it's pretty dark here now. Want me to walk you somewhere?" Dave asked again, but I shook my head no.

"You shouldn't hang around the beach after dark. It's dangerous."

"Why do you say that?"

"Why do they post lifeguards here, if it's not?"

"Go away," I laughed.

"Okay, but watch out for strangers," Dave said, disappearing in the dusk.

"Come on, girl," I said, and Stormy and I went back to pacing the beach. It got sort of lonely walking back and forth thinking. Stormy thought I was crazy, but she could tell I was upset, so even though she'd rather be walking through the woods full of rabbits, she behaved. Then she suddenly barked.

"You the resident ghost?" said a man's voice I didn't recognize.

"Come on, Stormy," I said, and hurried away from the beach along the footbridge over the dam.

"Going home?" Dave asked, when I stopped halfway across the bridge to pull out a splinter. I hadn't even seen him, he was so quiet.

"You scared me."

"Didn't mean to."

"What you been doing?" I asked. All I could see was the glowing tip of his cigarette, for it was finally dark.

"Oh, nothing much," he said. "Waiting for you."

"There's nothing I hate so much as waiting."

"It's not so bad. I like the woods," Dave said, still leaning on the railing. I stood beside him, listening to the patter of the tiny falls below.

"School starts tomorrow," said Dave.

"Yeah," I said, swatting my shoulder. The mosquitoes were murder. Beats me how Dave could stand it on the bridge.

The boards creaked and Stormy growled as Dave stepped closer.

"She's in her biting mood," I warned him. "It's a strong leash, but if she makes a leap for you, I might lose her. Better stay at least ten feet away."

"Can I walk you home?" Dave asked again. You had to hand it to Dave, he was brave.

"I have to run to the old Walters place for Mom."

"Sure you won't be scared walking alone?"

"Nah."

"Walk you to the road," he said.

"Sure," I answered. So Dave walked me to the turn-off and I headed on. There weren't many people out that night. Stormy and I walked all the way up Alma Place, then down Crescent Drive past the Baskins' and nearly made it to the Boulevard before I counted seven cars. We looked around the old Walters place, but it was empty, so we turned around and were halfway home before I heard Bruce's car.

Bruce looked awful. "Shit, Allie," he said.

I hadn't seen him since the night we walked around the lake before Dad choked me. I touched my neck. It was all right. My sweatshirt hood was up.

"Need a ride home?" Bruce said. "I think I'm drunk."

So I let Stormy loose and crawled into the car. Bruce threw his arms around me, almost crying, as we both sat there not knowing what to say.

"Are you okay?" Bruce said at last, so close his breath tickled my ear.

"Sure," I said, thinking how happy Mom would be that I'd found Bruce and how she would expect me to tell some lie that would smooth things out for a few hours. But I couldn't do it anymore. So I just said, "Come talk to Mom."

"Okay," Bruce said. I guess Bruce wasn't thinking all that clearly because he started driving straight for my house.

"Hadn't we better park someplace secret like the beach?" I suggested, figuring the parking lot there might be deserted.

The parking lot was all dark, with even the floodlights off, since the season was over. We pulled into a spot in the far corner half hidden by the fence around the tennis court.

"Now what?" Bruce said, his question reminding me of a morning ages ago when I searched half the neighborhood for him before I came home to find him stretched out napping in my own backyard. "All right, you've got me. Now what do you want?" he'd said, getting up light as a cat. And suddenly, there were all these things I had to tell him, just like with Howie, only completely different.

"Kids used to go parking here," Bruce said, turning to me. Have you ever sat all alone in a small car with just one other person, and not even the engine going for company? The funny stillness made me nervous.

"Look. I lost this," I said, pointing to the space left by my missing tooth.

"The girl of my dreams!" Bruce laughed. He must have been real nervous too, because he couldn't stop laughing.

"Come on, let's walk up the back path," I said, getting out of the car. Bruce followed me out of the parking lot, then strolled down to the water's edge and started pacing like I had earlier, only now we had a sky full of stars for company instead of just the sinking sun.

Bruce walked and walked, me trailing along behind like Stormy. Then Bruce stopped, turned to me, and said, "Allie..."

"I was here earlier, just walking," I told him. "I came to the beach in the morning and stayed past sunset. I haven't gone home even once all day." It was all that stillness that made me interrupt him.

I was scared Bruce might be mad, but he seemed to be thinking about what I'd said. Then he spoke real fast and quiet saying, "I remember what it was like being a kid, alone, walking along the empty September beach. School starts again the next day, and you're supposed to have grown and changed and be looking toward the future and wanting different things, only, somehow, you don't want them. All you want is to hold on to summer's freedom. But you can't."

"Why not?" I said.

"WHERE have you been?" Mom called as I walked in the back door. It was pitch-black outside. The kitchen clock said ten. Mom looked absolutely desperate. Then she saw Bruce.

"Dad's still here," Sam whispered. Bruce moved for the door.

"No," Mom said, real quiet. "You can help."

"Won't you come in?" Mom asked, like she was giving a party. Mom just looked at Bruce and there he was, trapped again. But it only seemed that way at first, for that was the strangest night, with everybody finally changing and no one changing more than Bruce.

"I'm through," Tad said, getting up from the kitchen table. A bowl of melted vanilla ice cream sat at each place like saucers of cream set for a family of big cats.

"Want something?" Mom asked me. Dad was wrong about Bruce being no good, but he was right about Mom's cooking. No wonder we'd all lived on ice cream and cookies since Ada left.

"You haven't eaten all day," Mom told me.

"I got a hamburger at the beach—Howie's treat," I lied, since I wasn't supposed to spend my allowance on junk.

But Mom wasn't listening to me. She was looking at Bruce, telling him that Dad was very sick.

"Don't tell me you've only just noticed," Bruce snorted.

"Boys," Mom said, "you'd better go up to your rooms and lay out your clothes for school."

"I want to go hunting for night crawlers after that," Tad said, not moving.

Mom looked at him. "We'll discuss that later, if at all," she told him.

Tad looked at Mom and shrugged the very same shrug she just gave him. She watched the boys disappear upstairs, then she turned back to Bruce.

"Allie's dad is terribly sick," she said. "I'm sure his appendix has burst, but he won't let me call for help."

"Not now," Mom said as Bruce reached over to touch her shoulder.

"My clothes are all ready," Tad said, racing downstairs. "I want to go hunting for night crawlers with Dave."

"You're not going anywhere but to your room!" Mom cried. "Take Sam with you," she added, seeing Sam had also strayed downstairs. So Tad went back upstairs, dragging Sam.

Mom leaned against the entrance hall archway all quiet, like she was waiting for it to grow hushed so she could reveal some great secret. I felt sure she was going to tell Bruce the whole sad story of her sister Alice-Marie dying when her appendix burst and they didn't take it out right away.

"Dammit, Jeanne, how long—" Bruce stopped when I touched his arm to show we were about to hear something important.

Mom looked at us both a moment in silence, but all she finally said was, "I don't know what to do."

Bruce groaned and shook his head.

"But what did you do when all this started?" he asked.

"You mean, tonight?"

"No, I mean years ago."

"You mean, after Tad was born?"

"I don't really care *when* it was. What I can't figure is what did you *do?*" Bruce asked, sounding so down I knew at once he meant Dad's drinking.

Mom looked puzzled by Bruce's question. She thought a moment. "Why, I did nothing. Absolutely nothing, beyond telling myself it wouldn't happen again."

"Only it did," Bruce insisted.

"Yes, but in the beginning he didn't always drink. And he used to be really nice the next day, which helped me not to think about it. But even back before he began drinking so much he had this way of literally *cornering* me. I was already trapped, yet he'd take both my hands in his and hold them together, like in a handcuff, just to mock me, and I'd say, 'Christ, don't!'"

"Then what would he do?" Bruce asked.

"Laugh and grip my hands tighter," Mom said, with her crooked smile.

"Hey, Mom!" Tad called, popping his head around the landing, but he disappeared when he saw Mom crying. Mom was so busy crying she didn't notice Tad or even look at Bruce and me. We stood there so long I felt like Mom waiting for Erich to get divorced. Then I went into the kitchen, came back, and handed her a Kleenex.

"I would have been all right if things had been normal. I just can't handle this," Mom sniffled, taking the tissue.

"Jeanne," Bruce said, running his hand along Mom's neck, acting like he didn't notice what he was doing. But they both noticed.

"He might die if we do nothing. Maybe it's a blessing. For years I've been too scared to stay and too weak to leave," Mom said, looking up at Bruce. "Perhaps we should go. Leave him just like he wants, then whatever happens, happens."

"Whatever happens, always happens," Bruce said, real flat.

"Be nice!" Mom pouted.

"I just can't believe it."

"I can't believe you! You men all hang together against us," Mom said, like she was going to get all angry. But Bruce just shrugged, so she got nice again.

"Let's go for a walk. A long walk," Mom said, giving Bruce that funny look of hers.

"Think of the children," Mom said.

"When have you ever thought of the children?" Bruce asked, so mean he was ashamed and touched Mom's neck again. "You're right to want to finally get it over," he whispered. "We'll call a doctor. Then, when he comes, we'll leave."

"You don't understand," Mom said. "Why should I have to give up everything? I want to stay. *He's* got to leave. But he won't leave on his own, so let them carry him out."

Mom paused to take a deep breath. "Well?" she said, looking up at Bruce.

Bruce looked at her, and I could see him trying to think clearly when all he could see was Mom. His fingers rapped her shoulders like you might a table, only this time he wasn't just pretending not to know what his fingers were doing.

Mom knew that she was winning, 'cause she just stood there smiling while Bruce stared at her like she was everything.

I didn't want to see it, so I walked out into the breakfast nook and picked up a magazine.

"Well?" Mom said. Bruce didn't answer. "Well?" she asked again more softly. Bruce still said nothing The only sound was me flipping through *Life*.

"I think I heard someone crying," I said. It sounded far off and muffled.

"Just ignore it," said Mom who looked at me like I was a traitor when I left to check it out.

Bruce followed me upstairs and we found Sam tied up

in the closet where Tad had left him after turning up the TV to cover his screams.

"That kid's a psychopath," Bruce said. But I told him Tad was only being such a pain so that Mom would be glad to let him go hunt for night crawlers—anything to get him out of the house. I know, because Tad called Dave as we were untying Sam.

"Of course it's okay," Tad told Dave, although he didn't even have permission yet.

"That kid," Bruce said, as Tad went back to watching a war movie where planes kept screaming into the ocean, exploding when they hit.

Tad forgot all about Sam in seconds, but Sam was still a little shaken because he hates being locked in dark closets, and Tad had locked him in a little one, which makes it even worse.

"Come on," I said, taking Sam with me to my room as Bruce went back downstairs. There is nothing greener than the leaves outside my window. There is nothing softer than the last night of summer.

"Oh, Sam," I sighed, grabbing his arm so sudden he jumped.

"What's the matter?" he cried.

"Nothing. It's way past your bedtime. Let's tuck you in," I said.

Sam's room was right next to mine. It also faced on the lake. You could hear the frogs and crickets through the open window. I used to like to sit on his bed telling stories about his trucks' adventures, smelling the flowers below. Yet there was something rotten in the sweetness from the garden now that the roses had all crumbled and their petals hid the ground.

After tucking Sam in, I suddenly realized I was starving, so I slipped down to the kitchen by the back stairs.

"Maybe I'm the one who should die," Mom said, pulling her hair back off her face, then twisting a strand the same way I did when she would say, "Don't play with your hair!"

Mom looked all pale and tired.

"I just don't know what to do," she said, shaking her head.

"Why don't you send Allie in there to hold his hand?" Bruce laughed, sort of mean. Then he turned around and saw me grabbing some cookies just behind him.

"God, I'm sorry," he said, trying to take my hand, but it was full of Oreos. Still, I could see he really was sorry, so I forgave him right away.

"Give us a smile. Have you seen this, Jeannie?" Bruce asked, putting his finger in my mouth to pat the empty space. "How much did the tooth fairy give you for it?" he asked, making Mom feel all guilty for forgetting to take the tooth from under my pillow.

"I'm sorry about the money," Mom said, starting to fumble in her purse. Bruce dug into his pocket and handed me a dollar which wasn't what I wanted, but he looked right at me and smiled so sadly I almost thought he knew what I was thinking about him and her and Sam and Stormy and Tad and Fluff gone and Dad lying sick upstairs; so I took it and thanked him, and I put it in my breast pocket and I swore to myself never to take that dollar out of my shirt.

"Why don't you run along and put that someplace where you won't lose it—right away," Mom said, since she still hadn't finished with Bruce.

I started upstairs to my room, but I kept going, up to the third floor, because that's where the groaning came from. I tiptoed to the door of my parents' bedroom. I didn't step inside. I just stood in the doorway looking through the shadows to where Dad lay in bed. His eyes were closed and he was sweating like crazy though he only had on his blue summer robe and a thin white sheet. Sweat can be real assuring, but this was not a good healthy, dripping sweat like Bruce's. Dad's sweat just sat on his face in beads like drops of rain stuck to a window. He was all scrunched up on the bed, so that his being tall only made him look more scrawny.

I took a small step forward and thought of taking Dad's arm and saying "Let Mom call a doctor," only Dad was already muttering and I was afraid. He looked all weak and sick, but you could never tell about Dad. If I came close he might still have the strength to grab me. So I went back downstairs.

"You know, Dad is very sick," I announced, walking into the kitchen.

"Big news," Tad said, digging in the freezer for Popsicles. "Where's she been all day?"

"Don't you two start!" Mom said.

"I don't want to fight with her. I just want to go hunting for night crawlers. This is the best time of the whole year for them," Tad explained. "They only crawl out of their holes when it's still warm, like tonight, but not too hot."

"School starts tomorrow," Mom said. "You're not going fishing. Why do you need worms?"

"Dad's really sick," I told Bruce, who was staring out the window.

"You need some help?" Bruce asked as I climbed up on the counter to try to reach the peanut butter and jelly. He reached them both for me while I got the cutting board. Then he just leaned against the counter thinking while I concentrated on spreading the peanut butter without ripping the bread.

"You can't go," Mom told Tad.

"I have to. Dave's coming over."

"At eleven?"

"That's the very best time to catch night crawlers," Tad assured her.

"Tad!" Mom said, so sharp even Tad stepped back.

"You know, we just can't leave him here," Bruce said, real sad, like he'd really tried to see things Mom's way but he just couldn't change his mind.

Mom turned on Bruce like he'd just ruined everything.

"Why do you always have to sit in the kitchen?" she screamed.

"That why you can't love me?" Bruce yelled back. Just then the phone rang, so Mom didn't hear him since she was already walking into the living room to take the call.

"Shit," Bruce said, yanking the refrigerator door open to look for a beer.

"I love you," I said.

Bruce just looked at me till rotten Tad walked in between us.

"You get out of here," Tad told me.

"You always leave the refrigerator door open where you live?" Tad asked Bruce, pulling out a can of Coke and waving it in Bruce's face.

"You get out!" Tad screamed, turning back to me.

"You'd better go," Bruce said. So I left them in the kitchen and went back up to the third floor, not because that's what I wanted, I just had to. I paused a second at Dad's door, then I tiptoed in.

I can't pretend life's a dream, but there's something good about not dying. Dad looked so sick lying there.

"Hey, Dad," I said. "Dad, it's important." But he didn't say anything. Maybe he couldn't hear me, or he just didn't care. His face was shiny as wax from the sweat.

It was always hot on the third floor, but Dad hated air

conditioning. I pushed my sweatshirt hood back since no one else was around.

"Dad?" I said, tiptoeing past Mom's big circular mirror where I could see the mark from Dad's hands around my neck. The bruises were red now, not purple. Pretty soon they would turn yellow and almost blend with my tan.

"Hey, Dad," I said. Still, I was afraid to go all the way over and touch him, so I just stood by the mirror trying to think of a way to sort of warn him without getting anyone in trouble.

I thought and thought. Then in the mirror I saw Mom standing in the doorway signaling like the room was already haunted and she was scared to come in.

I slipped out into the hall. "Go downstairs," Mom whispered. Then Mom went into the bathroom to fix her makeup, and I went downstairs.

When I got back to the kitchen Tad and Bruce were on opposite sides of the room, still so busy being nasty they didn't even notice Dave tapping on the glass door in the dining room.

"That you, Dave?" I asked, letting him in.

"Hey, Allie. Ready to go hunting for night crawlers?"

"She can't come," Tad said, walking in when he heard Dave's voice. "Mom barely let me."

"Mom didn't say you could go either."

"Dry up," Tad said. Then he and Dave went upstairs to get Tad's junk.

Bruce looked at me. "What happened to your neck?" he said. It was so embarrassing. I hadn't a clue what to say. I tried to make something up as Bruce pushed my hood all the way back to take a better look, only I couldn't tell Bruce a story, so I told the truth.

"Children?" Mom called, still on the stairs, but no one answered. Then she walked into the kitchen all pretty again with her mascara fixed and her lipstick straight.

"Allie, was there an earlier call you didn't tell me about?" Mom asked, her voice saying she already knew the answer.

"I'll take that walk with you now," Bruce told her. "You see what happened to Allie?"

Mom gave me a look. "She hurt her toes," said Mom, "It was one awful night."

"And the last," Bruce said, holding the door open.

But Mom had come back from taking that call with more than her face changed. "I've been thinking," she said, "You know, Allie's dad and I have been through a lot together."

"Yeah, you've stayed through so fucking much I begin to think you must be crazy. Your sweater is over on the counter," Bruce said, still holding the door.

"Just a minute. Let me think," Mom said, leaning back against the cupboard.

"I don't get it," Bruce muttered. "I'm ready to walk with you. Isn't that what you wanted?"

"But I can't just leave him here," Mom said.

"I guess I must have misunderstood you," Bruce laughed, shaking his head.

"I can't just leave him here to die," Mom repeated, twisting the rings on her hands. "I can't!" she said, her voice rising, all confused again.

"All right, fine. So just leave him here to sleep. After all, who says he's going to die?"

"I say so."

"I thought you were a doctor of letters, not medicine."

"I had a sister once who died of a ruptured appendix that wasn't treated," Mom said, real quiet. "He was in awful pain around noon. I think that's when his appendix burst."

"You *think*," Bruce said.

"He's been delirious for hours. Just like Alice-Marie. I tell you, Bruce, he's going to die."

"But you're not certain."

"I know," Mom said, walking over to the far corner to pick up her sweater. "It's hard to kill someone."

"You're killing me without much trouble."

"It's hard to kill someone you've lived with. You've never been married," Mom said, touching Bruce's hand.

"You're just being difficult," Bruce said. "What's the matter? Did your other guy call to say he'd take you away? Was that him on the phone?"

"Him? Who? No, of course not," Mom said, dropping her sweater. She really was the world's worst liar.

"But it's the opportunity of a lifetime," Bruce argued. "He won't let you call a doctor. Are you really so sure this other guy won't desert you? Think of the kids. Think of . . . Hell, it's a blessing in disguise, just like you said."

"That's easy for you to say, but I'll have to live with it," Mom answered, standing first on one foot, then the other.

"Better than living with him," Bruce said, looking at me.

"I just don't know what to do!" Mom cried, sick with worry.

"Do what you're good at—do nothing," Bruce said, sounding so much like Dad it made Mom want to let him have it. But I was closer, so she slapped me instead.

Now it was Bruce's turn to look sick. "How did I get here?" he asked, looking at Mom and me and the peanut butter sandwich still sitting on the cutting board untouched. Then he gave a choking laugh.

"I'm leaving," Bruce said, real quiet, as Tad and Dave walked in.

"Us too," Tad and Dave said, walking right through the kitchen, then out the door past Bruce.

Mom just ignored them as she held Bruce's arm, not

letting go while she and Bruce talked for what seemed hours, both talking at once even, neither one stopping, as if this time they both had to say everything.

"I'm going out for a long walk around the lake," Bruce said at last, though it was past midnight. Then he picked up his jacket and walked out.

"I'm losing my mind," Mom said, calm as you might tell someone you'd just lost an old sweater. It was only then I saw she had.

Mom walked to the door and hung there not saying anything for maybe a minute, then she followed Bruce. On her chair hung Tad's least favorite blue sweatshirt. I took it and ran out after them, then stopped at the end of the lawn and just stood there watching their shadows move along the path till they were just a couple of specks halfway around the lake.

"Take a picture, it lasts longer," Tad snickered, cutting through the yard to the kitchen for more worm cans. Tad and Dave already had two coffee cans full of night crawlers, some long as a ruler and thick as your finger. They were going to spend the night at Dave's because his father left for work at six thirty and would wake them up in time for fishing. We had to leave for school by eight fifteen.

"Mom will never let you get away with it," I told Tad.

"She'll never know. I'll be back before breakfast," he answered. Then he tried to stick a night crawler down my shirt, only he couldn't because I fought real hard, and besides, his heart wasn't in it.

"You'd better go home to bed," Dave said. Then the boys went off into the night and were just voices.

I didn't want to go to bed. As long as I stayed up it was still summer, so I walked down to our dock to watch the stars move and hear the fish kerplopping, thinking how I used to go out and wish on the night's first star. Have you ever noticed how you're never frightened when you're making wishes, even if you're all alone outside in the dark? I couldn't see many stars; still I sat dangling my feet in the water, sort of sleeping till I was waked up at dawn by two sunnies nibbling my toes.

You know that taste in your mouth when you first wake up? I wanted to go in and brush my teeth. Not that it would solve everything. The sore spot would still be there, but maybe this time when I rinsed out the scab, the bloody taste wouldn't come back.

I got up, brushed the dirt off my pants, and got halfway across the back lawn before I remembered about Dad.

I thought then of calling Stormy and just marching up the back path together till we came to something. I called a couple times, but the bushes didn't move. No one around, just the birds chirping their brains out. I looked back over the lake and saw the sun sneaking up.

"Hey, Stormy!" I called, looking around one last time. Then I walked back up to the house.

THAT was the summer after Marilyn Monroe killed herself and Bruce laid the patio, the summer *Life* featured Christine Keeler and we had the backyard re-landscaped—the summer Dad died—the summer before Dave took his father's rifle and bet he'd shoot the first thing coming up the back path. Frankie had stopped by our house to find Sam, but I was the only one home that day, out in the backyard waiting myself. I was lying in the hammock and Frankie sat out there with me sort of quiet while we waited together. The phone rang inside the house, but I just let it. I thought of going in to get shears to cut some roses for Frankie to give his mother, only I was too busy dreaming. Frankie was like Sam that way—most kids sit around whining, but you were always free to dream around Frankie and Sam.

"What time is it?" asked Frankie.

"Almost dinner time," I said, so Frankie headed on home up the back path. A few minutes later I heard a crack and a ping. That was when Dave shot Frankie. They say the police couldn't tell who it was at first, because Dave couldn't stop crying and Frankie's face was smashed. I was still out in the backyard waiting when I heard sirens far off, then so close they sounded like they were coming to our house. Eventually they did, and the police wanted to talk with me again. It was all very different from when Dad died, of course, but I was the last person to see Frankie alive too.

The second the police came in I recognized the nice detective who took me to the hospital after my accident. He took out a pen and spiral notebook and started acting very official, but his eyes still crinkled like Bruce's.

"Remember me? You found my teeth," I said.

The policeman smiled, remembering once I told him. "Hey, that's right. I see they've all grown back. So how you been, little girl?" he said.

About the Author

Blythe Holbrooke's work has appeared in a number of magazines, including *Vogue*, *New York*, and *The Washington Monthly*. She graduated from Yale, was a reporter for the MacNeil/Lehrer Newshour, and is the author of *Gossip*. *Baby Teeth* is her first novel.